Character by character, Sally Whitney expertly draws us into her story. We become part of this small southern town, diving into the viewpoints of multiple family members. We empathize with the volunteer basketball coach trying his best to resurrect a winning team. We feel for the brooding teens who train and play hard, while stoically struggling with broken homes, demanding dads, and adolescent self-doubt. Racial issues push their ugly way into the story, engaging the reader even more deeply. In all, a fascinating and thought-provoking read.

– Deborah Shouse, author of *An Old Woman Walks Into a Bar*

In *Circle of Adversaries*, a hit-and-run car accident shatters a Black star basketball player's bones, and his small southern town's sense of trust and community. With unfaltering empathy and honesty, Sally Whitney's gripping prose rips the facades off apparent long-standing friendships, exposing the jealousy, racism, guilt, rage and suspicion simmering under the surface.

– Merry Jones, author of Maincrest Media Award-winner *The Woman in the Cupboard*

CIRCLE OF ADVERSARIES

ISBN: 978-1-68313-277-6
First Edition
Printed in USA

Pen-L Publishing
www.Pen-L.com

Cover by Eliza Whitney
Interior by Kimberly Pennell

CIRCLE OF ADVERSARIES

By

Sally Whitney

Other books by Sally Whitney

Surface and Shadow

When Enemies Offend Thee

For Parker, Harlow, Julia, and Hayes

Children are the best hope for bringing us together.

Prologue

Small towns have a heart that beats as surely as the one in every person's chest. The beat is there long before the arrival of the first human beings. It starts with the dirt and water that shape the earth where the town will be and rises through wild grass and trees to envelop the people when they come. It gives of its own spirit and takes from each individual some of the good and some of the bad, making it richer and more palpable with each passing year. Townspeople may travel beyond the town's boundaries and may even stay for most of their lives, but the beat travels with them, never to leave them, often pulling them back to its source.

For those who stay, the heart is a source of identity and comfort, the beat keeping time in the daily rhythms of their lives. An interruption in the beat will eventually spread, sometimes quickly, sometimes not so fast.

For a boy lying next to his bicycle by the side of the road, his brain jostled, his pelvis cracked, and his femur fractured, an hour passes before a passerby is pulled into his racing heart rhythm, the first of many to be affected by the new beat.

1

The gymnasium at Tanner High School was older than most of the structure attached to it. The original classroom building and the gym had been erected in 1923 at the top of a hill overlooking the town's small commercial area and the river that had provided the original lifeblood of the community. Thirty years earlier, a young man named Arthur Galloway, newly arrived with his equally young wife, recognized that spot along the river as an ideal place to build a textile factory. Workers for the mill, which Arthur named Foxrow, came willingly, drawn by job opportunities and the beauty of the area, surrounded by the foothills of the North Carolina mountains. In 1895, the railroad arrived, bringing more people and eventually stores, houses, churches, and the school.

Main Street started at Arthur's mill and ran through the developing business district before rising up the hill to the school. Along the street between the stores and the school, new residents built stately Victorian and Arts and Crafts houses, some created with Sears mail-order kits. Both the houses and the gymnasium were larger than the school, which included eight classrooms and an office for the principal. The gym was the pride of Tanner, attesting to the townspeople's allegiance to physical fitness, but especially to basketball.

Basketball was the reason Paul Westover sat alone in the gym on a cold January day in 1985, the weight of the town's divided expectations squeezing him like a vise.

Around him, the gym formed a simple rectangle with long, narrow windows filling three of its four sides. Light pierced the immense windows and drifted down through the rafters to give the cavernous space an almost spectral quality. The coach of the Tanner High School basketball team had spontaneously started the first game there with a prayer because he said he felt in that space the presence not only of God Almighty but of the gods of basketball as well. When the first high school dance was held in the gym, the principal cringed because he feared it was a sacrilege.

Paul's prayer that day was a simple plea. *God, tell me what to do.*

In the past sixty years, basketball had climbed to the pinnacle of sports achievement and adoration in North Carolina. In 1921, the University of North Carolina and North Carolina State College became charter members of the pioneer Southern Conference. Ensuing rivalries between the North Carolina teams and their opponents from Georgia, South Carolina, and other nearby states ran hot, and the fans loved it. Tanner High School basketball games were attended by almost everybody in town. Many outstanding teams graduated from Tanner, all of them honorable white Christians.

As years went by, the gym continued to serve the community well.

In the 1950s and 1960s, the gym's bathrooms had to be replaced and the foundation needed repairs. Coaches, physical education teachers, and parents of athletes pleaded with the school board to build a new gym, but the response was always that the one they had was adequate and they could never afford to construct another gym that magnificent. The wood alone would break any budget. So, they would keep what they had and continue to revere it.

By 1984, the year the Tanner Terrors began practicing and playing games there, it had become almost a historical landmark. The original school was swallowed up by additions, but the gym stood out proudly.

The Terrors were equally proud. Their team of ten players had been accepted into the local Amateur Athletic Union organization when they were in sixth grade. Now, as eighth graders, they were determined to win the championship in the fourteen-and-under classification. They had practiced five days a week throughout the autumn months to be ready for the season, but two games in, six weeks before their coach sought God in the gym, they were zero and two. When the final buzzer sounded on game three, they were six points behind. Paul gathered the players in a back corner beneath one of the gym's towering windows, away from the celebrating opponents, but he struggled to find the right words to say. Working with the boys on the court, he knew exactly what to say. Talking to his legal clients, he knew exactly what to say. For him, practicing law was as much fun as sitting down to a big Thanksgiving dinner. Whether it was estate work, tax filings, property transfers, or even an occasional court case—they were all fun. But facing these youngsters with their eyes so full of disappointment was torture.

As he stalled for time, he couldn't be sure if their glistening cheeks were the result of sweat or tears. Their skinny adolescent limbs draped over the bleachers like spaghetti. The hardest ones to look at were the ones who had not yet gone into puberty. Their soft and childlike jawlines were on the verge of trembling. Paul had an urge to hug them all, but that wasn't his job as coach. He remembered football legend Bart Starr's remark that a quarterback's job is to be a coach on the field, and in that role, he should inspire his teammates to go with him to the gates of hell. Paul couldn't talk to eighth graders about hell. He cleared his throat.

"Chin up, guys," he said, making sure to hold up his. "We had some good moments in this game. Our plays worked most of the time. Some of you dropped outside shots that even surprised me. We had a couple of steals and a lot of good blocks. And all of you showed great hustle. I'm just sorry the final score didn't reflect that. But it's early in the season. We have plenty more games to show what we can do. And we will. Monday, we'll work exclusively on defense until nobody can get by us." He said the last words with a fervor that he hoped would warrant Bart Starr's approval. "Now go home and get some rest so you're ready for Monday."

The boys slowly lifted their arms and legs from the seats and rose to their feet. They wanted to believe Coach, but none of them could stir up even an ounce of optimism. Their dream of being undefeated was long gone. They thought they had been working as hard as they could, so where could they go from here? Paul's son, Benny, didn't want to face his father one-on-one. He felt like he had let the coach down. The whole team had let the coach down. But he was the only one who had to talk about it at home.

A serious boy whose eyeglasses gave him a studious appearance, Benny liked history and occasionally paid attention to politics, but he loved basketball. Because his favorite team was the NC State Wolfpack, it had been his idea to name the team the Tanner Terrors in honor of the Wolfpack's original name. He was already planning to go to State when he was old enough and then go on to law school in Chapel Hill to become a lawyer like his father. But in the meantime, he worked daily on his jump shot. He would never be tall enough to play any position other than guard, so developing an outside shot was important. Although he knew he was responsible for some of the outside shots his dad mentioned, he still felt he had let him down.

The boys resembled a funeral procession on their way across the gym to the front door. Assorted parents waited for them, their faces laced with sympathetic smiles. One by one, they gathered their sons, not certain whether to offer a hug or simply a few words of condolence or maybe nothing at all. All those adolescent feelings were so fragile. Benny was surprised to feel an arm around his shoulders. His dad wasn't the type to do that, especially in front of the others, but he understood the gesture when he realized the person next to him was Frankie Jessop, not his father.

"Let's go to my house," Frankie said. "We can play Atari if nothing else."

Paul saw the interaction, as glad as Benny not to have to discuss the game with his son so soon after the defeat. When Benny looked for his approval, he nodded, knowing that before the afternoon was over, the boys would be shooting goals in Frankie's backyard. Frankie was a natural athlete. He could run faster, jump higher, catch and throw balls better than anyone else in his class. In elementary school, he had always been the first one chosen for any team. Now, in middle school, he played football and baseball as well as basketball. Because of his ability to make sound decisions—and to pass the ball quickly and accurately—he was an excellent point guard, and the team depended on him.

Paul spoke to the other parents on his way out. Some of them helped with practices, so they knew how hard the boys were working. They believed in their kids, and most of them were sure something would turn around soon. The doubtful ones held their tongues for now. Their team had good seasons the years before, so this year shouldn't be any different, except some of the players on the opposing teams had gotten so big. The team today had been especially tall, towering over most of the Terrors' players except for their center, Jamie Parker.

Jamie ambled past Paul in the parking lot, causing him to marvel again at how many inches the willowy boy had grown over the summer. Maybe they'd all grow a little over Christmas break with more time at home to eat. Only one game remained before the break. Sure would be a boost to their spirits if they could win that one. And it would tee them up to do well in the holiday tournament the weekend before New Year's Day.

A nippy breeze caused tree branches to dance below the gray sky as Paul drove home. If the wind kicked up, there'd be dead branches all over his yard. His house was a 1960s split-level, but the trees had been there since before the Civil War. For all he knew, General Sherman had rested in their shade on his march to Richmond. Paul loved those trees, and he loved being outdoors. In the summer, he sported what he called a "farmer's tan," which was actually a golfer's tan. Even in the winter, his face retained a healthy glow, whether from his days in the sun or some inner fire, no one was sure. The ladies of Tanner said he could be a flirt, although they knew he meant nothing by it.

He was glad to see his wife's car in the driveway when he got home. She had missed the game because she had to meet with a new client. A lawyer like her husband, Meredith Westover had chosen to work part time in the county public defender's office and spend what time she could writing poetry. She was a quiet woman who often found herself studying the people in the room rather than talking to them, amused by the social mannerisms and clichés of her friends and acquaintances. Despite her preference for solitude, her blue eyes crackled with life and maybe mischief. No one knew for sure what was going on in that mind of hers.

From the expression on Paul's face, she knew the team had lost. She wrapped her arms around his waist and spoke against his chest, "It's all right. It's only a game. And they're just kids."

Paul pulled back and looked at her straight on. "That's why it matters." A lone ray of sunlight pierced the living room's bay window and illuminated her face against the dark wallpaper. "Learning to lose may build character, but these kids also need to be reassured that hard work pays off. I thought we'd have a winning season this year, but I cannot, for the life of me, pull this team together. I know we have the talent, but something's missing. Benny took it pretty hard. I told him he could go home with Frankie. It'll do them good to be together this afternoon. I'm going to spend some time figuring out new defensive drills. I think that's where we're falling short. We're letting them get too close to the basket, and we're not pulling down enough rebounds." He kissed the top of her head and walked toward the door. "But first, I'm going to pick up sticks in the yard."

Meredith knew there were no sticks in the yard yet, but she also knew he did some of his best thinking puttering around outside. She could tell him about her afternoon later. He was almost out of the house when he stopped and came back in. "How'd your meeting go?"

Meredith laid down the sweater and book bag she'd just taken from the couch. "It's a case I can't win. But maybe winning doesn't always mean having the judge decide in your favor. It's a child endangerment case, and you know how much I hate those. The mother is obviously guilty. A neighbor found her daughter locked in their apartment, where she said she'd been for three days. But she's only five years old, so it could have been longer. The only food in the place was a loaf of bread and a jar of peanut butter."

"Where was the mother?" Paul was almost always amazed by the people Meredith defended, the crimes they were accused of committing, and the circumstances that surrounded them.

"Looking for work, she said when she finally came home. Supposedly, the only job openings she could find were in Hickory, and for some reason, she wasn't able to go home at night. I'll learn more when I meet with her again. She'll be arraigned on Monday, and I can probably get the judge to grant bail because of the child, but I don't know how she'll get the money to pay it. Her daughter's with social services now, and I'm afraid she's going to be there for a while."

"No other family?"

"Not that we've found so far. The mother says there's an aunt in Charlotte, but the phone number she gave us is disconnected. They'll send someone to check out the address, and maybe we'll get lucky. That's what I mean by winning this case. The judge will find the mother guilty, but she'll probably get probation since it's a first offense. If we can find a responsible relative for the child to stay with until the mother gets her act together, then it's a win."

"What's the mother like?" Paul moved away from the door and into the living room, where Meredith sat next to the book bag on the couch.

"Young. Too young. She needs somebody taking care of her instead of the other way around. There's no husband or father in the picture as far as I can see." That was the case with so many of Meredith's clients. Lonely people, many of them young, needing support, guidance, and companionship, but looking in all the wrong places. These were the ones who kept her in the business. For the others— the repeat offenders, the sociopaths, the ones who got a thrill out of crime—she had to rely on her belief that every accused person deserves a good-faith defense. Otherwise, the justice system wouldn't work.

"She's lucky she has you," Paul said. "And I'd suggest you check with the unemployment office and see if she's getting any help there. I know that's not your job, but it can't hurt." He returned to his mission in the yard just as the wind was picking up.

At five o'clock, Meredith arrived at Frankie's house to collect Benny for supper. Exactly as Paul had guessed, the boys were outside shooting basketballs at a goal erected by Frankie's father when he realized he'd never interest his son in his favorite sport, bowling. Well-liked around town, Frank Sr. often joined the pickup games at the horseshoe pits in the town park, where he was known for his dead-eye aim. But he was even better aiming at the tenpins with his beloved custom bowling ball. He'd been captain of his bowling team for five years, leading them to top standing in their league. It was easy to see where Frankie got his athletic ability, but he referred to horseshoes and bowling as sports for old men.

When Benny saw his mother, he ran to the car and pleaded through the open window, "Just ten more minutes. Please. We need to finish this game."

Meredith agreed, followed by, "And put your jacket back on. It's cold out here." After parking the car close to the house, she went to the back door and knocked. The Jessops were the kind of people who liked guests to come in through the kitchen. Meredith was glad Benny asked to stay longer because she wanted the chance to talk to Frankie's mother, Suzanne, a tall, buxom woman mostly known for her irreverent comments and brash wit. When the church secretary reminded her she hadn't paid her son's summer Bible school fee, she explained she was waiting to see if he learned anything before she paid. Most of the people in town either liked her, or they didn't. There was no in-between.

Suzanne opened the door wearing an old-fashioned bib apron, her red hair tied at her neck with a paisley scarf. At her request, Meredith stepped inside into a cloud of aromas, a mixture of cinnamon, vanilla, and maybe something peachy.

"Taste this," Suzanne said as she crammed a spongy square into Meredith's mouth, then stared with eyebrows pinched while Meredith chewed. "Smells like heaven, tastes like shit," she said before Meredith had swallowed. "I knew it." She grabbed the pan of turnovers and held them over the garbage disposal.

"It's not that bad," Meredith said. "Put a little whipped cream on top, and they'll be fine."

Suzanne moved the pan back to the counter. Because she always said exactly what she thought, she expected other people to do the same. "Good idea about the whipped cream. Frank and Frankie could eat that with a spoon. Here. Have some ice tea to get the taste out of your mouth."

She filled a tall glass from a sun-tea jar and handed it to Meredith, who leaned against the kitchen table and asked, "What did you think of the game today?"

Suzanne shrugged. "They were a little flat-footed. Not enough spark. You know, always a second behind."

"So what's going on with them?"

"Who knows? They're kids."

"What did Frank say about it?"

"Just that he knew the kids were disappointed, like he was. He likes to win, if you haven't noticed. He said maybe they need to work on their stamina, that they seemed to let down more in the second half. I said, 'So how do you do that?' He said, 'Run 'em. Run 'em up and down the court at the end of practice and then make 'em shoot foul shots when they're drop-dead tired. That's what Dean Smith would do.' As if he had any idea what Dean Smith would do."

"Can't hurt," Meredith mused. "Maybe he'll suggest that at practice on Monday. Paul thinks the problem is defense." She paused before she asked the question she had come to ask. "With the bad start to the season, are any of the parents doubting Paul's ability to coach? I think he's beginning to doubt himself." There was something in the slope of his shoulders and the droop of his head as he'd piddled around the chilly yard that made her concerned.

Instead of giving her the immediate answer she'd hoped for, Suzanne continued putting peach turnovers into a Tupperware container. To her, the idea of blaming Paul for the team's problems was ridiculous, but she had to think about anything that others had said so she could answer honestly. "Nope," she said as she tucked the Tupperware away in the refrigerator. "I can't remember anybody blaming Paul, not specifically anyway. But this is an important year for people who care about those things. The high school coach is watching, and Frank said a couple of AAU coaches from other schools are looking to build their teams. Depends on what you want for your kid, I guess."

Several of the Terrors' parents wanted a basketball future for their sons, or so it would appear from the phone calls Paul sometimes received. "Equal playing time" was a phrase thrown around a lot. County leagues encouraged it, but AAU was thought to be more competitive, a place where the best players could hone their skills and prepare for star status on varsity teams. Those players couldn't give up playing time in games just so every player got a chance to be on the court. The next step was the big prize, a basketball scholarship to a Division 1 college.

Meredith let the conversation drop there. She just wanted Benny to be happy, although Paul often had other ideas. But she wasn't worried about Benny. She was worried about Paul. "Thanks for the information," she said. "I need to get Benny home and finish up supper. See you at the game next Saturday."

Outside, the boys were gulping water from a garden hose. Meredith shook her head in exasperation that they never tired of playing basketball but were too lazy to walk inside for a glass of water. "Let's go, Benny," she called. "See you next Saturday, Frankie."

The ride home was mostly silent. Benny took the safety strap off his eyeglasses and tucked it into his pants pocket but otherwise stared straight ahead. About three blocks from home, Meredith said, "I'm sorry about the game. The next one'll be better."

"You weren't even there, Mom," Benny said, continuing to stare out the front window.

"I couldn't help it. I had to meet with a client. I promise I'll be there next week."

Benny knew she meant what she was saying, but something could very likely come up at the last minute, and she wouldn't be at the game. He wasn't sure she liked basketball. It was his thing. His and his dad's. He would have to talk to his dad about the game when he got home, but he wasn't going to talk to Mom.

Paul was waiting for him, watching a golf tournament on TV. "C'mere, Benny," he said. "Tell me what you think went wrong this afternoon."

Reluctantly, Benny dropped his jacket on top of the sweater and book bag still lying at one end of the couch and sat at the other end, near Paul's easy chair. "I don't know what went wrong. We just weren't good enough. Or big enough."

"So how do we get better?"

"Grow some."

Paul smiled, since that had been his first idea too. But there had to be other ways. "We're going to work on some new defensive drills and practice rebounding," he said. "But I want to keep up everybody's spirit. Any ideas on that?"

Benny groaned inwardly. Why did adults think they could change everything with a good pep talk? "Everybody will be happier when we start winning games." He stared at the soles of his worn-out sneakers, remembering to make sure his dad had put his good pair of Chuck Taylors where they belonged. He was saving money to buy a pair of Nikes, but he had a long way to go.

"Okay. Unless you have any other ideas, we'll work on defense. I know we can turn the season around."

"Sure, Dad. Can I go now?"

"Go ahead. See if your mother needs help setting the table." Paul turned up the sound on the TV, but he'd lost interest in the tournament. He knew Benny loved basketball, but he sure wasn't seeing any of that zeal with him. The only reason he'd taken the coaching job was that Benny asked him to. It wasn't like he didn't have enough to do already with work and the house and the yard and trying to squeeze in a few rounds of golf here and there. Benny could at least act like he appreciated the time Paul was putting in with the team and be willing to talk with him about it. Maybe this was the wrong time to talk. He'd wait until after church the next day and ask Benny to shoot foul shots with him in the backyard. Maybe doing something physical would start the conversation naturally.

Paul's favorite part of a meal was dessert, so he was annoyed when the telephone rang just as Meredith was slicing up large pieces of pie hot from the oven. Pecan pie was her specialty, made from her grandmother's recipe with plenty of butter, sugar, and white corn syrup. Usually, it was a delicacy that the family was treated to only around holidays, but Meredith figured Christmas was close enough to warrant it, and she wanted to see Paul and Benny smile.

"Don't answer it," she said, but Benny was already halfway there. He talked for a minute and then pointed the receiver at Paul.

Reluctantly, Paul took it from Benny's hand. With his back to the table, he spoke quietly. Benny took a detour to the kitchen to retrieve a can of spray-on whipped cream from the refrigerator and proceeded to create a grapefruit-sized mound of white on top of his pie before shooting a squirt into his mouth, which caused his mother to quickly remove the can from his hand. They both laughed, and Benny almost choked on the whipped cream, but it was a good moment, one Meredith wished Paul could have shared in, although he probably would have been too concerned about his son's gross behavior to see the humor in the situation.

When the phone conversation ended, Paul returned to the table, his eyebrows pushed together, and his lips skewed to one side. "What's up, Dad?" Benny asked.

"It's about the basketball team," Paul said. "That was the commissioner. He said a new boy in town wants to try out for the Terrors."

"That's good news, isn't it?" Meredith asked.

"I hope so. Depends on the boy." Paul sat down in front of his slice of pie.

"Can he play?" Benny's voice was flat, hiding his hope that they were getting a ringer and his fear they'd get stuck with a loser.

"The commissioner didn't say much about him. His family moved here from Greensboro, and he was on an AAU team before, so the commissioner there put his father in touch with the one here. He's in eighth grade, so he's with us."

"At least he's played AAU before. Sounds good to me." Meredith laid her fork beside her half-eaten pie. "Why do you look so concerned?"

"I'm not concerned, but this will be something new for us. He'll be the only Black player on our team and one of very few in the league."

"Who cares?" Benny asked. "As long as he's a good player. Maybe he can pull us out of this slump."

Paul hoped Benny was right about everything.

2

After some deliberation, Paul decided to ask Marcus Thomas to bring his son, Quentin, to the gym early on Monday so he could assess the boy's skills before introducing him to the other players. If Quentin didn't play at the same level as the Terrors, he could suggest he play with the county league without embarrassing him in front of the team.

Marcus and Quentin arrived for the meeting fifteen minutes early. A few high school players were still straggling out of the gym, taking one last jump shot or talking with their friends. The air was warm from the previous practice, laced with the faint odor of adolescent sweat. Marcus paused at the entrance, like a ranger on reconnaissance. He was a big man, tall and barrel-chested, with the sharp eyes of a person who met life head-on. With one hand on his son's shoulder, he steered Quentin, who was nearly as tall as his father, across the court to the spot where Paul was taking a basketball out of the large bag of balls he had brought with him. Benny, whom Paul had brought along to run drills with Quentin, sat on the lowest bleacher, wary but eager to see what this new kid had.

"Welcome," Paul said in his formal lawyer voice. He extended his hand to Quentin first, then Marcus. "I'm Paul Westover, and this is my son, Benny." He motioned to Benny, who unfolded off the bleacher and offered a small wave.

"It's a pleasure to meet you," Marcus said. "This is Quentin." He nodded at Quentin, who smiled shyly and murmured, "Hi."

Paul tossed the ball he was holding to Benny. "You boys go shoot a few shots while I talk to Quentin's father. Then we'll run some drills."

Benny caught the ball and dribbled toward one of the baskets. Quentin followed with a slow, graceful lope, his arms and legs moving with the fluidity of a dancer. Paul made a mental note to have him run some sprints up and down the court. One of the famous basketball coaches once said that the sign of a natural athlete is the way he runs. "You can teach a player how to shoot, pass, and strategize, but you can't teach him how to run. That's either God-given or it isn't." Paul had no reason to doubt that was true.

"So when did y'all move to Tanner?" he asked as he gestured for Marcus to have a seat on the bleachers. He was surprised Benny hadn't said anything about seeing Quentin at school.

"I've been here since Labor Day, but it took us a while to find a house, so the family didn't move until last Saturday. Now we're living in a maze of boxes. I thought about leaving a trail of socks when I got up this morning so I can find my way back to bed tonight, but by then, my wife will've moved stuff, so it wouldn't do me any good." Marcus chuckled, displaying a friendly smile that drew Paul in immediately.

"Where'd you decide to buy?"

"We're on Pine Street. We picked it because it's close to the elementary school, and we have two daughters younger than Quentin. We figure they can walk to school and won't have to ride a bus."

Pine Street was one of the older streets in town, which was why the elementary school was located there. Its tree-lined sidewalks passed in front of classic middle-class houses with small porches and good-sized yards. Homeowners were mostly empty nesters who originally moved there for their children or young families who had come when earlier owners died or moved to the nursing center. Paul couldn't think of a single Black family who lived there. The Thomases were the first.

"That's a nice neighborhood," Paul said. "And you're working at the mill, right?"

"I'm in the industrial engineering department." After Marcus's degree from North Carolina A&T landed him a job with Cone

Mills, he expected to stay in Greensboro, so he was surprised when the head of the department at Foxrow invited him to interview. What he didn't know was that so many advances had been made in textile equipment in the past decade that the top brass at Foxrow knew if they wanted to stay on the cutting edge of the industry, they had to invest in new machinery and increased efficiency. Cone was finishing a nine-year program of plant modernization that involved Marcus, so he was an ideal candidate for the Foxrow job.

Paul nodded. "I know a few guys in that department. They're good people, but then almost everybody in Tanner is good people." He looked back out at the boys on the court. "Tell me about Quentin's basketball experience. What position does he usually play?"

"He was a power forward on his old team. He's not afraid to rush the basket. But he can move around wherever you need him."

Paul was already thinking if Quentin had the skills, he might try him at center and move Jamie to forward. Like Quentin, Jamie's arms and legs turned to flowing water on the court, gliding like smooth streams around obstacles, including members of the other team. But Quentin had more meat on his bones and would be a more formidable presence in the lane.

"I'd like to see him in action," he said, "so if you'll excuse me, I'm going to get that started." He left Marcus to join the boys on the court and was pleased to see they seemed to enjoy working together. Benny was often shy around people he didn't know, so the situation could have been awkward, but Quentin had his father's easy laugh, and any ice there might have been was undoubtedly broken. Paul wanted Quentin to be as much at ease as possible before he started evaluating him. After a few passing and layup drills, in which Quentin showed the same ease in getting the ball into the basket that he had in running, Paul had them play against each other one-on-one. Benny managed to sink a few long jump shots over Quentin, but there was no way he was going to get around him to get to the basket. Quentin was agile as a cat, anticipating Benny's every move.

"Let's try two-on-one," Paul called, signaling for Benny to pass him the ball. As father and son snapped passes back and forth, Quentin didn't miss a step maneuvering from one to the other. Finally, Paul widened the distance between Benny and him enough to make it impossible for Quentin to guard them both, allowing Benny to slip around him and go in for a layup.

"Gotcha," Benny called with a grin as the ball slipped through the net. Quentin smiled too, because he knew there'd been no way for him to prevent the basket.

Paul was happiest of all because he could see that Quentin was going to be a great addition to the team. He'd forgotten to have Quentin do laps so he could watch him run, which wasn't necessary now, but he decided to do it anyway, just for the beauty of it. "Give me four laps now," he said. "I want to see some speed and stamina. You too, Malcolm," he called to another teammate who'd just arrived. "Good warm-up for you."

Malcolm was followed into the gym by his mother, Lydia Colton, a divorcée who shared custody of Malcolm with his father, Jeff, one of the doctors in town. Most of the parents dropped their sons off to practice and picked them up afterward, but during the weeks that Malcolm lived with her, Lydia stayed for every practice. Paul wasn't sure if she was an overprotective parent or just wanted to spend as much time with Malcolm as she could. The way Paul remembered it, her divorce from the doctor had been less than amicable, strictly one-sided, with Lydia filing the papers, but that was twelve years ago, and their lives seemed to have settled into a non-contentious pattern now.

Today, she took her usual seat on the fourth bleacher midway down the side of the court, her shoulders squared, her eyes following the running boys. Paul studied her face to see if she had any reaction when she spotted Quentin. He hadn't phoned the parents to tell them there'd be a new player because he wasn't sure Quentin would be joining the team and didn't need their approval. But maybe he should have given them a heads-up.

As he expected, Lydia's expression never changed. She, of course, noticed the new boy and wondered who he was, but she knew Paul would explain it when he was ready. For the moment, she was more interested in seeing what Malcolm did. He was a friendly boy, comfortable with most people, probably because he'd had to make a lot of adjustments in his young life. Having a home with each of his parents and regularly moving between them wasn't easy. He seemed well-adjusted, but Lydia was always alert to signals about his personality. In this case, he fell into running with Benny and Quentin as if nothing new was going on.

Paul continued to scrutinize the boys and the adults as they arrived. Instinct told him he would likely be able to spot any sources of trouble based on what happened at this first meeting. Frank Jessop, his assistant coach, frowned at the sight of Quentin, but it was more a frown of inquisitiveness than disapproval.

James Parker, Jamie's dad, arrived next. While Jamie made his way toward the boys, who by that time had stopped running and were sitting on the floor catching their breath, James strode straight toward Paul. Whenever James entered a room, everyone felt his presence, even though he wasn't unusually tall, large, or loud. He took each step as if he knew exactly where he was going. His arms moved slightly at his sides, giving the impression that they had chosen the destination and were propelling his body in that direction. Lydia stopped watching Malcolm for a second and smiled at James. Marcus took him in with some apprehension. Paul and Frank braced for the impact.

"Who's the new player?" James asked, his expression non-committal. His tone, as usual, was confident but not domineering.

"He's Quentin Thomas, and this is his dad, Marcus," Paul said, gesturing toward Marcus, who sat four rows up on the bleachers. The introduction included Frank, who came forward to shake hands with Marcus as James did. "They just moved here from Greensboro," Paul continued. "Quentin's joining the team."

"Can't wait to see what he's got," James said as he climbed the bleachers to sit next to Marcus. "I hope y'all like our little town."

Frank turned to face the court and spoke to Paul in a muffled voice. "We already have ten players. Can we carry another one?"

"Rule book says we can carry up to fifteen, and when you see this kid play, I think you'll want to stretch our team to eleven. He may be the jumpstart we've been looking for." Paul walked out on the court to join the group of boys, which had now increased to ten. "Okay. We gotta get started. I hope you've all met Quentin. He just moved here, and he's a new member of our team. Make him feel welcome, you hear? Since several of you are already warmed up, the rest are going to luck out today and skip that. We'll go straight into drills. Grab the cones and set 'em up leading to the basket on both sides." The boys leaped to their feet and went to get the cones.

Paul realized he was missing a player. "Hey. Where's Adam?"

"At the beauty shop," Frankie called out.

"Stop that," Paul said. He couldn't tolerate that kind of remark, even though he understood why Frankie said it. Some of the women in town, especially Adam's mother's friends, were always going on about his "movie-star looks," which embarrassed him to no end. He thought he looked like everybody else, but people were always pointing out his wavy dark hair, even darker eyes, and Al Pacino cheekbones. Girls hung around him in droves, which caused his male friends to tease him incessantly. He tried shaving his hair to a buzz cut, but that only evoked teasing of a different sort. He currently resorted to wearing a green knit cap pulled as low on his forehead as possible, except when the girls were around, and no one was there to tease him. Mostly, he was confused by it all and preferred to concentrate on basketball.

The team was well into the drill with the cones when Adam, green cap low as ever, dashed through the narthex-like entry to the gym. He was breathing hard when he spoke to Paul.

Sorry, Coach. My mom made me wait while she finished

making notes for her committee meeting at the church. Do you want me to run laps?"

"Not this time. Go on out on the court. We've got a new player. His name's Quentin. Introduce yourself."

Adam dropped his coat on the bleachers. As he turned for the court, Paul snatched the cap off his head. Adam sneaked a glance at Paul's frown. He knew he wasn't supposed to wear the cap on the court.

When the practice finally wound down, Paul gathered the boys for a final talk like he always did. "Good practice, guys," he said. "Next time, we're going to try some changes in our lineup." He looked at one of the second-string guards. "Carson, I want you at shooting guard, and Jason, you'll be power forward. Quentin—I hope all of you met Quentin—we'll give you a turn at center. We're going to be switching around a lot for a while to find the best combination possible for our next game. We want to go into the holiday break with a win." Carson's father had been pestering Paul for a while to give Carson more playing time, so now, when he was trying to work in Quentin, was a good time to see what Carson could do.

The team split up and headed for their parents or the door. James chided Jamie to put on his coat before going out into the cold. On the ride home, he asked his son what he thought of the new guy.

"He's okay," Jamie said.

"But not as good as you." James flashed a big smile, hoping Jamie would return it, but the boy just shrugged. Getting him to smile sometimes seemed to require an act of God, but when he did, divine radiance seemed to illuminate his face. That's what James was looking for as he worked to instill confidence in Jamie's basketball skills. He knew his son had a future in the sport because the high school coach had already said he was looking forward to having Jamie on the varsity squad, maybe even as a freshman.

Back at home, Jamie plopped down in front of the television, and James went looking for his wife, Elaine. He never knew for sure where she'd be. Her slender body suggested she was always on the move, which she pretty much was, making her the family's link with the town. As secretary of the First United Methodist Church, she came into contact with a large portion of the local population. She was also leader of her daughter's Girl Scout troop and a member of the PTA. That night, James found her in their bedroom writing invitations to a luncheon she was hosting right before Christmas.

"Dinner's in the oven," she said as he kissed her cheek. "We're having lasagna. How was practice?"

James sat on the bed and removed his coat and tie, even though he often seemed more comfortable in a suit than casual clothes, which befitted his position as manager of the main office at the mill. "There's a new kid on the team," he said. "Every bit as tall as Jamie and heavier too. Paul said he was going to try him at center."

"What did Jamie say about that?'

"Nothing. But I watched this kid play. He's really good."

"Maybe Jamie could play forward."

"The varsity coach is looking for a center."

"Give it time." Elaine put her note cards back into the desk drawer. "Let's see how things work out."

"There's one other thing about this kid," James said. "He's Black."

Elaine raised her eyebrows. "That's a first."

Over at Adam Campbell's house, his mom, Laura, was busy preparing chicken Florentine for dinner. She was grateful her husband made enough money (barely) for her to stay home and devote her energy full time to her children and her church. She went to church at least twice a week—once on Sunday for worship and again on Wednesday night for choir practice. Once a month, she chaired education committee meetings on Monday night and met with members of her United Methodist Women's circle on Thursday morning. The softness of her plump face and midsection suggested a woman living in contentment. Her friends knew she was always willing to listen to their concerns and would hold everything in confidence. They suspected she overcame the urge to spill secrets by telling everything to God. Unfortunately, her children didn't share their inclination to confide in her.

"How was practice?" she asked Adam after Lydia Colton dropped him off.

"Fine," he said. "When's dinner?"

Laura knew this lack of response would never do, but she decided to wait until Adam, his father, and his sister were gathered for dinner to pursue it. As the family served up the creamy chicken, she asked again, "Did anything exciting happen at practice?"

Adam knew he wasn't going to get out of answering this time, so he offered the one item his mother might really be interested in. "We got a new kid on the team."

"Oh!" Laura couldn't help showing her surprise. She hadn't heard anything about a new family in town. "What's he like?"

"He's a good player. And he's tall. His name is Quentin Thomas. I like him."

"We'll have to find out who his parents are," Laura said, "so we can invite them to go to church with us." Her mind was already spinning with possibilities for the new family.

Her husband, Richard, spoke up. "Take it easy, Laura. Let's not swarm over these folks like a bunch of bees." Richard respected his wife's devotion to Christ, although he didn't share it. His family were Baptists in name only. He had few memories of going to church except to Bible school during the summer, which he knew was his mother's way of getting him out of the house. His loyalty was to ideas rather than a deity. John Locke was his hero. Most of his students at the community college enjoyed his lectures, which were more like discussions than presentations. Richard wanted to teach them to think, and what better way to do that than by analyzing the ideas of modern philosophers?

"Besides," Richard continued, "they may prefer a different church. Quentin's African American, isn't he, Adam?"

"Yeah. How'd you know that?" Usually, Adam's parents never knew anything.

"I met Quentin's mother about a month ago at the college. At least, I think she's his mother. She said she had a son named Quentin, and that's an unusual name, so it's probably the same one. She hadn't moved here yet, but she was in the dean's office applying for a job as a teaching assistant next semester. I just happened to be there. Don't you think Quentin and his family might prefer the AME church?"

"Oh!" Laura said again. "That's even better. They can help us with the Cultural Bridge program."

Richard sighed. "Give 'em a break. You're not ready to launch that Cultural Bridge thing anyway, are you?" He knew his wife loved to devise elaborate plans for ambitious projects, but they often were never realized.

"We certainly are," Laura retorted. "Elaine and I and the rest of the committee have some great ideas for ways to celebrate Martin Luther King, Junior's birthday in January. Just because North Carolina doesn't celebrate the new holiday and probably never will as long as Jesse Helms is around, that doesn't mean we can't celebrate it. In fact," she smiled sweetly at Richard, "we have our first planning meeting Wednesday night, and I'd like you to go with me."

"Sorry I mentioned it."

Laura smiled again. Richard might complain, but she knew he'd go with her. He always did whatever she asked.

Lydia and Malcolm finished dinner around seven thirty. While Lydia cleaned up the kitchen, Malcolm escaped to his room under the pretense of doing homework. Totally shunning his school backpack, he stretched out on his bed and opened the novel he had started reading the night before. The book was *The Outsiders*, and even though Malcolm had seen the movie version, his English teacher encouraged him to read the novel. Malcolm was glad she had. He liked Ponyboy, and he felt sorry for him because his parents had been killed in a car crash.

Malcolm had parent problems of his own. He'd never known what it was like to live with both of them. When he was four, he got his first calendar to help him remember which days would be spent at which parent's house, and he'd had plenty of those calendars since. Whenever he asked a friend to sleep over at his house, he had to be sure to specify which house, especially since his father lived out in the country, away from town. He wished he could be like other kids with two parents who lived together.

Lydia came upstairs to check on him when the dishes were done. "Don't forget your homework," she said gently as she sat on the edge of the bed. "What do you think of your new teammate?"

"He's okay. I think he'll be good for the team."

"Well, be nice to him. Especially when you see him at school. It's not easy being the new kid." Lydia knew what it was like being a newcomer to Tanner. When she'd arrived twelve years ago, the only two friends she'd made right away were Suzanne Jessop and Nancy Galloway, both of whom her husband considered less than ideal companions—Suzanne because she was so outspoken and Nancy because she was the very sheltered daughter of the most powerful family in town. But Lydia had insisted on maintaining the friendships and was still close to both women twelve years later. She'd lost her husband but kept her friends.

After her divorce, she thought she'd eventually leave Tanner, but she didn't want to make any hasty decisions, so she'd taken a job in the dye development department at the Dixie Underwear Company, where Nancy worked. Her two motivations for staying in town were to keep Malcolm close to his father, who wanted to play an active role in his son's life, and to be close to Nancy. Although nearly the same age as Lydia, Nancy had the mental capacity of a child. Lydia had helped her find a job at the underwear company and sometimes went with her to group meetings at the social services center.

Nancy had become largely independent, and Malcolm had a solid relationship with his father. A restless urge in the back of Lydia's mind told her it was time for her to move on.

3

Delia Thomas had a busy week unpacking the many moving boxes scattered around the house. Although she'd made several trips to Tanner in early autumn to try to find a job, nothing had panned out. The high school administrators had all the math teachers they needed for the year, and the nearby community college had very few teaching-assistant positions, all of which were filled. But maybe it was for the best, at least for a while. There was a lot of unpacking to do, and she wanted to be available to her children in case they had any problems getting settled in their new schools.

Delia hadn't wanted to move to Tanner. Although Greensboro had been through a lot of racial turbulence in the past decade, she was certain the Black residents were better off because of it, and she didn't want to start over again in a small town, which was surely filled with bigots. She knew when she met Marcus at A&T that he was a man of ambition and courage who would stop at nothing to succeed, but was moving their son and two daughters to a place with fewer resources and less diversity really a step forward? A sturdy woman who was as tall as her husband, Delia often made decisions for the family, but she knew she wasn't going to win this argument. So she made up her mind to find her place in Tanner.

For the time being, the only opportunity she had to meet other adults in town was through her children, so she was looking forward to Quentin's first basketball game that afternoon. She hoped the mothers of the other players would welcome her, though she knew from Marcus that she'd be the only Black woman there.

"Come on, Quentin," she called up the stairs. "We need to

leave. Dad said warm-up starts at two thirty." Marcus had gone with Quentin to practices all week and had posted the game schedule on the refrigerator, but he still started prodding the family at noon to get there on time.

"Don't want anybody to accuse us of living on 'colored people's time,'" he whispered to Delia as soon as they finished lunch.

Quentin stood in front of the mirror in his room, looking at himself in the new basketball uniform. It wasn't what he wanted to see. He shared his mother's thoughts about the move. Why should he have to leave his friends? A few of the boys he hung out with had been his friends since kindergarten, and his basketball teammates were poised to win the league championship this year. He was doing well in school with teachers who liked him. Now he had to start over with strangers everywhere. His parents thought making friends was easy for him. With his quick smile and ready conversation, adults and peers seemed to gravitate to him, but no one knew it was all a front. He'd learned early on that people like you better if you're happy. Although his sunny personality had worked for him in his large elementary and middle schools, he had doubts about this tiny school he was in now. With its smaller, more intimate culture, they might see right through him. Reluctantly, he pulled on his socks and shoes. Before lacing up the left shoe, he slipped a tiny arrowhead on top of the sock below the shoe's tongue. He'd found the arrowhead in his backyard in Greensboro, and it had become his secret talisman. He believed it gave him strength and courage, and he put it into his shoe whenever he was afraid.

"Quentin!" Marcus was the one yelling at him this time. He put on his sweatpants and warm-up jacket and followed his parents and sisters out the front door. Practices had been fun, but now it was showtime, and everybody in the gym would be looking at him.

Paul was afraid Quentin might be nervous about his first game with the Terrors, so he took him aside before the buzzer and told him to pretend it was another practice and play like he had all week. "I'm going to let things get rolling and then put you in with the first subs," he said. "Don't feel any pressure. The first string will carry the weight."

At the beginning of the second quarter, the Terrors were down by six points. Paul motioned to Quentin and two other players to take the court. Jamie, Benny, and Malcolm dropped onto the bench and reached for their water bottles. James climbed over a few bleachers to grab Jamie by the shoulders. "Don't let them get those rebounds!" he said in his son's ear. "You grab those balls and put them right back in." Jamie nodded as he slurped water as quickly as he could.

Out on the court, the subs slid into their positions as Frankie passed the ball inbounds to Adam, who sent a quick pass to the other forward. The first shot on goal bounced around the rim and appeared headed to the eager hands of the opposing team's center, but Quentin stepped in front of him at the last minute, seized the ball, pivoted, and executed a perfect layup. The Terrors' fans cheered, and the teams ran to the other end of the court.

After a few passes around the foul circle, the point guard sent the ball to the center under the basket, but when he let the shot go, Quentin was in his face and batted the ball to Adam, who hurled a pass to Frankie, who was already down the court. A dash for the fast break, and Frankie gently laid the ball in the basket. The Terrors' fans were on their feet.

In the bleachers, four rows up from the team, Richard Campbell reached around Laura and slapped Marcus on the shoulder. "That's quite a player you've got there." Marcus smiled, pleased at the recognition but hoping the adults wouldn't raise their expectations for Quentin too high.

The opposing team's possession ended with an intercepted pass, and the Terrors were soon back under their basket. Adam sank a short jump shot, and the score was tied. Frank Jessop, sitting next to the team on the bench, could feel the boys' enthusiasm building. One more basket, and they'd be in the lead. Another shot block by

Quentin sent the Terrors back to their goal. Quentin ran in and out of the lane, waving for a pass. "Get it to Quentin!" Paul yelled, and Frankie tried, but the other center got a hand on the ball, deflecting it into the midst of the players. A swarm for the ball ensued, and Adam came up with it. He lobbed it over to Frankie, who got off an outside shot. The ball hit the edge of the rim, and Quentin tapped it in. Terrors were now up by two points.

"C'mere, Jamie," Paul called. "We need somebody taller to get the ball in to Quentin under the basket. I want you to go in for Adam at forward. Tell Frankie to pass you the ball, and then you fire it to Quentin under the basket. You got it?"

Jamie jumped up and ran to the scorers' table. The referee blew his whistle and motioned for him to come in. The opposing team threw the ball in play to their point guard, who faked out one of the Terrors, dribbled to the basket, and executed a neat layup. Back under their basket, the Terrors set up for the play Paul wanted. Frankie passed the ball to Jamie, who sent a bullet pass to Quentin, who laid the ball in the basket. "I knew that would work!" Paul punched Frank's arm and returned his assistant coach's huge grin.

At halftime, the Terrors were up by four points, a lead they managed to maintain until the end. When the buzzer went off, players and parents were all on their feet cheering. The team finally had a win. Paul gathered the boys together and breathed a sigh of joy at the expressions on their faces. Their eyes sparkled above their damp cheeks, but this time, Paul knew the moisture wasn't tears. "You see what we can do?" he said. "We're going to start our season right here and never look back."

"It's all because of Quentin," Frankie murmured.

"No." Paul looked first at Frankie and then at the others. "Having a new player may have given us a fresh spark, but you all had that spark today. You played like I know you can play. And we're going to work on some new plays next week that capitalize on that energy. Now, be proud of yourselves and enjoy the rest of your weekend. But before you go, bring your parents over here to meet Quentin and his parents."

"My dad already met them, and my mom's not here," Jamie said.

"Bring your dad over anyway. I want us all together for a few minutes."

"My mom's not here either," Benny whispered to his dad, "but you know that already."

"Everybody just gather 'round for a few minutes."

When the group had assembled, Paul pulled the Thomases to the front. "This is Marcus and Delia Thomas and their son, Quentin. I want them to meet all of you, and I want you to make them feel welcome. I'll start by saying I'm the coach, Paul Westover, and this is my son, Benny." He slapped Benny on the back and continued, "I'm sorry my wife, Meredith, couldn't be here today, but she had to work. She'll be here next time." A few folks clapped loudly. "Hold your applause 'til the end," Paul said.

"And that's my assistant coach, Frank Jessop," he pointed at Frank, "and his wife, Suzanne." Suzanne offered a deep curtsy.

"Where's Frankie?" Paul looked at the younger faces.

"In the head!" one of the boys yelled.

Paul nodded. "Our point guard, Frankie, is their son." He moved on to Lydia. "You probably remember Lydia Colton. I think Marcus met her at one of the practices this week. Her son is Malcolm, one of our forwards." Malcolm brushed his shaggy blond hair from his eyes and raised his hand. "Malcolm's father, Jeff, isn't here today, but he's a doctor, so maybe he had an emergency." Suzanne scowled at that remark. Jeff Colton wasn't one of her favorite people.

Paul ignored her and looked to see who was next. "Delia," he said, "this is James Parker. He's already met Marcus. His son is Jamie. You can spot him easily 'cause he's the tallest kid on the team." Jamie ducked his head in sort of a half nod. "His mom, Elaine, isn't here today, but she usually comes to the games. Laura and Richard Campbell"—he indicated who they were—are Adam's parents."

"Pretty boy Campbell," Benny said, causing Paul to grab him by the shoulders. Adam snatched his green cap from the bleachers and crammed it onto his head.

"Jason McBride is another forward," Paul said, "and this is his father, Sam." And on he went to introduce the other four players on the team and their parents. After the group dispersed, James and Frank were waiting for him.

"Nice to have some new talent," James said. "So, how do you plan to use him?"

"He's used to playing forward, but he did a good job at center today. I think he could play either position."

"Uh-huh. So, what about Jamie? Where do you see him?"

"I don't know. It's early yet." Paul shook his head. Why couldn't these parents enjoy the win and worry about the next game later?

"Don't worry, James," Frank said. "Jamie's one of the best players on the team. He'll always get plenty of playing time."

James shrugged. "See you at practice." And then he was gone.

"Shit," Frank said. "He's going to be at every practice, isn't he?"

"Yep. That he is."

Walking toward the door of the gym with his family, Quentin wasn't sure how he felt. He was glad they'd won, but they weren't his team. Just like this wasn't his gymnasium. As his gaze followed the dark, aged wood on the walls up to the towering ceiling and then slid back down the gleaming windows, he remembered the white walls and small windows of his school's gym in Greensboro. That gym was friendly and welcoming, whereas this one felt over-whelming and hollow. He hurried to get outside into the cold, clean air while his parents herded his sisters behind him.

In the car on the way home, Marcus and Delia raved about how well Quentin played, although he offered only the responses that manners required. At home, he went straight to his room, closed the door, and flopped onto his unmade bed. The walls of the room were bare, still showing nail marks from whatever the person who lived in the room before had hung there. Quentin's posters and photographs were still in a box in the corner. He told his mother he wasn't going to hang them yet because he wanted to repaint the room, but that wasn't the real reason. If he hung them, that meant he was there to stay, and he couldn't face that yet. Maybe what he needed was to put nothing from his old room in this new space. Then maybe he wouldn't miss the old room so much.

The only thing he liked about this room was the dormer that jutted out beside his bed. It provided a perfect lookout window for his brown and white beagle, Rambler. They'd been together six years, and Quentin couldn't imagine life without him. But you couldn't build your life around a dog.

After following Quentin upstairs, Rambler jumped on the bed beside him and lay with his head nuzzled against Quentin's thigh. Quentin absentmindedly rubbed the dog between his ears. Then he reached into the drawer in the bedside table for the latest issue of *Mad* magazine. Before long, Marcus knocked on the door. "Quentin, son, can I come in?"

"It's a free country."

Marcus opened the door and took a seat in the swivel chair next to Quentin's desk. Quentin continued flipping through the magazine. "What's wrong?" Marcus asked. "Your team won today. Why aren't you happy?"

"It's not my team," Quentin said. "My team's back in Greensboro. I mean, these guys are nice and all, but I don't fit in." He continued to flip through *Mad*.

"I know it's hard being the new kid." Marcus felt a pain in his stomach like he always did when one of his children was unhappy. "But give it some time. You'll get to know the other boys better, and they'll get to know you. Pretty soon you'll be just one of the guys."

"Dad! Are you blind?" Quentin hurled the magazine onto the floor. "I can never be one of the guys on this team. There's not another kid that looks like me."

Marcus went to the bed and sat next to his son. "Okay, so you're different in one way. But you're the same in a lot of others."

"I'm still their token Black guy. On my old team, half of us were Black. We had each other. I don't have anybody here."

"Let me tell you something. When I came to Foxrow Mills for interviews, the first thing I noticed was the lack of Black engineers. There were plenty of Black hourly workers out in the mill and a few in the offices, but no engineers. I hoped the company wasn't interested in me just because they needed diversity, but then I decided I didn't care. Even if that was the case, the job was an advancement for me with a better salary, and I was going to take it. And so far, it's worked out well. I don't know if I'm one of the guys yet, but I have friends, and they respect my work. The same thing will happen for you. Having the wind at your face isn't always a bad thing." Marcus put his arm around Quentin's shoulders and gave him a gentle hug.

Quentin shrugged himself free. He'd heard variations of these ideas most of his life, but this was the first time his dad had made them personal. Whether that made him feel better or worse, he wasn't sure.

4

With Christmas less than a week away, Lydia drove out to Foxrow farm to give Nancy Galloway a Christmas present. Nancy was the granddaughter of Henry Galloway, whose father had named the farm the same as his mill. Most people in Tanner referred to the mill as "the mill," so if anybody mentioned Foxrow, they usually meant the farm. The house on the farm hadn't changed much in the twelve years since Lydia first laid eyes on it, and it still impressed her with its genteel grandeur. The century-old oaks leading to the broad wraparound porch had grown even more majestic. Some of the boulder-sized boxwoods in the yard had died and been replaced by smaller bushes, but the flower garden was still radiant with season-appropriate flora, including winter jasmine and Christmas roses.

Lydia climbed the worn steps to the front door and twisted the vintage buzzer. The door flew open immediately. Nancy, dressed in a bright red turtleneck, beamed on the other side of the threshold. "Lydia, I've been waiting for you. Come see the new Christmas tree."

"Well, don't you look like Christmas itself?" Lydia said as she gave her a hug. Nancy took her hand and led her down the wide entry hall, past the living room, where Lydia caught a glimpse of the huge Christmas tree she was used to seeing at Foxrow. But Nancy kept pulling her farther down the hall, through the dining room, and into the large kitchen at the back of the house.

"See!" Nancy exclaimed. "This is the tree for Pansy and Marie. And me when I come in here after work to eat cookies. We're decorating it today, and you can help." The tree stood next to the fireplace at the rear of the room. About six feet tall, it was beautifully shaped and filled the space usually occupied by a ladder-back rocking chair, which had been moved to the other side of the hearth. Seeing the empty chair always made Lydia a little sad because it reminded her of Stella, who had been Nancy's caretaker when the women first met. But Stella had been at Foxrow since Nancy's father was a baby, and soon after Lydia got to know her, she retired. Marie, a woman not much older than Nancy, had taken her place.

Pansy, the Galloways' cook, was unpacking boxes of ornaments, mostly balls painted with winter scenes and cheery sayings. "Look at this one," Nancy said as she lifted a fragile sphere decorated with a horse and sleigh gliding through the snow. "It says 'Merry Christmas 1984.'"

"Don't you go taking 'em off the tree quick as I put 'em on," Pansy chided good-naturedly. The Afro-style halo of hair she'd had when Lydia met her was now a cap of tight curls.

Just as Lydia reached for an ornament, Nancy's mother, Caroline, came into the room. Lydia and Caroline's relationship had run hot and cold since the beginning. At first, Caroline suspected Lydia would take advantage of Nancy and end up hurting her, but she had warmed to her daughter's new friend as time went by. Her biggest objection to Lydia—the insistence that Nancy was capable of holding a job and should have one—turned out to be unfounded. Nancy loved her job at the "bloomer factory," as some townspeople called the underwear company. While Caroline wasn't wild about Lydia, she tolerated her. "I didn't know we had company," she said. "Hello, Lydia."

Lydia nodded in reply as Pansy asked, "How's Mr. Henry?"

"Resting, finally." At ninety years old, Henry was short on energy but not on fervor. His mind was still sharp, and his capacity for petulance was very much intact. Pansy's failure to cook his lunch hamburger to a perfect medium rare had brought on one of his usual tirades. Caroline had spent nearly an hour getting him settled down. Now she slid over to Nancy and kissed her cheek. "The tree is beautiful, darling. That was a great idea to put one in the kitchen."

Nancy beamed at the compliment, as she did whenever anyone was kind to her. "Help us decorate it, Mama."

"Not now. Getting Grandfather to bed has eaten up a lot of my time this afternoon, and it seems you have plenty of decorating help." Marie had finished with the lights, and now all four women were hanging ornaments.

Lydia wished she could stay longer, but she had to pick up Malcolm from basketball practice. She stayed another fifteen minutes, and after giving Nancy the Nancy Drew mystery book she had brought her, she left, letting herself out through the stately double front doors.

Basketball practices for the Terrors continued through the Saturday before Christmas. True to his word, James attended all of them. Lydia attended all except the Saturday practice. She needed that day to get ready for Christmas because Malcolm would be with her until noon on Christmas Day when he would go to his father's. Marcus had been to a few, but being new to his job, he had to put in long hours at work, which made it difficult for him to get away in time for practices. A surprise arrival at the Saturday practice was Jeff Colton, Malcolm's father. He came occasionally, but usually not on the same days Lydia came. Paul wondered how he knew she wasn't going to be there that day.

"I told him," Frank said. "She asked me to give Malcolm a ride because she couldn't make it, although she'd pick him up afterward. So, when Jeff wanted me to have a beer with him this afternoon, I asked him to meet me at practice. I thought Malcolm would enjoy having him here." His eyes followed the boys running drills under the basket.

"I didn't know y'all were buddies."

"We aren't, really, but he wants me to run for town council. He's been on it for several years now, and he says they need younger members. It's all a bunch of wrinklies."

"Wrinklies? That's a new one, but I'm sure it's true." Paul laughed. "So are you gonna do it?"

"Run for council? Probably. I'll see what he has to say about it today. Suzanne thinks I'm crazy to do it, but I think it would be good for my career at the mill. Get involved in town politics and all."

Paul had a hard time envisioning Frank as a politician, but you never know. Jeff was coming toward them now. Although he was a doctor by profession, he was a natural politician. He shook hands with Paul and Frank, flashing a warm grin. "Good to see you both," he said. "Congratulations on your last game. It was a stunner. You kept the lead through most of the second half. Looks like you've got quite an asset with your new player." He nodded toward Quentin.

"He's definitely an asset, but the whole team played better last Saturday. That's what we're working toward for the tournament." Paul turned to see if the boys were slowing down on the drills. "Excuse me. I think I'm needed on the court." He walked toward the team just as Malcolm gave his dad a discreet wave.

"Glad you could make it," Frank said to Jeff. "Have a seat with the other parents, and when practice is finished, we'll go over to the pool hall and have a beer."

"Sounds good." Jeff immediately spotted Marcus in the bleachers and climbed up to the third row to introduce himself. After introductions and a firm handshake, he climbed even higher to sit next to James. He and James had known each other since high school. Both Tanner natives, they'd gone to different colleges and ended up back in their hometown by different routes. James had been Jeff's first choice as a possible candidate for town council, but James wanted nothing to do with politics of any sort. "I'm better off playing straight down the middle," he'd said when Jeff tried to pressure him into running, "just like on the golf course." He also avoided any company politics at the mill. He saw his next career move as manager of operations, and he couldn't afford to make any enemies.

"What's new?" Jeff asked as he took a seat on the bleacher.

James shrugged. "Not much." He paused, undecided whether to say what was actually on his mind.

"How 'bout the new player? What do you think of him?"

Given an invitation, James couldn't help responding. "He's good, but I'm worried he's going to dominate the team. He's taller than most of our boys."

"Not Jamie."

"Yeah, but he's heavier."

"So what? I bet Jamie's faster. And if this new kid helps us win games, it makes all our guys look better." Jeff glanced at Marcus and hoped he couldn't hear their conversation.

"Or it could go the other way. He could be so good he makes the others look shabby. In any event, some of them are going to spend more time on the bench. Watch what Paul does when he has them scrimmage." Out on the court, the boys divided into two teams, with Quentin as center for one and Jamie as center for the other. "See. You can't have two centers on game day."

Still worried about Marcus, Jeff looked for a way to turn the conversation. "How's Elaine? I haven't seen her in a while."

"She's fine. To see her, though, you'd have to hang out at the church or with the PTA, and I doubt you do either." James smiled for the first time since Jeff sat down. "And now Laura Campbell's got her all involved with this project to get the people at our church to be friends with the people at the AME church in Copeland." He shook his head. "Oh, look. Speak of the devil. Here she comes now."

Jeff turned, expecting to see Elaine, but instead, Laura was making her way around the court. She waved at Adam, who was too busy playing to see her. After a brief pause in front of the group of parents scattered on the bleachers, she took a seat next to Marcus. "So good to see you again," she said. "We met at the game last Saturday. I didn't get a chance to talk with your wife, though. What's her name?"

"Delia," Marcus said. "I'm sorry you didn't get to speak with her. Maybe at the next game."

"Yes, yes. I hope so. I want to welcome you all to Tanner and invite you to attend Sunday morning church service with us. Have you found a church family here yet?"

Marcus suppressed a groan. "Delia and the kids have been here only a few weeks, and we've been spending all our time getting settled in. Also, the kids are busy with their new schools. I'm sure we'll visit churches eventually."

"Our church is Methodist, but we also have a Baptist church, a Presbyterian church, and a Catholic church in Tanner. There's an AME church over in Copeland, but that's a bit of a drive. To find a synagogue, you'd have to go to Charlotte, I think, but I doubt you're Jewish. You aren't, are you?"

"No, we're not."

"Then I hope you'll come to church with us as soon as you can. We'd love to have you in our congregation, and we're just starting a new program that I bet you'll like. We call it Cultural Bridge because, you see, we don't have much diversity in our church"—Laura could feel her cheeks turning pink at that admission—"and we're hoping to do something about that. We're joining together with members of the AME church I told you about to get to know each other. If you and Delia join this group, you'll get to know some of our members as well as some AME members. What do you think?"

Marcus knew this was going to happen. As soon as his family moved to town, people would be tripping over each other to put out the welcome mat. They certainly couldn't let anyone think they were less than congenial with this particular family. He didn't want to be ungracious, but he didn't want to rush into things, either, especially since Quentin felt so uncomfortable with the basketball team. Give the boy time to get comfortable with one group before pushing him into another. And Laura had made it pretty clear they'd likely be the only Black family in her church. Still, he worried about Delia. Since she hadn't been able to find a job, she'd be stuck at home for a while. "That's very nice of you," he said. "I'll talk it over with Delia and see what she thinks."

"Tell her I'll look for her at the game next Saturday. And Merry Christmas!" Laura smiled and left him to his thoughts. She didn't want him to feel like she was smothering him. Plus, Lydia was standing just inside the gym door, waiting for Malcolm. It would be nice to have a chat with her. They hadn't talked in a while. Practice would be over soon, so Laura hurried to catch her before she got away.

Marcus watched Quentin slip in and out among the other players, passing and catching the ball. He seemed to work well with them on the court. Now if he could just extend the teamwork off the court as well.

5

Two days after Christmas, Meredith Westover went to see her newest client in the county detention center. Just as she predicted, the judge granted the woman bail, but there was no one to pay it. She had spent the holiday in jail, and her daughter had spent it with a foster family in the next county. Being in another county meant she had to change elementary schools, but at least she was attending now. According to her first teacher, she had been absent more than present, which didn't bode well for her mother.

Social services workers had gone to the Charlotte address where the aunt supposedly lived, but the people in the house said they didn't know her. "What about Clarinda Morgan?" the workers had asked, offering the mother's name, but the people said they didn't know her either.

"She lived there a year ago," Clarinda insisted when she heard what happened. Her already sullen face had grown more mournful. "Guess she doesn't want any more to do with me."

Since her last visit, Meredith had followed Paul's advice and contacted the unemployment office, but a counselor told her there was nothing they could do for Clarinda until she was out of jail. She had to be ready to go to work. Meredith expected that, but she had to ask. Now she had to tell Clarinda.

The county detention center, known informally as the Valley Street jail, was a one-story, nondescript brick building on the outskirts of the county seat. Until she joined the public defender's office, Meredith had driven by there dozens of times and never really noticed it. Its only distinguishing characteristics were an American flag on a pole out front and the words "In God We Trust" emblazoned above the main entrance. The hallways inside were narrow and dark, leading past the administrative offices to the gray room where inmates could talk to their lawyers. The only spot of color in the room was a series of yellow daffodils painted along one wall as if someone had tried to add a little brightness to a really dismal atmosphere. Meredith wondered if the idea for the flowers came from a compassionate guard or an activist attorney. Whoever had done it, she was surprised, given what she knew of the rules in the jail, that it had ever been allowed. The first time she saw it, she smiled.

The room was empty when she arrived. She settled into her usual chair across from the video camera and waited. Clarinda, handcuffed, her thin red hair hanging about her face in stringy strands, entered a few minutes later, led by a guard. After removing the handcuffs, the guard, a slight woman whose khaki uniform seemed too large for her, said, "I'll be outside if anybody needs me." Then she left and closed the door.

Clarinda immediately turned her searching gaze to Meredith. "How's Lucy?" she asked. "Have you seen her?"

"No, I haven't seen her since the last time we talked. I imagine she's fine, though, just missing her mother. I'll check with Child Protective Services to make sure everything's all right. But in the meantime, we have to figure out a way to get you out of here. Have a seat, and let's talk."

Clarinda shuffled to the chair across the table from Meredith. Her pale complexion appeared sallow under the harsh fluorescent lights. "You promise you'll check on Lucy?"

"Yes, I promise." Meredith offered what she hoped was a reassuring smile. "Now tell me again why you left Lucy alone for what appears to be three days."

The only sound in the room was the hissing and popping of the lights. Meredith waited for Clarinda to construct her answer. All she'd said previously was that she'd heard there were better-paying jobs in Hickory and wanted time to check them out. Meredith needed more.

"Okay," Clarinda finally said. "I'll tell you again. One of my girlfriends said the restaurants in Hickory pay a lot more than restaurants around here, so I went over there to find a job." She slid down in the chair with one arm slung over the back. "I can't hardly take care of Lucy and me on what I make here."

"When was the last time you had a job?"

"I don't know. Six months ago, maybe."

"The unemployment office said they hadn't heard from you in over a year. They said you applied for unemployment in 1982, but they never heard from you again. No follow-up visits or phone calls to show you were looking for work, so they had to stop your payments. Why was that?"

Clarinda sat up straight, her expression stern. "What does that have to do with getting me out of here and back with Lucy?"

"Because we have to convince CPS you can be a responsible parent."

"Okay," Clarinda drawled as she slid down in the chair again. "I never called them because I had a job for a while."

"What were you doing?" Pulling information out of Clarinda felt like a tug-of-war.

"Working at Belk's."

"What happened to that job?"

Clarinda swallowed softly. "They fired me."

"Why?" Meredith continued to pull.

"I took a pair of pink socks for Lucy. She wanted to wear 'em to the first day of kindergarten. I was gonna pay for 'em with my next paycheck, but one of the other salesgirls saw me put 'em in my purse and reported me. They said they wouldn't call the police, but they fired me."

Thank God they didn't call the police, Meredith thought. *We don't need a shoplifting charge to contend with too.* Maybe there was some way she could use the incident to illustrate Clarinda's concern for Lucy, but it would be tricky. "So you haven't worked since Belk?"

Clarinda shook her head.

"Have you ever applied for a job at the mill? They seem to be hiring regularly."

"I can't do the same eight-hour shift every day. I need hours here and there so I can get my friends to keep Lucy. They can't always do it the same time every day."

Meredith shook her head at the irony of caring about child care for several hours each day and apparently not caring about child care for three whole days. "Why didn't you get your friends to keep Lucy while you went to Hickory? And what about your neighbor? She's the one who heard Lucy crying and called the police."

"I didn't think I'd be gone that long. And I did ask a few people, but nobody could."

"Why were you gone that long?"

"Nobody would hire me."

"Where were you staying?"

"With a friend." Clarinda hardened her defensive stare.

Meredith studied her client carefully. "Clarinda, do you do drugs? Is that why you couldn't come home for three days? Were you high the whole time?"

Clarinda stood up and turned toward the door. She liked Meredith, but she wouldn't let anybody accuse her of doing drugs. That was one thing she held tight to and was proud of. Her parents had used everything from marijuana to heroin to LSD. One of her earliest memories was pricking herself with a syringe she found on the bathroom floor. When she was eight, her father disappeared, and she never saw him again. Her mother said, "Good riddance," but Clarinda knew she missed him. In addition to the drugs, there was a lot of alcohol. When her mother got drunk, she would cry and talk about him. They'd never lived in one place long, but after he left, it seemed to Clarinda they moved every month, always to a smaller, darker apartment. Once, they got lucky and snagged a tiny house out in the country. A shack is how most people would have described it, but to Clarinda, it was a palace because it had a big yard where she could run and climb trees. Clarinda always hoped the drugs and alcohol wouldn't follow them to the next place, but they always did.

Her mother had gone from job to job with long stretches of unemployment, during which the drug use multiplied. Sometimes there was no money for food, but there was always money for drugs, or else a boyfriend would bring them over. At thirteen, Clarinda suffered a brutal case of pneumonia that forced her mother to take her to the emergency room. In addition to an antibiotic, the ER doctor gave her strict instructions to eat more. She was severely underweight. Horrified by what had happened, her mother cleaned herself up enough to get a job in the weave room at the mill in Tanner.

Two years later, Clarinda thought she should drop out of high school and get a job at the mill too, but her mother wouldn't let her. It wasn't long, however, before she got pregnant and had to drop out anyway. Somehow, through all her travails with her parents, she had managed to avoid the drugs that littered her home. Instead of seeing them as a way out, a way to ease the pain, she'd recognized them as the root of her mother's suffering. Once, when she was ten, she'd gathered up everything she could find, including a pouch of marijuana, a bag of heroin, two syringes, and a pint of gin, and thrown them into the trash. Furious when she came home and couldn't find any of her stashes, Clarinda's mother had torn through the apartment, screaming and slamming drawers and cabinet doors. Finally, she dragged Clarinda out from under the bed and demanded to know where her things were. Clarinda cried and said she didn't know, until her mother threatened to leave and never come back. Terrified at the prospect of being left alone, Clarinda came clean and pointed to the trash can. "But she didn't hit me," Clarinda later told a neighbor. "She never hit me."

"Where are you going?" Meredith asked as Clarinda moved toward the door.

"To get the guard. I want to go back to my cell."

"Wait a minute. We have other things to talk about. Just please tell me about the drugs. I can't help you unless you're honest with me. I have to know why you left your five-year-old daughter alone for three whole days."

Clarinda paused. "Well, it sure as hell wasn't because of drugs."

Meredith waited.

Clarinda slowly turned around. "Like I said, nobody would hire me. And then I got sick. Vomiting and diarrhea. I couldn't go home. I couldn't hardly stand up. Soon as I could drive, I went home, and Lucy was gone. My neighbor told me what happened, even admitted she was the one who called the police. I'll never speak to that bitch again. Now, can I go? You let me know when I can see Lucy. I mean that."

"Can anybody besides your friend vouch that you were sick? Did you see a doctor? Did you buy medicine at a pharmacy?" The friend would be a questionable witness, but a third party, particularly a doctor, would likely be believed.

"I was too sick to go to any doctor or drug store. If I could've done that, I'd have driven home. I told you I couldn't get off the couch. Now, when can I see Lucy?"

"I don't know when you'll be able to see Lucy. It depends on what the judge says. He could send you to prison, you know—child endangerment's a serious charge—but I'm going to try to get you probation. Even then, you won't get custody back right away. That's why we need to find you a job. And dependable child care. Is your rent paid up?"

"For now, but we'll most likely get kicked out soon." Tears began to trickle down Clarinda's cheeks. She wiped at them quickly with the rough sleeve of her prison sweater.

"Let me see what kind of relief I can get for you. I'll be back on Monday, and I hope I have something new for you. We should have a trial date by then. Stay optimistic." Meredith smiled as encouragingly as she could.

Clarinda knocked on the door, and the little guard led her away. After gathering her folders and notebook, Meredith left the jail. Her heart ached for Clarinda. She seemed so young and frightened behind the bursts of bravado. She couldn't be capable of deliberately leaving her daughter alone like that. Something had happened.

Maybe she really had been too sick to come home. But the little girl must have been terrified. The thought of Benny being in that situation almost made Meredith sick. She'd have to find out more about Clarinda.

When Meredith got home, Paul was in his office reading through the Terrors' playbook. He heard the door close and waited for her to pass by the office. "C'mere," he said. "See what you think about my ideas for Saturday." She tossed her coat and briefcase on the sofa and drifted toward his desk. "I've been going over these plays," he continued, "and I think some will work better with Quentin at center, and some will work better with Jamie. Some need bulk, and some need speed. What do you think of that?"

"You're the coach," Meredith said. "Do whatever you think is right." She laid her hand on his shoulder and began to massage the tense muscles. Sometimes she wished he had never agreed to coach this basketball team. It stressed him a lot more than his job did. He wanted to quit smoking, but as long as he was coaching, he never would.

"Well, Quentin's fast too, but I'm trying to figure out a way to rotate the players, at least the first string, so they all get to play a good part of the game." Paul lifted the cigarette from his horseshoe ashtray and took a drag.

"So Quentin and Jamie each get to play half the game?"

"No, I'll move them into forward positions for part of the game."

"Then Adam and Malcolm get less playing time." Meredith smiled. "I can tell you right now which parents you're going to hear from if you do that."

"Yeah, I know." Coaching the kids was often the easy part of Paul's job. Managing the parents was harder. "I'll see what Frank thinks. But I've got a feeling he's going to want to do whatever it takes to win."

"Well," Meredith said, "he's a parent too. And his son's a guard."

6

Regional holiday tournaments were a big deal for North Carolina AAU basketball teams. They were always played on the weekend between Christmas and New Year's Day unless the holidays fell on a weekend, and then tournament games were played during the week. Locations were moved around among middle-sized colleges in the area so as not to give a home-court advantage to any team. This year, the Terrors' tournament was being played at Lenoir-Rhyne College, a coed liberal arts school about thirty miles from Tanner.

Adam Campbell was the first team member to arrive at Lenoir-Rhyne on the day of the Terrors' first game. Wearing his trademark green cap, he followed his parents and younger sister from the two-acre parking lot into a large red-brick building. They entered the building through a brick archway directly beneath a bright sign that proclaimed "Home of the Bears." Inside, the gym was as bright as the sign. The floor and bleachers were painted red and black, obviously the Bears' colors. An array of championship banners hung above the bleachers, which were dotted with parents and friends of the two teams currently on the court.

Laura Campbell looked for other members of the Terrors and, seeing none, led her family to seats behind one of the baskets. "Watch these teams," she said to Adam. "You may be playing one of them next. See if you can figure out what their forwards are doing so you're ready to guard them. There! Watch number 42 on the red team. His team's winning." Adam glanced at number 42, a tall boy with blond hair, but wasn't impressed. He'd wait until he was actually facing an opponent on the court before he tried to figure out what the guy was doing.

Jamie and his parents arrived next, followed by the rest of the team, each with one or two parents in tow. While they waited for the final buzzer on the current game, Paul gathered the players around him. "Keep up the spirit from our last game," he said. "Stay sharp and play like a team." Ten minutes later, they were out on the court warming up. The parents moved to the center-court bleachers, and Paul and Frank positioned themselves where they could watch the Terrors and the opposing team on opposite sides of the court.

"So, are you gonna run the new substitution plan?" Frank asked.

"Why wouldn't I? It's what we practiced."

"Just brace yourself for afterward."

"Yeah. Shit."

The referee blew his whistle, and the game began. Paul started his usual first-string lineup and kept Quentin on the bench. Halfway through the quarter, he sent in Quentin at center, moved Jamie to forward, and pulled Adam out. At the end of the quarter, the Terrors were ahead by six points. To start the second quarter, he put in Quentin at center, Adam at forward, and held Jamie out. Three minutes before the end of the half, he put Jamie in Malcolm's position as power forward. When the buzzer sounded for halftime, the Terrors were up by eight.

While Paul and Frank spoke with the team, the other parents moved around to talk with each other. Laura made a beeline for Delia Thomas. "I'm so glad y'all moved to Tanner," she said. "I think you'll be a great addition to our town."

Because we're Black or because my son is a good basketball player? Delia wondered. "Thank you," she said. "We're enjoying getting to know the townspeople. Tell me something about you. Please remind me which boy on the team is your son."

"Adam," Laura said. "The one with the wavy dark hair." She pointed at Adam's back in the team huddle. "Number 15. He's one of the starting forwards."

Delia nodded. "And what about you? What are your interests?"

"I guess you could say I'm a professional volunteer." Laura chuckled. "I spend a lot of time helping out at my church. That's what I want to talk with you about. Would you and your family like to come with our family to Sunday morning service next Sunday? We go to First United Methodist on Hill Street. I'd ask you for tomorrow, but this weekend is going to be so busy with the tournament and all." She laid her hand lightly on Delia's arm.

Delia wanted to refuse, but the expression on Laura's face was so eager she couldn't bring herself to do it. And she didn't want her family to get the reputation of being standoffish. "We'd be delighted," she said. "I assume it's an eleven o'clock service. We'll meet you there around ten forty-five. Will that be good?"

"Excellent!" Laura said. "And I'd also like to tell you about our new Cultural Bridge program." Marcus had already told Delia about Cultural Bridge. It sounded good in theory, but Delia wondered what it would actually accomplish if the two congregations were located so far apart. She guessed she shouldn't judge without knowing more about it, so she listened while Laura detailed the plans for the group.

Meanwhile, Suzanne and Lydia, who'd been sitting together throughout the first half of the game, talked about Lydia's visit to Foxrow. They'd been close friends ever since Lydia moved to Tanner, and Suzanne had been a witness to Lydia's up-and-down relationships with the Galloway family. When her description of the tree decorating began to wind down, Suzanne brought up her conversation with Meredith before Christmas. "She asked me if any of the parents doubted Paul's ability to coach since we lost the first three games. She's afraid he thinks they doubt him, and it's really bringing him down. Nobody doubts him, do they?"

"You know this crowd. If they did, they'd probably tell him about it. If you ask me, I think the league's way too competitive. I didn't want Malcolm to play, but he begged me to let him. Paul was one reason I gave in. I didn't think he would be as rough on the players as some coaches are. Some of these men shouldn't be working with children at all!" Lydia felt like the temperature in the gym, which was already warm, had gone up a few degrees.

"You don't think that of Frank, do you?" Suzanne was horrified that her friend might think her husband was cruel to kids.

"No, but you know how some guys are, even some dads. Even Malcolm's dad sometimes. Remember when the soccer coach asked Jeff to stop yelling at Malcolm so much? I think that may be why Jeff doesn't come to many of Malcolm's games. He gets so wound up."

When the buzzer sounded to begin the second half, Paul sent his starting lineup onto the court. The Terrors got the ball first, but when Adam missed his shot, the center from the other team grabbed the rebound and sent a powerful pass to the point guard down court. With a few quick passes, the ball was in to one of the forwards under the basket, who dropped it through the net.

Frank sat with his chin resting on his fist. "They're cold," he said to Paul, who had moments earlier been calling out which play to run. "Something drained out of 'em during halftime. We gotta get it back."

"You think I don't know that?" Paul said, a little testier than he intended. Then he signaled to the referee. "Time-out!" In the brief huddle, he went over with the boys the plays they needed to run. "And Jamie, don't let that center get in your face!"

Back on the court, the opposing team was still in command. The Terrors managed to make a few baskets, but they couldn't answer all the points from the other side. Soon they were down by six points. "You know what you gotta do," Frank said to Paul. "Send in Quentin. It's his turn, anyway."

Paul wanted to wait a little longer before subbing, but Frank was right. He had to do something, or it might be too late. "Quentin," he called. "Go in for Jamie."

Quentin took off, and Jamie plopped down on the bench, his face red and angry. "That center's all over me," he said. "Why don't they ever call a foul?"

"It's okay," Paul said. "Get some water."

Out on the court, Frankie brought the ball down for the Terrors. He passed to Benny, initiating one of the "Quentin plays." The next pass went to Malcolm, who sent it over to Quentin. The other center tried to get between him and the basket, but Quentin was a step ahead and put the ball through the hoop. For the next few minutes, the teams exchanged baskets until Frankie sank a three-pointer, and Quentin intercepted the inbounds pass, whirled around, and banked the ball off the backboard into the goal. The Terrors were up by three. Paul and Frank were on their feet, cheering along with most of the other parents.

As the game continued, the Terrors barely managed to hold on to their slim lead. With two minutes left, Paul said, "I guess I'd better put in the subs."

"Don't do it," Frank said. "Not if you wanna win. Not now. They've got a rhythm going, and if you substitute, you'll ruin it."

Paul looked at his subs, especially Jamie, sitting forlornly on the bench. Well, maybe they weren't all forlorn since they were watching the game intensely, but he felt their longing. Was it better to boost team morale by doing everything he could to ensure a win or to give everybody a taste of the battle they had trained for? Gazing at the subs, he also caught a glimpse of James Parker in the stands, glaring at him and Frank. *I can't worry about the parents right now*, he thought and turned back to the game. When the Terrors' lead dropped to two, he made his decision. No subs. He called one more time-out to go over the best plays again and saved his last time-out in case he needed it at the end. Fortunately, he didn't. The Terrors finished the game two points ahead, which advanced them to the semifinals that night.

"Good game, Coach," Frank said as he slapped Paul on the back. "Let's go eat."

Their next game was at 6:30, which gave the team and parents a couple of hours for dinner. They'd made reservations at a small pub not far from the college. The Campbells and Thomases arrived first, with Laura still chattering about the church. Marcus moved closer to Richard to find something else to talk about, and they settled on the history of Tanner until the waiter came and Richard ordered pizzas for everyone. Paul and Frank stayed behind to sign the scorebook and double-check the time of the next game. As they were leaving, Paul saw James waiting under the brick arch. "God-damn," he whispered to Frank. "Do you think he'll go after both of us or just me?"

"Don't care," Frank said. "We did the right thing."

"Got a minute?" James said to both of them as they drew near. They stopped in front of him and waited. "What are you doing to my son?"

"Nothing," Frank said. "What do you think we're doing?"

James looked at Paul. "You kept him on the bench the whole second half, and he's the best player you've got."

"I don't know about…" Frank started, but Paul interrupted him.

"The team was doing well the second half, and I didn't want to interrupt that. Jamie will get to play tonight."

"Let's hope so," James said. "This team needs him." He pulled the hood of his parka over his head and walked away.

"Was that a threat?" Frank asked when James was far enough away not to hear.

"Who knows?" Paul said. "I guess the worst he can do is take Jamie off the team, but he won't do that. He just likes to talk big."

"If you say so, but I'm not sure."

The sun was sinking below the horizon when the men arrived at the pub. Pink streaks in the sky announced a chilling drop in temperature as the warm rays disappeared. Paul pulled open the heavy door and welcomed the rush of heat from inside. The pub was filled with basketball players, their families, and friends. Fortunately, the college students who usually packed the place on Saturday nights were at home on winter break, or there'd be no room for the basketball crowd. Paul and Frank squeezed through the wall-to-wall bodies and found the tables where the Terrors sat. Their wives had saved them seats with the other parents. A gentle wave of applause arose when they sat down. They nodded their appreciation and asked for the pizza to be passed.

The noise in the room was so loud that conversation was difficult, but the parents all tried to talk with each other—all, that is, except James, who sat in silence at the far end of the table, away from the coaches. His wife, Elaine, kept telling him to snap out of it, but he couldn't. Jamie had worked too hard to be ignored. He knew this was coming the minute he saw Quentin play. He tried to believe Paul knew what a talent he had in Jamie, but he couldn't be sure. And he hoped the high school varsity coach hadn't been at the game. Probably, he wouldn't come until the final game tomorrow. He was chewing on a slice of pizza that tasted like straw when he saw one of the other AAU coaches working his way toward him. *Oh, shit,* he thought because he knew what was coming.

"Sorry I didn't get to see Jamie play more," the coach said when he finally popped out of the crowd. "Is he hurt?"

"No, he's not hurt," James murmured. "You'll see him play more tonight."

"I hope so." The coach smiled and turned back into the crowd. His team was one of the ones James was considering trying to move Jamie to next year. He had a solid reputation as a molder of good players, and James wanted that for Jamie.

The pizza was gone, and Paul was rounding up the players to return to the gym. "No, we're not ordering more. You don't want to overeat, or you'll be barfing all over the court." The team let out a collective groan and put on their coats.

Inside the gym, the current game was starting the fourth quarter. The Terrors had forty-five minutes before their game, so Paul told them to rest. Quentin sat down on the bleachers next to his dad, but Marcus told him to go join his team. "Go on," he said. "Y'all have to be a team off the court as well as on." Quentin shook his head and did what he was told.

"Don't push him," Delia whispered to her husband. "Let him make his own way."

"He has to accept this," Marcus said. "We're not moving back to Greensboro."

Meanwhile, Paul and Frank sat alone, strategizing for the next game. Or maybe *agonizing* was a better word. "So what's our substitution plan?" Paul asked.

"Do what you have to do to win," Frank said. "This team has a better record than the last one."

Paul knew that to win, he needed Quentin in as much as possible. But Jamie deserved to play. "I'm going to try a combination that worked well in Quentin's first game with us." His mind was made up.

When the buzzer sounded, Paul sent in Quentin at center and Jamie at forward, which meant keeping Adam on the bench. "Why isn't he starting Adam?" Laura Campbell muttered to her husband, Richard.

"Relax," Richard said. "Adam'll get to play." Having Adam on the bench actually worked for Richard because he could read the paperback book he'd brought without feeling guilty, as long as Laura didn't keep interrupting.

Six minutes into the game, the Terrors were up by eight. Paul pulled Jamie, Malcolm, and Benny to send in three subs, including Adam. *I told you so,* Richard thought, but he didn't say it. Quentin was playing a stellar game, which helped keep the Terrors ahead, so Paul left the subs in until halftime.

While the team rested, the parents talked to each other, but most stayed where they were. Maybe they had said everything they needed to say to each other during the first game and dinner, or maybe they were just tired. Laura was the only one who left her seat when she climbed over the bleachers to get closer to the team and motioned to Adam to join her. "You're doing great," she said. "I don't know why Coach didn't start you, but you're showing him what you can do now. Just keep it up."

James Parker leaned back on his elbows, propped on the

bleacher behind him, and silently fumed. Finally, he said to Elaine, "Why's he keeping Quentin in all the time?"

"He didn't sub for Frankie, either," Elaine replied.

"Yeah, but Frankie's our point guard. We need him to call the plays."

"Don't second-guess Paul. He's the coach. Let him do his job."

"Let's see how he does his job in the second half."

Paul started the second half with the same lineup he had at the beginning of the game. Seven minutes in, he sent Adam in for Jamie, but four minutes later, the Terrors' lead began to slip. Quentin was getting open, but Malcolm and Adam were having trouble getting the ball to him. "Go in for Malcolm and get the ball to Quentin!" Paul yelled at Jamie. Jamie did what he was told, and the Terrors held the lead until the end.

"Congratulations, guys!" Frank shouted as the team came off the court. "We're headed to the finals. This tournament's ours!" Tired as they were, the boys clapped and punched each other in the arm as they put their clothes on over their uniforms.

Paul gave them all high-fives and hugged Benny. "The season's looking up, isn't it?" he said to his son.

James and Elaine collected Jamie and started for the door, but Jamie ran ahead to walk with Malcolm and Frankie. "See," Elaine said when he was gone, "Jamie got to play a lot in the second half."

"You know why, don't you?" James said. "Paul sent him in to make Quentin look good. And that's what he did. I'm sure Quentin was high scorer again, but that's what happens when you play the entire game, and the other players set you up."

Later that night, Marcus and Delia Thomas sat alone in their living room. Their daughters had gone to bed as soon as the family returned from the basketball game, and Quentin was in his room watching television. They had sworn they would never let their kids have TVs in their rooms, but the twelve-inch Zenith was a consolation prize for making him move. "Give him something to be excited about," Delia had told Marcus, "and he'll need more entertainment at home until he makes a few friends."

They looked for something to watch on the TV in the living room, but when *Fantasy Island* and *Saturday Night at the Movies* didn't catch their interest, they sat in the soft light of the table lamps, glancing through magazines. Before long, Marcus was staring at the wall. "Quentin played well today, didn't he?" he said.

Delia folded her magazine, knowing he was asking for a longer conversation. "He did. I just wish he was happier about it."

"He's happy. Didn't you see the smile on his face?"

"During the game. But not so much afterward. It would almost be better if he wasn't such a good player. Then he wouldn't stand out so much. I know he feels like an outsider."

"How do you know that?"

"Mothers just know. A mother's only as happy as her saddest child."

"Now don't you go getting all depressed. This move is going to be good for all of us."

Don't go getting depressed. Delia had heard some form of that command more times in the past year than she cared to remember. Whenever she told her mother about her concerns, her mother always said, "The Lord won't give you more to deal with than you can bear. You need to pray on it." Praying was fine, but so far it hadn't gotten rid of Delia's negative feelings. Sometimes she was so tired of having to be the strong Black woman that everybody thinks of when they think of Harriet Tubman, Rosa Parks, Toni Morrison, and so many Black grandmothers with their abundant love and perseverance.

"Do you think being the standout player today was good for Quentin? Will it help him adjust to being here?" she asked.

"I think it's better to be the best player than the worst."

"I don't want the other boys to resent him."

"They won't," Marcus said. *Unless it drifts down from the parents,* he thought, but he wouldn't say that out loud. "I was proud of him today, and I think being a good player will win more friends for him than it'll lose."

"They better not mistreat him."

"Delia, he's thirteen years old. He's faced insults before, probably worse than anything he's going to hear from these kids. It's good they can't criticize him about his ability. And they won't mistreat him." *Because if they do, they'll have me to answer to.*

7

Because Regional AAU holiday tournaments were a big deal in North Carolina, coaches and players from teams that had been eliminated or played in other age brackets often came to the final games. Local people from the area where the game was played sometimes came too. Thirty minutes before the 1984 fourteen-and-under final game began, the Lenoir-Rhyne gym was nearly half-filled with spectators. Malcolm looked around the bleachers and shuddered. He'd never played in front of that many people before. Lydia heard the deep breaths he was taking and put her hand on his shoulder. "Don't be nervous," she said. "It's a game just like any other."

Malcolm was beginning to get his breathing under control when Jeff Colton entered the gym. He had told Malcolm he would try to make the game, but Malcolm was never sure if he would show up or not. As a doctor, he had a lot of last-minute responsibilities, or so he said. Malcolm couldn't help feeling more pressure to play well when his dad was there. Jeff liked sports and sometimes took Malcolm to Durham to see his alma mater's Blue Devils play. Malcolm loved those games and wished he and his dad could see more of them.

Jeff was headed toward Malcolm and Lydia when Paul told the boys to start warming up, so he had to settle for a brief slap on the shoulder before Malcolm dashed out onto the court. Lydia found a seat higher on the bleachers so she could have a better view of the game, and Jeff joined her there. "How was your Christmas?" he asked.

"Nice," Lydia replied. "Especially since Malcolm doesn't get up at dawn anymore. I was actually up before he was this year." She smiled gently, causing Jeff to wish that he had been there with her. He had never gotten over losing her, and he never completely understood why she left him. If anything, he should have been the one who no longer wanted to be married to her. But he did, at least until enough years had passed that he could accept his fate, and the longing subsided into a chronic melancholy. For a while, he considered moving out of town so he wouldn't have to see her, but that would mean leaving Malcolm, which would create another hole in his life. He also loved his small-town medical practice, and finding another one of those wouldn't be easy. So, he stayed.

"We had a good time after Malcolm came to my house," he said. "I think he liked the present I gave him."

"Air Force Ones? Of course he did." Lydia still couldn't believe Jeff had given their son such an expensive pair of basketball shoes. "He's hardly had them off since Christmas."

"Maybe they're bringing him luck. The team's done well to make it to the finals. I heard from James, though, that Paul's depending a lot on the new kid. How's Malcolm been playing?"

You'd know if you'd been here, Lydia wanted to say, but she didn't. "He's playing well. He scored eight points in the last game."

"That's good. How many did the new kid score?"

"The new kid's name is Quentin," Lydia said. "And I don't know how many points he scored. Probably a lot."

"Well, he's got a lot going in his favor. Look at him. He's tall and heavy, and he's Black, which means he has a lot of natural athletic ability."

Lydia sighed at Jeff's last remark but said nothing. The referee had called for starting lineups to take the court, and she wanted to see who Paul would send in. Jamie led the way, followed by Malcolm, Frankie, Benny, and Quentin. The opposing team wasn't any bigger than the Terrors, but some of them looked like they were already well into puberty. Paul had heard that several of them were ninth graders with birthdays late in the year, so they could be as much as a year older than his players. Maturity meant more muscle mass, so they could be stronger.

They obviously had something going in their favor because they won the opening jump, brought the ball down the court, and didn't bother to run a play. The point guard flipped the ball over to the shooting guard, who got off a perfect jump shot that was all net. "Jesus!" Frankie couldn't help saying. It seemed like a bad omen for the game to start that way.

"Benny!" Paul yelled at his son. "Get in that guy's face. Why'd you let him get that shot off?" Benny nodded and looked to Frankie to see which play he was going to call. He hoped Frankie didn't expect him to pull off a jumper like the other shooting guard did, especially since the guy was tracking him like a dog. Instead, Frankie called a Quentin play, which meant a quick pass to Jamie, a fake, and then a bullet pass to Quentin, who jumped above the opposing center and put the ball in the hoop without ever touching the ground.

"Al-l-l-l right!" Frankie cried.

The game went back and forth, up and down the court, with each team scoring when they had the ball.

"We have to force them into some errors," Frank said to Paul. "Or intercept a pass. We need a way to get ahead." Just then, the opposing team made their own attempt to break out of the rut. One of their forwards dropped back behind the three-point line, leaving his defender in the dust with the help of a well-placed pick. A short pass from the point guard, and he let fly a beautifully arced shot. Only problem was it hit the rim and bounced back into play. Quentin timed his jump perfectly and pulled the ball out of the air, elbows pointed to ward off any would-be stealers.

"Now's our chance," Paul said. "Stay calm, guys, and get it in the basket."

Whether they heard what their coach said or not, they followed his command. A smooth play worked the ball into Jamie, who laid it right in. The Terrors were up by two.

"See what he can do if you give him a chance?" James said to Meredith, loud enough that he hoped Paul could hear him.

A few rows up in the bleachers, Laura said to Richard, "Maybe now they'll put in Adam. The others have to be tired, especially Quentin."

"Let me know if he does," Richard said and continued reading his magazine.

Suzanne Jessop sat with Meredith Westover, two coaches' wives with more invested in the game than anyone else. They weren't talking much, however, with each engrossed in her own thoughts. With so many spectators at the game, Meredith knew that whether the Terrors won or lost, Paul's coaching would be scrutinized and commented on for days to come. Suzanne knew some of that scrutiny would fall on Frank too, but not nearly as much as on Paul. And Frank wasn't as sensitive to what other people thought as Paul was. No, she was thinking more about Frankie and what winning this game would mean to him. Sports, especially basketball, were Frankie's whole world. He struggled in school. His happy disposition and gregarious personality often hid his difficulties from his many friends, but not from him. He knew he was different. Officially, he was diagnosed with a learning disability in reading and language arts, but to him, his difference meant he had difficulty keeping up with all the assigned reading in English and history classes. Even in science, which was his favorite class, the textbook sometimes stumped him. He needed achievement in his life, and winning this regional tournament would be a big deal for him. Just before halftime, when Frankie intercepted a pass and dropped the ball into the basket, Suzanne's heart raced because she knew Frankie's was racing too.

During halftime, Paul chose his words to the boys carefully, praising them for their four-point lead but reminding them they'd have to work hard to make sure the lead didn't slip away. Adam almost asked if he was going to get to play this half, but he backed down at the last second, afraid he might make Paul angry. He just wasn't used to sitting out an entire half. He was running his fingers through his wavy hair in short, jerky movements when Paul called up the players to start the second half.

This time, it was Jamie, Adam, Frankie, Benny, and Malcolm. "Why aren't you putting Quentin in?" Frank hissed at Paul. "We're only up by four. We can't afford to keep our best player on the bench."

"It's only the beginning of the half," Paul said. "We've got lots of time. I may send in a few other subs for a minute or so to save our regulars' energy for the end."

Frank usually trusted Paul's judgment, but not this time. "Are you crazy?" he asked. "If we play this game right, we can win the tournament, which would be a first for any Tanner team since I can't remember when. Plus, this is the best chance we're going to have for the best coaches from the older teams to see our really good players play. They'll be looking for recruits next year."

Paul smiled a sly smile. "You're not just talking about Quentin, are you? You're talking about Frankie."

"Of course I'm talking about Frankie. And about Benny too. We want them to get on good AAU teams in high school. The college coaches always look there."

"Benny'll never play college basketball," Paul said.

"He could. And if he doesn't, then you want him to have the time of his life in high school. You want him to win!"

"We can win this game. Just watch."

Up in the stands, Elaine Parker sat between her husband and Laura Campbell. The ball was moving up and down the court so fast that the three of them looked as if they were watching a tennis match instead of a basketball game. Both teams were scoring with each possession and wasting no time getting down to their goal when they got the ball. Finally, the referee called a foul, which brought the game to a halt, and the scorekeeper sounded the buzzer to let in two substitutes for the Terrors. "Don't sub," Elaine said softly. "Please don't sub."

"Don't sub," Laura repeated in a louder voice.

The fresh players ran into the game, sending Malcolm and

Benny to the bench. Jeff Colton nudged Lydia. "Must be giving Malcolm a rest. Saving him for the big finale."

"Or maybe he wants to give the other boys a chance to play," Lydia fired back.

"Not in this league. In fact, I can't figure out why he's keeping the new kid on the bench."

"His name is Quentin," Lydia said.

The shooter sank both free throws, cutting the Terrors' lead to two points. The game moved ahead at a slower pace, and the Terrors began to slide behind.

"I told you not to sub," Laura said and nodded at Elaine. Richard Campbell looked around to see if the parents of the subs were sitting nearby. He was relieved to see that they weren't.

Realizing it was time to do something, Paul called up Quentin and Benny to bring the subs back to the bench. "Tell Jamie to move to forward," he said to Quentin. "And tell Frankie to run the Quentin plays."

On the court, Frankie called the first play, which sent Benny and Malcolm to screen for Quentin and Adam near the foul circle. Quentin and Adam used the screens to pop outside the three-point line, followed by Benny and Malcolm moving to the left side of the goal as Frankie passed the ball to Quentin, who was already moving toward the goal on the right side, about a half step ahead of his defender. Two seconds later, he gently laid the ball in the basket.

"Atta boy, Quentin!" Frank yelled.

Marcus patted Delia's hand and smiled. No matter what she thought, he was sure being the best player on the team was good for Quentin. It would motivate the other boys to accept him. Delia was waiting for what she considered to be a true sign of acceptance—an invitation from one of his teammates to a pickup game or a movie. So far, he hadn't heard from any of them.

The next play Frankie called sent Adam to screen for Quentin near the basket. Quentin rolled away from the screen and executed a perfect hook shot.

"Damn good player," Jeff said. "But I thought Paul gave Malcolm a rest so he could put him in at the end. When's he going to do it?"

Lydia wished Jeff would go sit with one of the other men. "Paul's trying to win the game," she said, "and he'll do it however he wants to."

With two minutes left, the Terrors were up by two points until the opposing team intercepted a pass and capitalized on a fast break to tie the score. "Run your plays!" Paul yelled.

"So only one person gets a chance to shoot?" James said. "What about the rest of the team?"

Richard looked around Elaine and Laura and said, "Shut up, James."

Minutes slipped away as the Terrors fought to keep the score tied. "Watch your defense!" Paul yelled. "Don't let 'em score." Finally, one of their players missed his shot, and Quentin immediately had the rebound, but there were only thirty seconds left in the game. "Play for the last shot!" Paul yelled as the clock ticked down. With twelve seconds left, a player on the opposing team slapped at the ball in Benny's hands and deliberately hit him on the arm.

"They picked Benny because they think he's the least likely to make the free throws," Meredith said to Suzanne. Thinking of all the practicing he did in the backyard, she added, "They may be surprised."

"Come on, Benny. Come on, Benny," Frank chanted as he paced in front of the bench. Fans of the opposing team began kicking the bleachers to throw off Benny's concentration. Benny adjusted his glasses and wiped sweat from below his eyes. He made himself stare just at the basket because if he saw any of the crowd, some yelling, some standing in tense silence, he'd panic. There were so many of them. The referee blew his whistle, and Benny released the ball. The other players jumped into the lane for no reason because the ball bounced off the backboard and straight into the basket, just like Benny's dad had taught him to do. Now the noise rose to a roar.

The referee tossed Benny the ball for his second shot. Benny adjusted his glasses again. Maybe that was his good luck charm. The ball went up toward the basket, but it was a hair to the right and bounced off the side. Quentin grabbed it and put it right back up. This time, it hit where it was supposed to, dropping through the net for two more points. The opposing guard took it out of bounds as quickly as he could and hurled it down the court, but it was too late. The buzzer sounded.

The Terrors on the bench jumped up and ran with Paul and Frank to embrace their teammates. Jamie seized Benny, lifted him off the ground, and whirled him around. "You did it, man. You did it, man," he kept saying. Benny couldn't believe this was happening to him. He was never the star, always the guard in the shadows.

Caught up in the moment, Quentin hugged Frankie and Adam and then backed away, surprised at what he had done. For a few seconds, he stood frozen until Malcolm grabbed him from behind. "Way to go, Quentin!" he shouted. "We couldn't have done it without you."

By that time, the parents were on the court too, congratulating the boys and the coaches. Quentin slid over to Marcus and Delia, who hugged him at the same time. "That's the way to show your stuff when it counts," Marcus said.

Over the loudspeaker, the tournament chairman asked everybody to remain in the gym for the presentation of trophies and for the winning team to stay on the court. The Terrors' parents retreated to the sidelines as Paul said, "You accept the trophy, Frankie. You're our leader." Frankie was happy to comply, and the photograph of the moment showed Frankie, who was one of the shortest players on the team, holding the trophy high above his head as his teammates clustered around him.

When the boys returned to their parents, a group of men surrounded Marcus and Delia. "Who are they?" Jeff asked

"Don't you know?" James's frown pulled his eyebrows closer together. "They're coaches of older AAU teams, and one's from the high school."

Just then, Quentin walked up, and the group absorbed him too.

"I knew this was going to happen," James said. "It was only a matter of time."

While the men talked to Quentin and Marcus, Delia slipped to the edge of the group. Laura immediately came over to her. "You must be very proud of Quentin," she said. "He's so talented. And in basketball, of all things. It could be a great ticket to college and other successes for him."

"We think he'll have a lot of avenues to success," Delia said.

"Of course he will. Don't forget you're joining us for church next Sunday. We're looking forward to it."

"We are too," Delia lied. When she told Quentin they were going to church with the Campbells, he said he wasn't going. "We'll be like five grains of pepper in a salt shaker!" Delia told him he had no choice. This was a command performance.

"See you Sunday," Laura said and went to join Richard.

As they left the gym, Richard asked, "What the hell's the matter with James?"

"What do you mean?"

"The past few games, he's been all over Paul. Yelling at him, making snide comments."

"If I had to guess, I'd say he's upset about the favoritism on the team." Laura looked around to see where Adam was.

"It's not favoritism. James just can't handle the fact that Jamie's not the star player anymore."

"You can't be the star if you don't get to play. Looked what happened to Adam today."

"Adam did fine. He scored a few points, and his team won. It's supposed to be a team sport, not a showcase for high-pressure parents and their kids."

"I just hope one of those high-pressure parents doesn't explode," Laura said.

8

Laura considered inviting Marcus and Delia to the second Cultural Bridge meeting but decided attending church was a better way to begin their relationship. She'd told them about Cultural Bridge so they'd have time to think about it. She didn't want to push them too hard. Plus, Elaine said it was better to do their initial planning for the group with the original members who had come up with and agreed to the idea.

The meeting was held at the AME church because the first meeting had been in Tanner, and Elaine thought having the second meeting in Copeland would be a good way to show the AME members that the United Methodist members wanted everything about the group to be on equal footing. Laura told Richard he should go with her, but he said he didn't need to be in on the planning. He'd go when the real meetings started. "The only thing I would suggest is that the group needs to have a project. Social psychology shows people who have a common goal reduce tension and bond together."

"We have a project," Laura said. "We're planning a Martin Luther King Day celebration."

"Okay. I guess that's enough, but you might think of some service project too."

"I thought you didn't want to be in on the planning." Laura gritted her teeth. Richard could be so annoying with his philosophical, hands-off approach to life.

James told Elaine the group smacked too much of politics for his tastes, not in the sense of government but as in trying to force something on the community, but he might change his mind after he saw more of what they planned to do. So, Elaine and Laura drove to Copeland together.

The church was an old-fashioned place of worship built in the 1920s. As such, the two front doors opened directly into the sanctuary, a dimly lit room with deep red carpet, dark oak pews, and an intricately carved chancel rail. The space in front of the rail was strewn with assorted metal music stands.

Sharon Robinson, a large older woman, met Elaine and Laura at the back pew and led them through the sanctuary to a smaller room on the other side. A young Black couple, still in their twenties, Elaine guessed, were sitting in folding chairs at a round table. They hadn't attended the first meeting, and when the women from Tanner sat next to them, they introduced themselves as Erlene and Alfred Duncan. Sharon went back to the sanctuary and soon returned with four more members from Tanner. A few minutes later, another AME couple, Candice and Darnell Washington, joined the group.

"Looks like we're all here," Sharon said, "so let's begin."

Elaine, the leader of the group, pushed back from the table and stood. "I want to welcome two new members of our group"— she nodded at Erlene and Alfred—"and tell them a little about our purpose and plans. After Simon Atkins shot Ike Davis over a parking place dispute last fall, some of us recognized an urgent need to reduce racial tension in our communities, and we thought the best way to do that was to get to know each other better. After all, I know I can go for weeks and hardly see a Black person, much less talk to one."

"Not anymore," Laura murmured, but Elaine ignored her and continued talking.

"We're hoping our group can foster friendships not only among ourselves but among the members of our congregations. We think we can do that through projects and social gatherings, and we're starting off with a bang—a celebration of the Reverend Martin Luther King, Junior's birthday."

The biggest decision the group had made at the first meeting was to hold the celebration in Tanner because the church was larger, and they hoped to attract a large crowd. The ministers from each church would speak, and they hoped to find an outside speaker as well. The rest of the program would be musical selections from the combined choirs followed by a social hour with refreshments.

When Elaine paused, Sharon jumped right in. "I have great news about our speaker! I contacted Glenn Griffin's office, and after a few phone calls, he agreed to come. Since we're celebrating on Sunday instead of the actual birthday, his schedule was clear, and he's coming." Sharon's smile covered her entire face.

"Who's Glenn Griffin?" Alfred asked, and Erlene poked him with her elbow.

"He's a justice on the North Carolina Supreme Court, appointed just a little over a year ago, and he's Black," Sharon said. "We're very lucky to get him."

"He better know some good jokes," Alfred whispered, but no one heard him because they were all clapping.

As the applause died down, Elaine said, "Thank you, Sharon, for all your work on securing Justice Griffin. Now, what about the music? Have we made any progress on that?"

"I talked with both choir directors, and they're selecting the songs now," said Julia Harris, one of the committee members from Tanner. "They have a joint rehearsal scheduled for next week. I think the music is going to be magnificent."

"Are they going to do 'Lift Every Voice and Sing?'" Alfred asked.

"I'm pretty sure they will." Julia beamed a reassuring smile.

"What's 'Lift Every Voice and Sing'?" Laura asked.

"It's sometimes called the Black national anthem," Erlene explained. "James Johnson, an NAACP leader, and his brother wrote it around the turn of the century."

"It's a beautiful hymn," Sharon said.

"And it'll get your blood pumping," Alfred added.

Driving back to Tanner, Elaine asked Laura how she thought the meeting went.

"Smooth as molasses," Laura said. "Sounds like we've got a good speaker, and I never doubted the music would be good. The big question is whether anybody will come."

"Why wouldn't they?" Elaine slowed the car to take one of the nearly hairpin curves in the two-lane road between the two towns. Many an accident had happened on that road, particularly at night when it was hard to see how sharp the curves were. "We've been advertising it in the church bulletin and the newsletter since before Christmas. A lot of people at our church have told me they're coming." But now she began to worry.

"They better come," Laura said. "It'll be embarrassing if we host this event and the people from our own church don't come."

Elaine thought about how hard she'd worked to convince the Tanner church pastor that this was a good program for the church to support. She couldn't let it fail. Laura was right. "I'll make sure they come," she said with more vigor than she expected. She was already thinking about the people she would call.

"I'm more worried about the people from Copeland," Laura said. "They're the ones who'll have to drive to get here."

"They'll come," Elaine said. "They're used to spending most of Sunday in church anyway. What did you think of that new couple, the Duncans?"

"He seemed a little scattered, but she could be an asset to the group. We need to get more young people involved."

"Yeah. They're the ones who can really benefit from this. Before they get too set in their ways."

The next morning, Meredith Parker changed the blouse she was wearing three times. She had selected her skirt suit carefully, but none of her blouses seemed right.

"What's up with you? Are you meeting the Queen of England today?" Paul asked.

"No. It's more important than that. Clarinda's trial is at ten o'clock, and she and I both have to make a good impression on the judge. I went to her apartment and picked out the best dress I could find for her. Now I have to live up to my part of the image."

"Then I pick this." Paul pointed toward a burgundy silk-knit bow-tie blouse. "It says respectable and smart. Just the kind of lawyer whose client should get probation."

Meredith figured that one was as good as any of the others, so she put it on and drove to the courthouse. Clarinda was waiting for her inside the courtroom. She had worn the dress Meredith brought her and tied her thin hair into a loose ponytail at the nape of her neck. Her cheeks showed more color than usual, whether because she was sleeping and eating better in jail or because she was nervous, Meredith didn't know, but she looked older. The earrings Meredith had brought her helped.

Meredith gave her a hand a squeeze as they waited for the judge to appear. "We got a good judge," she said. "He's not known for being particularly strict, and, frankly, we're lucky you're white. His record shows he's more likely to give probation to white defendants than Black ones."

The judge arrived, and everyone stood. When they were seated again, he asked the attorney for Child Protective Services to begin the prosecution. A sharp young man with his sights definitely set on the District Attorney's office, the lawyer called as his first witness Rebecca Goodman, the neighbor who found Lucy and called 911.

"How did you know the child, Lucy, had been left alone?" he asked when Rebecca was sworn in and seated. Looking back at him, she squirmed slightly.

"I heard her crying through the wall and went to check on her. I knew she must be in trouble. It took a while before I could get her to let me in, but when she did, I immediately realized she'd been alone for a while. The apartment was a mess, with an open jar of peanut butter and a spilled loaf of bread on the kitchen table. There was also water on the kitchen floor where the linoleum had begun to buckle, so I knew the water had been there a while. Her little face was dirty and flushed."

"Bitch," Clarinda said. Meredith put her finger to her lips and gave Clarinda a stern look.

"Where did Lucy say her mother was?"

"Looking for work. But she didn't know where. She's too little to know those things. She did have a pretty good idea of how long she'd been there, though. She said her mom left after they saw Santa at city hall. Santa was only there one day, and that was three days earlier."

"Had you seen the defendant during that three-day period?"

"No. I hadn't. And now that I think about it, that was unusual. We usually ran into each other at least twice a week."

"Did the defendant ask you to look after Lucy while she was gone?"

"No. She did not. She had asked me one time before, but I work different shifts at the grocery store, and I take care of my mother, so it's hard for me to babysit too."

"More like ten or twenty times, and she always said no," Clarinda murmured as she made a mental note to slug Rebecca the next time she got near her.

Meredith was up next for cross-examination. "How long have you lived next door to the defendant?" she asked Rebecca.

"Three years or so, I'd say."

"And how well do you know her?"

"Like I said, we talk in the hall a couple of times a week. She's always complaining about how hard it is to find somebody to stay with Lucy."

"And yet she only asked you once in three years to look after her?"

"Well, maybe it was more times than that. I can't remember. Like I said, I'm really busy with work and my mother and all."

"As far as you know, has the defendant ever left her daughter alone for an extended period before?" Meredith asked.

"No."

Well, at least she told the truth about that, Clarinda thought, but she still intended to slug her.

The CPS attorney called the police officer who was given the case after the 911 call as his next witness. "Officer Clemmons," he said, "when did you first talk with the defendant?"

"She came home soon after the child was taken into DSS custody. When she couldn't find her daughter, she called us. We questioned her at the apartment and then brought her to the station for more questioning. After hearing her story, we knew we had grounds for child neglect, so we charged her and held her for arraignment."

"Did she tell you why she left Lucy?"

"She said she was looking for a job in Hickory when she got sick and couldn't drive home."

"Did she see a doctor?"

"No."

"Was anyone with her in Hickory?"

"She gave us the name of a friend, Jill Jones.

"Did you talk to Miss Jones?"

"Yes. She said the defendant was at her apartment for at least three days."

Meredith declined to cross-examine the officer. When her turn came to call witnesses, she said, "The defense calls Jill Jones to the stand."

A small, mousy-looking woman with a boyish haircut stood up in the back row of the gallery. Clarinda turned and smiled at her. She'd been afraid Jill might not show up. A totally free spirit, Jill was unpredictable that way.

"When did the defendant, your friend Clarinda, arrive at your apartment?"

"Around noon on December fourth," Jill said.

"What did she do after she arrived?"

"She went out to look for restaurants that were hiring waitresses, but when she came back that night, she went straight to the bathroom and threw up. She was sweaty and feverish and kept puk-ing until there couldn't have been anything left inside her."

"What did you do?"

"I told her to go lay down. She went to sleep, but she woke me up around midnight, still puking, and she said her stomach hurt like hell. The next day, she was mostly dry heaving, but she was still in pain. I tried to give her a little water, but she couldn't keep it down. And then she got the runs."

"Officer Clemmons testified that she didn't see a doctor while she was staying with you. Is that true, and if so, why didn't she see a doctor?"

Jill's face showed how embarrassed she was to answer, but she forged ahead anyway. "Neither one of us had any money to pay for a doctor, so we decided to wait it out together."

"What happened next?"

"She spent the day on the couch, limp as a dishrag, clutching her stomach. I gave up trying to give her water because it just came right back up. Finally, late that night, she managed to keep some water down. The next day, I gave her some beef broth I had in the cabinet. I like to keep that on hand for making vegetable soup with my leftover vegetables, and it was lucky I had some that day." Jill smiled for the first time since she started testifying.

"And then what happened?"

"The next day, I added some soda crackers to the broth, and she kept that down. Her fever was lower too, and the pain seemed to have gone away. But she was still weak."

"When did she leave to go home."

"That was the next day, I think. It's been a while ago, so I can't be for sure about everything. When I gave her some cereal, and she kept that down, she said she had to go home. I didn't think she was strong enough, but she can be bullheaded that way, and she left."

Meredith said she had no further questions, and the CPS attorney asked only two. "At any time while she was staying with you did the defendant say she had left her five-year-old daughter home alone?"

"No," Jill said.

"And did she ever ask you to take her home?"

"No." Jill knew how bad that sounded for Clarinda, but she had sworn to tell the truth.

Meredith had wrestled for weeks about whether or not to put Clarinda on the stand. She wanted the judge to feel sympathy for her and to realize that she was not a bad mother, just a very young mother who made a mistake and then got caught up in some bad circumstances. But she also couldn't be certain that Clarinda wouldn't get angry and alienate the judge. She finally decided to ask her only three questions and hope she didn't explode under cross-examination.

"When you left home that day, what time did you plan to return?" she asked when Clarinda had been sworn in.

Clarinda straightened her thin shoulders and adjusted her pony-tail. Her body seemed to stiffen with the delicate layer of steel she kept just beneath her skin. "No later than seven o'clock. I told Lucy to take a nap, and I left a peanut butter sandwich and an apple for her supper. I also told her not to open the door until I got home."

"When did you actually return home?"

"As soon as I could hold my head up and not vomit or have to rush to the bathroom."

"How long was that?"

"I didn't know until the police told me it was three days. I was so sick I lost track of time."

"What did you think when they told you'd been gone for three days?"

"I cried. I couldn't believe I left my baby for that long." Clarinda looked like she might cry then, and Meredith prayed that she wouldn't. Tears would seem staged at that point. Clarinda sniffed and pulled herself together. "It was an accident. I promise I'll never do it again."

The CPS attorney started his cross-examination with a glare that could have made almost anybody cry. "At any time while you were at Miss Jones's apartment, did you try to call Lucy?"

"No. I was too sick to think straight."

"Did you ever try to call Mrs. Goodman while you were away?"

"If I was too sick to call Lucy, do you think I'd call anybody else?"

Meredith took a deep breath. She could feel sparks starting to fly in Clarinda's brain. This was what she was afraid of.

"I'll take that as a 'no,'" the attorney said. "So, you didn't try to call anyone for help, and you didn't try to get Miss Jones to drive you home."

"Objection." Meredith was on her feet. "Counsel is testifying."

"I apologize," the attorney said. "No further questions."

When Meredith said she had no additional witnesses, the judge called a thirty-minute recess to consider his verdict. "How'd we do?" Clarinda asked.

"If the judge decides to convict you, I think we have a good chance for probation. You and Jill made a good case that circumstances got beyond your control."

"And I can take Lucy home?"

"That's up to CPS. We have to convince them you can take care of her before they'll give you custody. They'll be in touch with you right away, I'm sure."

The color paled in Clarinda's cheeks, taking years off her appearance. Once again, she looked like a frightened teenager.

After twenty agonizing minutes, the judge returned. "Thank you to all of you for coming here today, but I find no crime has been committed. This is truly a case of bad judgment and unfortunate circumstances. The case is dismissed. The defendant is free to go."

Meredith grabbed Clarinda around her shoulders and held her close, surprised at how fragile she felt. "What about parole?" Clarinda cried into Meredith's neck.

"This is better than parole." Meredith pulled away and held her at arm's length. "This means you're innocent."

"And I can have Lucy back?"

"Not yet. But you will. If you work hard and do what social services tells you to do, you'll get her back."

Clarinda looked skeptical, exacerbating Meredith's fears that the girl's hardest battles might be yet to come.

9

At the Terrors' game on Saturday, the group of parents and friends in the stands had nearly tripled in size. Word had gotten out that the team won the regional holiday tournament, a rarity for Tanner teams, so many of the local basketball enthusiasts had come to see what this team had. The elegant old gym rang with the sound of boisterous conversations among townspeople (mostly men) who hoped to see a game worth watching. Paul wished they'd all stay home and watch the Tar Heels play on TV. He didn't need the added pressure, and neither did the boys. Frank, on the other hand, thought the attention was grand. "The more people who see them play, the better their chances for a basketball future," he said.

Paul had finally hit on a plan that he thought would enable the team to win and give all the boys at least a little playing time. Frank said it was a ridiculous idea and he should simply play to win and forget everything else. Paul ignored him and did what he pleased, which meant rotating Quentin and Jamie at center and occasionally subbing each of them in at forward for Malcolm or Adam. When he could, he put in the second-string players for short periods of time.

The second time Jamie was pulled to sit on the bench, James pounded the bleacher. "Give him a chance!" he yelled.

Laura, sitting in front of him, turned around and said, "You're right. Give him a chance," but Richard, sitting next to Laura, glared at James and told Laura to calm down. The tension in the stands was making him uncomfortable.

At halftime, the Terrors were down by six. "I told you this wouldn't work," Frank said. "You have to play Quentin more. Put

Jamie in at forward and pull Adam out. He's our weakest first-string forward."Paul groaned and waited for the players to gather around him.

"Let's get some fresh air," Richard said to Laura. When she gave him a puzzled look, he told her to grab her coat and come on. They made their way through the throng of spectators crowded around the tiny refreshment stand in the corner of the gym's entry area. Back when the gym was built, fans didn't think they needed sustenance during a game, so trying to squeeze in a place for drinks and snacks to please modern expectations had been difficult, but when school administrators realized how much money they could make off refreshments, they found a way and made it a student-council project.

Outside, small groups gathered in various spaces, smoking, eating, and talking. Richard stopped several feet away from everyone else. His first words were, "We have a problem."

"Who has a problem?"

"This basketball team, and it's not the kids. It's the parents. James is undermining Paul's coaching, and you're not much better."

"Nobody's undermining Paul. We just want to win, and we want our sons to play." Laura wanted to shake Richard. His obtuseness could be so frustrating.

"What if the two are mutually exclusive? Then what?"

"They aren't mutually exclusive. Our original first string—Jamie, Adam, Malcolm, Benny, and Frankie—that's who we should be using to win."

"But Quentin's the best player we have. You know that. What about him?"

"He's no better than Jamie and Adam and Frankie. And he came late to the team. He should be a first sub, that's all."

Richard pulled his coat tighter around his throat. The wind had picked up, sending a chill down the back of his neck. This was a side of Laura he hadn't seen before. She'd always been protective of Adam, but she didn't usually deny reality in his defense. "Remember the three games we lost this year before Quentin joined the team?" Richard asked. "With Quentin, we haven't lost a game."

"Our boys realized they could lose their spot on the first string if they didn't shape up. So they did what they had to do, and they deserve to be the team leaders. We don't need an outsider pushing them aside." Laura knew she should go back into the gym before she said something she regretted. She was trying to be a good Christian and not be critical of anyone, but God helps those who help themselves, and she had to set an example for Adam to stand up for his rights on the team. For his rights anywhere. The only way she'd gotten anywhere in life was to insist on not being pushed out of the way.

As the middle of five siblings, she had had to fight for any attention she got growing up. She wasn't one of the smart older siblings, and she wasn't one of the cute younger ones. She figured out early on that the only way she'd ever get new clothes instead of her sisters' hand-me-downs was to gain enough weight so that their clothes would never fit her. She spent her childhood in pleasant plumpness, resisting any attempts her mother made to restrict the calories she ate.

When she met Richard at college, she knew immediately that he was the man for her. "It was like a vision," she told her sister. "I saw him standing across the room at a fraternity mixer, and I said to myself, 'I'm going to marry him before we graduate.'" Richard was not similarly smitten. He liked all the girls and had no interest in limiting himself to one. For Laura, he became a mission. She limited her calorie intake herself and shed a few pounds, which she thought would make her more attractive. Then she cajoled one of his fraternity brothers, whom she knew from high school, to introduce them. "He's clever and cute," she reported to her roommate. "We make a perfect pair."

"So, what's your next move?" the roommate asked.

"I have his class schedule," Laura said. "I'll make sure we bump into each other a lot on campus." Which is exactly what she did, especially when he was talking with other girls. Before long, he asked her to a frat party and then another one. And then they were pinned. "He never knew what hit him," Laura announced when she showed off the pin.

Richard knew what hit him. He just didn't care. He loved Laura and decided it was time to settle down and concentrate on the world's great ideas. He gave her a diamond at Christmas of their senior year. They married the summer after graduation, and Richard went straight into graduate school. When he secured his first teaching position, Laura gave birth to Adam and set out on her career as a professional church volunteer. And God help anybody who stood in her way.

"I'm going back inside," she said to Richard as the other basketball spectators crushed out their cigarettes and threw their paper cups into the bin. "But before I go, I'm going to say a prayer that the Lord will grant Paul the wisdom to do what's right." She bowed her head for a moment and then walked away.

"Promise me you'll keep your prayers and your thoughts to yourself," Richard called after her. He shook his head a few times before he hurried behind her to make sure she did just that.

To start the second half, Paul did what Frank wanted. Jamie and Quentin took the court while Adam sat on the bench. Sensing Laura's muscles tightening, Richard put his hand on her thigh. He had deliberately steered her away from James so they wouldn't feed off each other. The only parents sitting close to them were Lydia and Suzanne, and he didn't expect any fireworks from them.

He was almost right, but not quite. Two minutes into the third quarter, momentum picked up among the Terrors. Malcolm intercepted a pass and hurled it to Frankie while the rest of the team dashed down the court. By the time Frankie brought the ball to the foul line, Quentin had set up under the basket, ready to receive the ball and drop it through the hoop. Suzanne jumped to her feet and yelled, "Way to go, Quentin!"

Frank looked back at her and smiled. He had told her before the game that the spectators needed to show support for Quentin to counter the negative comments. A few plays later, Benny missed an outside shot, but Quentin was right there to tap the ball in when it bounced off the rim. Suzanne was on her feet again. "Great save, Quentin." This time, Delia smiled at her, a shy, appreciative smile. Laura looked at her too, but she wasn't smiling. Sitting next to James, Elaine silently prayed that he wouldn't make a nasty remark. Jamie was in the game, even though he wasn't scoring much. She hoped that was enough to keep James quiet.

When Suzanne sat down, Lydia asked her, "What else did Frank say when he asked you to show support for Quentin?"

"He said James is getting out of hand, and Laura isn't far behind. Even Jeff, when he's here, isn't helping the situation. Frank wants me to cheer for all the boys, especially Quentin."

Suzanne kept her voice low because Laura was so close, but she didn't keep it low enough. "Did you hear that?" Laura said to Richard. "It's a conspiracy to make Quentin the top player on the team."

Richard exhaled a long breath and told her to move farther down the bleacher. Next week, he was going to insist that she not come to the game.

Watching the Campbells change seats, Lydia wondered how so much animosity had built up among the parents. Well, not all the parents, but certainly some of them. Except for the Thomases, they'd all known each other since their sons started playing basketball in third grade. That's how it was when your kids were in elementary and high school. Your friends were the parents of their friends. You spent so much time at the kids' activities, where you invariably saw each other, that you hardly had any time left to do anything with anybody else. If you were lucky, the other parents were nice. If they weren't, you tried to avoid them, but that wasn't easy. You could only move so far down the bleachers.

"I guess we upset them," Suzanne said.

"We upset her," Lydia said. "I don't get it. Laura's usually pretty even-tempered. You can tell her anything, and she doesn't flinch. Just absorbs it all and keeps going. Why does a change in the basketball team bother her so much?"

"Maybe there's more to it than just a new player on the team. And what about James? What's bringing out the bear in him?"

"He's done a lot of yelling before, but usually he yells at Jamie, not another player, and rarely at Paul. Is he giving Paul and Frank a hard time off the court, as well?"

"Frank says he and Paul know it's coming after every game. And often at practices. He's come to most of the practices since Quentin joined the team. I heard he was an excellent basketball player in high school right here in Tanner, but he never played college ball. Maybe he's trying to relive his basketball career through Jamie and have it turn out better this time."

Lydia thought about that idea and decided it was disgusting. Parents needed to grow up before their children could. "Whatever it is, it needs to stop. If it doesn't, it's going to affect the kids. And it's uncomfortable for all of us. What must Marcus and Delia be thinking?"

"That we're a bunch of selfish parents at best. Or a bunch of racists at worst. And poor Paul can't win. Meredith told me he was worried that the parents were doubting him when the team was losing, and now they're angry with him when we're winning. I'm afraid he's going to quit, and it's all going to fall on Frank's shoulders."

"He won't quit. He's coached these boys for five years, and he'll stay with it for Benny's sake, if nothing else. But he deserves better from the parents. We have to do something about all this resentment, and I don't know what the hell it's going to be." Lydia looked at each of the adults huddled on the bleachers behind the players sitting in the first row. James with his perpetual scowl, Elaine looking poised for some shock even though she didn't know what it might be, Marcus with a slight smile of pride, Delia with creases of worry around her eyes and mouth, Meredith leaning forward with intense interest, Richard and Laura in their place of exile, both with almost no expression, and Suzanne staring expectantly at Lydia, waiting for her to continue. Only Jeff was missing, a blessing in Lydia's opinion, but his strong opinions were undeniably part of the mix. Something or somebody had to bring this group together the way it used to be.

"Maybe we should have a parents' meeting," Lydia said. "Talk things out."

"Scream things out is more likely," Suzanne said. "It's better to keep the lid on."

Out on the court, the Terrors had regained the lead. Quentin had maintained his shooting streak, and Jamie had dropped a few baskets. Paul sent in Adam for Malcolm and hoped he could maintain that lineup until the end of the game. At the end of the third quarter, however, Jamie went up for a shot and came down on top of the boy who was guarding him. The two of them landed in a pile. When Jamie stood up, he had trouble putting weight on his right ankle. Malcolm went in for him immediately, and James and Elaine met him at the sideline after Frank helped him off the court. Elaine wanted to take him home, but Jamie insisted on staying with an ice pack on his ankle.

The Terrors maintained their lead to the end, chalking up their fifth win and giving them a five-three record. For their end-of-game huddle, the boys clustered around Jamie, who sat with his foot propped up on the bleacher next to him. After congratulating the team on the win, Paul told Jamie he was excused from practice for as long as it took for the ankle to heal. "It's probably a sprain," he said, "but you should get it examined."

"He'll be fine," James said. "A few days of rest, and he'll be good as new."

"Yeah," Jamie said. "I'll be good as new."

On the drive home, Lydia wondered if Malcolm was feeling any of the tension in the stands. "Great game," she said. "But too bad about Jamie. I hope he'll be better soon."

"Yeah. Me too. But he should never have taken that shot. The guard was in his face before he ever left the ground. He should have passed the ball. Quentin was open, and so was Adam." Malcolm stared out the window at the houses rolling by.

"Why do you think he did it?"

"His dad's been yelling at him about scoring more points. And Jamie's afraid that Quentin's taking his place on the team."

"Do Jamie and Quentin get along?"

Malcolm shrugged. "I guess so. They don't argue or anything. Jamie just doesn't talk to him much."

"Does anybody talk to Quentin?"

"Sometimes. He's kind of quiet. Keeps to himself a lot."

"Do you talk to him?" Lydia feared she was getting the answer to her concern about hard feelings on the team.

"Yes, Mom." Malcolm turned to give her an exasperated look.

"Remember when you and I talked about how hard it is to be the new kid? I think it may be twice as hard for Quentin. Why don't you invite him over to shoot baskets in the backyard after school one day?"

There was almost nothing Malcolm hated more than having his mother orchestrate his life, but shooting baskets with Quentin wouldn't be so bad. Scrimmaging one-on-one with Quentin could only improve his game.

When the Thomases arrived home after the game, Delia made a ham sandwich for Quentin and gave Marcus a beer. The three of them sat around the kitchen table until Quentin finished eating and went to his room to watch TV. When they were alone, Delia told Marcus, "I don't think I can face going to church with Laura and Richard Campbell tomorrow. She has something against Quentin, and I don't know if I can deal with it."

"Are you sure it's Quentin she's angry at? Seems more like it's Paul to me." Marcus took a swallow of his beer and pointed the bottle toward Delia in a gesture that asked if she wanted one. She didn't drink much because of the antidepressants she was taking, but today she nodded yes.

"If she's mad at Paul, it's because of Quentin," she said after Marcus handed her a beer.

"If she doesn't like Quentin, then why was she so eager for us to go to church with her?"

"Because she asked you to come and bring us before she realized Quentin was going to shake up the basketball team, and now she can't uninvite us. Besides, bringing us to church shows she's a good Christian, no matter how she really feels inside."

"That's not a very Christian thing for you to say."

"It is if it's the truth, and you know it is." Delia looked at her half-empty bottle of beer and debated whether to finish it. After one more swallow, she pushed it a few inches away from her. "How long have we been here? How many weeks? It feels like an eternity."

Marcus counted backward to the day Delia and the kids arrived. To him, time had dragged in the weeks he spent in Tanner alone, but since the family joined him, it had flown. "Five weeks, maybe?"

"It feels like twenty-five. I came here determined to try to fit in, even though I knew it would be hard, but I didn't expect it to be like this. If these people don't want Quentin on their team, let's take him off. I don't think he likes it, anyway. And he could get hurt. Disturbed people can be dangerous."

"I think you're blowing things out of proportion."

Delia leaned forward as she spoke. "Think about all the young Black men who've been assaulted by angry white people, even by the police."

"But that wasn't here. This is a peaceful town."

"Until it isn't." Delia couldn't believe Marcus was so trusting. "Let Quentin sit this year out. Try it again in high school. Maybe things will be different then. At least give the kids—and the parents—a chance to get to know him as a person instead of an athletic stereotype."

"If we encourage him to do that, we'll be teaching him to back away from things the rest of his life. I promise I won't let anything happen to him."

Delia wished he had the power to make good on that promise.

10

L aura made sure her family went to church early the next morning so she could be standing on the front steps with open arms when the Thomases arrived. Built in 1970, the white brick church building was notable for its Georgian Colonial architecture and large windows made of handblown, slightly tinted antique glass. It was the third church to house the Tanner congregation. After starting out in a small wooden building that served as a school during the week in the late 1800s, the congregation grew until they couldn't fit there anymore. They built a second church close to the Main Street retail section of town and later added a parsonage next door. But Tanner continued to grow, and so did the congregation, until they decided to build the current church with its fellowship hall, Sunday school classrooms, and chapel on what were then the outskirts of town. The congregation was proud to be the second largest in Tanner, outsized only by the Baptists. Their church was a noble church, remarked one of the congregants on the day it was dedicated.

Laura looked noble as she stood on the steps with Richard, Adam, and her daughter, Annabelle—Laura's entourage, as Elaine once referred to them. When one of her church friends asked her what she was doing there, she said she was waiting to welcome a new family who she hoped would soon become members. "Wait just inside," she said, "so you can meet them. I know you'll like them."

"Don't you think you're overdoing it?" Richard asked as the friend and her family moved through the door.

"No. Our church needs diversity." Laura removed Adam's green cap from his head and put it into her purse. He scowled at her but said nothing.

"I agree with that. I'm just surprised at you in this particular instance."

Laura gave him an angry look that quickly changed to a smile when she saw the Thomases approaching. "I'm so glad y'all came," she cried as she threw her arms around Delia. "I have a lot of people I want you to meet." Delia backed away as swiftly as she could and murmured a polite reply. Richard shook hands with Delia and Marcus while the children smiled shyly at each other.

"Hey, Quentin," Adam said. "What's up?" He ran his fingers through his hair, feeling very naked up there.

"Not much." Getting Quentin to come that morning had required a stern talking-to from Marcus and a bribe from Delia. She promised to bake his favorite dessert, chocolate crème pie, for dinner that night if he cooperated.

On the other side of the twelve-foot-tall front doors, Laura's friend waited with her husband. Laura was just finishing her detailed introductions when the husband exclaimed, "I've heard about you all! This young man"—he nodded at Quentin— "is an excellent basketball player. Frank Jessop told me he's the reason the Tanner team won their division in the AAU holiday tournament. He said I should come watch you play sometime, and maybe I will."

Embarrassment flooded through Quentin. He didn't even know this man. Richard smiled slightly, and Laura looked shocked. "Well, I'm sure the team would be delighted to have you," she said. "But right now, we'd better get to our seats."

"So nice to meet you," Marcus managed to say before Laura ushered them all into the sanctuary.

As they walked down the center aisle, Laura smiled and waved at people in every pew, drawing curious glances and perplexed acknowledgments. Delia sighed when she saw James and Elaine Parker. How much worse could this get? Their daughter was with them, but not Jamie. Likely, he was home nursing his ankle, Delia thought. Elaine smiled and waved while James gave a half-wave.

When Laura's expanded entourage reached the pew where she wanted them to sit, she said, "Adam, you and Quentin go in first. Annabelle, you sit with the girls, and the adults will sit at the end." They all did as they were told, causing a young couple who were already sitting in the pew to slide to the end.

After Adam and Quentin were seated with their three sisters separating them from their parents, Adam whispered, "Did your mom and dad make you come today?"

Quentin nodded. "Yeah."

"Mine made me come too. Why didn't you wanna come?"

"'Cause I knew we'd be the only Black people here."

Adam considered this fact and decided Quentin had more reason to want to stay home than he did. "That must= be tough."

"It is. Just like on the basketball team."

Adam was stunned. He thought Quentin was king of the team, and he couldn't imagine his being unhappy there. Being un-happy somewhere like church made sense, but on the basketball court when you played like Quentin? If Adam were as good a player as Quentin, he'd feel like he was in heaven. What was wrong with Quentin? Before he could put his thoughts into words, the choir started filing into the loft. Then the minister entered, and the con-gregation rose. "Welcome to the house of the Lord," the minister said, and the service began.

After the benediction, numerous churchgoers gathered around the Thomases, much to Laura's delight. She got to introduce them again and again as if they were her special project, making her feel important, except when a few mentioned that they had heard of Quentin's basketball prowess. Even the minister, as he shook their hands at the door and invited them to come again next Sunday, said he was glad to meet the young man who'd become the talk of the town.

"I hope you will come again," Laura said as they parted ways in the parking lot.

"We'll certainly consider it," Marcus said. "We hope to visit several churches in the next few weeks."

"Well, you're always welcome here. And don't forget our Cultural Bridge group. I want to take you to that next. And we certainly want you to come to our Martin Luther King Day celebration," Laura said.

Marcus and Delia nodded and were finally able to get away. When they were a safe distance across the parking lot, and their kids had run ahead to the car, Delia asked, "What's with that woman? She's all happy to have us here, but she sure as hell doesn't want Quentin on the basketball court."

"We don't ever have to go to church with her again," Marcus said. "We'll find our own church. Let's go to the AME church in Copeland. If we join this Cultural Bridge thing, we'll join with them."

On Monday, Jamie's ankle was still swollen, so Elaine took time off from her job at the church to take him to get it X-rayed. James went to work at the mill and promised to call Elaine at noon to see what the X-ray showed. Around ten o'clock, he was just finishing a call with a major customer when one of the account managers came into his office. "What can I do for you, Bill?" he asked.

"I just wanted to say I'm sorry about Jamie's ankle. Looked like he came down pretty hard."

"You were there?" James didn't remember seeing Bill at the game.

"Yeah. I go to a lot of AAU games. I like to see the talent coming up for the high school team since we haven't won a state or even a county championship in years. And it's always fun to see if there're any stars that might make Tanner proud at Carolina or NC State." Bill pushed his floppy bangs out of his eyes. Although his hair was tinged with gray, he still wore it long in the front, giving him the appearance of an aging teenager. "I hope Jamie won't have to miss any games. He has promise, but I have to say that I haven't seen him playing as much as usual lately. Seems like he's sitting on the bench more than he used to."

"I hope he doesn't miss any games too. He's getting the ankle X-rayed today, so we'll know more after that." James didn't like the way the conversation seemed to be going.

Bill nodded. "But what's the deal with him not getting as much playing time?"

That was exactly the way James feared the conversation was going. Anger bubbled in his chest, but he fought to keep it down like a bad case of indigestion. "If you haven't noticed, there's a new player on our team. Makes it harder for the other kids to get as much playing time."

"Of course I noticed. It's the Black kid. He's good, but so is Jamie. Doesn't seem fair that he's keeping Jamie and some of the others off the court."

"I agree, but there's not much I can do. I've told the coach how I feel about it, but I don't want to beat up on him too much."

"Maybe you should." Bill turned to go. "And let me know about the ankle. Tell Jamie I hope he's back on the court soon and more often."

When he was gone, James went to the water cooler. His luke-warm cup of coffee had become even more unappetizing. Dealing with the situation at practice and at games was bad enough, but now he was having to deal with it at work. He dumped the coffee down the water-cooler drain and filled the cup with water. Back at his desk, he began reviewing recent orders for Foxrow fabrics, grateful to have something else to think about. As he promised, he called Elaine at noon.

"Good news," she said. "The ankle's not broken. Just a bad sprain. The doctor suggested we rent crutches to help Jamie get around at school. And lots of ice packs."

"Crutches? Does he really need crutches? It didn't seem that bad yesterday. He'll be fine in a few days."

"Whatever happens, I got the crutches, and he'll have them as long as he needs them."

"What does Jamie say about it?"

"He says the ankle hurts, and he's happy to use the crutches for a few days. He thinks they'll attract girls with lots of sympathy hugs."

James laughed. "Okay, but he has to be ready for the game on Saturday. Where is he now?"

"I dropped him off at school with the new crutches, and he hobbled happily away. See you tonight."

"See you tonight." James hung up the phone, shaking his head. *Poor Jamie*, he thought for several reasons. *I hope he gets those hugs.*

At seven o'clock on Tuesday night, Frank met Jeff in the lobby of the YMCA for his first Kiwanis Club meeting. The Galloway family had built the YMCA building to serve as a community center for Tanner in 1927, not long after the high school gym was erected. In 1961, they refurbished the inside but kept the impressive columns of the structure's neoclassical facade. The Y had its own gymnasium, but it was used mostly for children's after-school gym classes and an evening gymnastics club for teenagers. The third floor was filled with meeting rooms, one of which had the Kiwanis crest on the door.

As Frank and Jeff climbed the stairs to the third floor, Jeff talked about the men he wanted Frank to meet that night. "They're all movers and shakers in town," he said. "We've got doctors like me, lawyers, prominent merchants, and a few bigwigs from the mill."

"I'll bet I already know a lot of them," Frank replied. "This town's not that big."

"You may know them, and they may know you, but not like this. That's the point of joining Kiwanis. We want the men of the community to know you as a leader before you run for town council."

Frank thought about the logic of Jeff's remark. "I'm a leader at the mill," he said. "Being in charge of production planning and sequencing is nothing to sneeze at." During his twenty-three years working at Foxrow Mills, Frank had risen from being a loom operator to his current position, and he was very proud of his success.

"But only the people at the mill know that, and not all of them do, at least not the ones who matter. At Kiwanis, your job will come up in conversation, so you'll be able to tell the guys what you've done."

"It sounds like the purpose of Kiwanis is networking."

They reached the third floor, where other men were going into the Kiwanis room or chatting in small groups in the hall. "Wait a minute," Jeff said. "I want to tell you a little about the club before we go in. Kiwanis started out as a networking club for businessmen, but after a few years, the organization changed its focus to service, especially service to children. We do several big projects a year and donate to smaller ones, but that doesn't mean we still don't look to help ourselves and each other through our associations here. Even if we don't always talk about it, success often depends on who you know, not what you know."

Frank was familiar with the adage about who you know, so he didn't need Jeff's explanation about networking. He just wanted to know more about Kiwanis and how it was going to help him get elected to town council. He was about to ask what the club's current project was when Ralph Peterson, who owned one of the drugstores in town, approached Jeff and him. After Jeff made the introductions, just as he'd promised, Ralph asked Frank about his job. Frank felt good talking about his accomplishments, and he was enjoying hearing about the growth of the drugstore after Ralph inherited it, so he was surprised when Ralph suddenly changed the topic. "Tell me," he said, "don't you and Paul Westover coach Tanner's eighth-grade AAU basketball team? The one that just won the regional holiday tournament?"

"Yes, we do," Frank said. "We've coached the boys for six years. My son, Frankie, is the point guard. They're a fine group of kids."

"If you've been coaching for six years, you certainly did something right this year." Ralph flashed a wide-open grin.

"My son, Malcolm, plays on the team too," Jeff interjected. "He's a forward."

"So, what's your secret this year?" Ralph asked. "I heard this is the first time any Tanner team has won the tournament."

"The culmination of years of good coaching," Frank said with a laugh, "and we have a new player who's really talented."

"We have a lot of talented kids, including Malcolm and Frankie." Jeff's frown sucked the earlier enthusiasm from his face.

"Yeah, but this kid's tall and Black, just the kind of power-house we need to win the division. After we lost our first three games, I didn't think we stood a chance, but now I think we do, especially if some of the other teams suffer a few losses." Frank realized for the first time that he truly believed that was the case, and the realization gave him a spirited sense of pride. He was a leader on a lot of different fronts. These Kiwanis guys had nothing on him.

"Good luck," Ralph said. "I'll be watching the *Observer* to see how you do. Y'all could put Tanner on the map." He patted Frank on the shoulder and turned to go into the room.

"We better go in too," Jeff said. "The meeting's gonna start soon. I'll introduce you to more of the guys when it's over."

"Your mood sure took a left turn when I mentioned Quentin. What's going on?"

"Nothing's going on. I just don't want him to get all the credit when our team wins." Jeff hadn't recognized how much praise for Quentin bothered him until now. "Just forget about it. That's not what we're here for. You need to meet more people."

Inside the room, Frank scanned the men's faces and was glad to see that he knew most of them, maybe not personally, but at least he knew who they were, and some of them knew him. "Frank! Hey. Good to see you here." George Simmons, vice president of Frank's division at the mill, was already seated in the row of chairs Jeff led Frank into. "I didn't know you were interested in community affairs."

"I'm interested. It's just been hard to find time to do anything about it. Work keeps me pretty busy." Frank hoped George saw that as dedication and not a complaint.

"Well, it's good to see you here tonight. We need more young-bloods like you. I'm worried about some of our older members. I understand Henry Galloway's been under the weather for the past two weeks. At his age, that can be serious." George shook his head.

Frank couldn't hide his dismay. He wanted to ask George for more details about Henry's health, but the meeting started, and after it was over, George left before he could ask.

When Marcus arrived home from work Wednesday night, Delia was nearly bursting with good news. "Guess what?" she exclaimed. "I have a job!" She threw her arms around his broad shoulders, and although he was somewhat stunned, he hugged her back.

"Where? How?" he asked with his mouth against her ear.

Delia pulled away and took hold of one of his hands. "The high school," she said. "The superintendent called this morning to tell me one of the math teachers is pregnant. She thought she was going to be able to finish the school year, but she's had some problems, and her doctor put her on bed rest for the rest of the pregnancy. I feel terrible being so happy about her misfortune, but things will likely work out for her, and this is so good for me."

She squeezed Marcus's hand before she let it go. Then she took a breath and continued. "I'll be teaching Algebra I, Algebra II, and plane geometry. Another teacher teaches the higher-level courses, but this is just perfect for me."

Marcus returned her bright smile. "I'm really happy for you," he said. "When do you start?"

"On Monday. They have a sub for the rest of the week, so I can 'put my affairs in order,' as the superintendent said. Sounds like I'm dying, doesn't it? But I'm not. I'm starting to live in this town. Maybe I can fit in after all." Delia wasn't sure that would happen, but at least this was a start.

Marcus said a silent prayer that this job would turn out to be all that Delia hoped it would. And he prayed even harder that it wouldn't backfire.

11

Saturday's basketball game came before Frank was ready. He'd gone to practice on Thursday and Friday, but his mind hadn't been on the drills and scrimmages. After hearing the news about Henry, he worried about the future of the mill. He had worked so hard to build a career there, and now his future was uncertain. Suzanne reassured him that it wasn't just a family business anymore, and if anything happened to Henry, the board members would take care of the employees, but Frank still worried. Fortunately, Paul didn't have that worry, so he was ready to play.

And so were the boys, all of them, including Jamie. At least, that was what James insisted. "He's fine now," he told Paul. "As long as he keeps the ankle wrapped, he's fine."

"He may be," Paul said, "but he hasn't practiced all week, and until I see him practice, I can't be sure he's ready to play. And if I were you, I'd get the doctor to sign off that the ankle's okay." James had more to say, but Paul cut him off. "If he feels like practicing on Monday, that's great. But for now, he's on the bench. I can use him to spot the other team's plays."

As James skulked up the bleachers to sit with Elaine, Benny overheard Paul explaining the plan to Jamie. After Paul moved on to talk to other players, Benny told Jamie, "That's tough, man. We need you in the game today."

"You bet we need me in the game today. The guys we're playing are really good. But Coach doesn't appreciate me enough now that he has his pet player." The scowl on Jamie's face made him resemble his dad.

Benny was immediately defensive. "Quentin's not his pet player.

He's just another good player like you and Frankie, and my dad's trying to use him to help us win. Obviously, it's working."

"What's up, guys?" Malcolm asked. He was sitting near Benny and could feel the tension rising between his teammates.

"Jamie's mad because my dad won't let him play today," Benny said.

"Or any other day," Jamie muttered.

"Oh, cool off." Malcolm was annoyed at the argument. "You play as much or more than any of us. You're not playing today because of your ankle, and that's your fault."

"It is *not* my fault. That guard was all over me and then knocked my feet out from under me."

"Then why did you shoot?"

Anger radiated from Jamie's eyes, and Malcolm's expression was just as menacing. "Come on, Malcolm," Benny said. "We gotta go warm up. The other guys are on the court."

"Think about it, Jamie," Malcolm said as Benny pulled him off the bleachers. "Don't let your head mess up your game."

"Shut up, Malcolm," Jamie said, but Malcolm's back was turned, and he didn't reply.

Jamie was right about the opposing team's being especially talented. Paul had scouted them earlier and was grateful to have the home-court advantage. The crowd was nearly as big as it had been the week before and included more of the team's classmates, who were already getting rowdy. The aged wooden walls of the gym didn't amplify the sound the way concrete or tile would have, but they didn't absorb it, either. Even though the weather outside was cloudy, the huge windows let in enough light to keep the feeling inside energetic rather than gloomy.

Paul tried to spread some energy among his players, especially Benny and Malcolm, whose expressions were still glum. "Go get 'em, Terrors!" he yelled as he sent Adam, Quentin, Frankie, Benny, and Malcolm onto the court. "This is your turf. Protect it!"

The Terrors won first possession and made the most of it.

Frankie brought the ball down the court and passed it to Benny, who darted toward the basket while Adam and Malcolm pulled the defense out. He was ready to take a close jump shot, but the opposing team's center was in his way, so he tossed the ball over to Quentin, who dropped it into the basket. A resounding roar rose from the crowd. Meanwhile, Jeff Colton scooted down the sideline to take a seat next to Richard Campbell. "What'd I miss?" he asked.

"Not much. Quentin just scored for our team."

"That's what I've been hearing, that Quentin scores a lot, much more than anybody else." Jeff's voice had an edge to it.

"I wouldn't say that necessarily. He's a good player, but we have other good players too."

"Yeah, I came to see for myself what's going on with the team. Seems like everywhere I go, I hear about Quentin."

Lydia was sitting a few rows in front of the men, and Richard realized it was unusual for both Jeff and her to be at the game. They usually attended alternate games. "Today's not a typical game because Jamie's out with a sprained ankle," he said, "so Quentin and the other forwards will likely play more."

"I'll get the full picture because I'm going to come to every game for a while. I want to make sure Malcolm's getting to play."

Richard sighed. Who else was going to get caught up in this parental competition? It didn't used to be like this.

Out on the court, the Terrors worked to build a six-point lead. The game was moving fast, with the opposing team hustling to catch up. Paul kept signaling to Frankie to slow down the pace because otherwise, the team was going to get tired soon, and their bench wasn't very deep. But if Frankie and Benny spent too much time dribbling, they were likely to lose the ball since the other team's players had very quick hands. Maybe the best solution was to substitute now. "Carson," he called, "go in for Benny, and Jason, you go in for Adam." Carson's and Jason's faces exploded with smiles, but Laura Campbell's face crumpled when Adam left the court.

"Relax," Richard said. "None of these kids needs to play the whole game."

The Terrors' lead was cut to four points when halftime arrived despite some excellent shooting by Quentin. James was sure they wouldn't have any problems winning if Paul would let Jamie play. He started to say that to Elaine, who was sitting next to him, but when he turned to her, she had moved a few rows up to talk with Meredith and Suzanne, who often sat together since their husbands sat with the team. "Good game so far," Elaine said lightly as she joined them next to Suzanne. The other women nodded, and Elaine moved on to the reason she had come. "There's a big celebration coming up at our church on Martin Luther King, Jr. Day."

"Martin Luther King Day isn't a holiday in North Carolina," Suzanne said.

"I know, but that doesn't mean we can't celebrate the man on his birthday, or actually the Sunday after his birthday. James and I would love it if you all would come."

Suzanne and Frank were not active churchgoers. It wasn't that they were atheists or even agnostics. Frank would have gone with Suzanne if she'd asked him to, and he was beginning to think he might have to start going if he ran for town council, but Suzanne thought she could be just as good a person without church. And for her, that was probably true. Although she was proud of her caustic personality—if anyone asked her the secret to staying trim into her forties, she would say she was too stubborn and ornery to get fat— the people who liked her knew that she could be truly kind. If she suspected a person was in need, she was the first to take care of the need if she could. "I'll grant you the Reverend King deserves to be celebrated," she said, "but how did your church come up with the idea for something like that?"

Delighted to be asked about her pet project, Elaine said, "It's only one part of a great program we've started with the AME church in Copeland. It's called Cultural Bridge. People from their church and people from our church get together so we can get to know each other and do things together. It's an idea I got from some friends in Kansas. Their church has a program like this that's been going for a couple of years. They love it." The idea sounded better to her every time she talked about it. "We've met some really nice people at the first meetings. I know you'd like them."

"I probably would like them, but why do we need a program like that?"

"How else are we going to meet them? You know the AME members are all Black, don't you? We need more association with Black people in our lives."

"You say that, but look at the animosity it causes when one joins the basketball team." Suzanne almost laughed at the irony of the situation, but because she knew Elaine was being sincere, she didn't. "What does James think of this Cultural Bridge program?"

"Don't pay any attention to James. He has his heart set on Jamie being a high school and college basketball star, and he doesn't want anybody, Black or white, to get in the way."

"It's hard not to pay attention to James. What puzzles me is he didn't used to be so mean. Until this year, we were all friends supporting the team, but now it feels like we're working against each other."

"You're making it sound worse than it is. After all, it's only an eighth-grade basketball team." Elaine wondered how the conversation had gotten so heated when all she wanted was for more people to come to the Martin Luther King, Jr. Day celebration.

"Tell that to James."

Meredith couldn't stay silent any longer. "That's enough. If there's friction on the team this year, it's not any one person's fault. As for the Martin Luther King celebration, I think it's a good idea. Paul and I would like to come if you'll accept a couple of Baptists at your Methodist meeting."

"Of course you can come. The celebration is open to everyone."

Unlike the basketball team, Suzanne wanted to say, and she would have too, but this wasn't the place to take the conversation any further. They needed to get all the parents together to iron this out before the kids got more involved. "I'll see if I can get Frank to go to the celebration," she said. "Maybe you should invite the whole team."

"I think I will," Elaine said, although she had no intention of doing it.

The Terrors continued to hold their own during the second half of the game. Paul called a lot of "Quentin plays," which were designed to work the ball in to the center, and Quentin never let them down. Toward the end of the third quarter, however, he began to drag on his way down the court. "Is he okay?" Delia asked Marcus, but he patted her knee and assured her Quentin was fine.

Paul knew what was happening. They were depending on Quentin too much. He needed a rest. "Jason," Paul said, "go in for Quentin. Tell Malcolm to move to center, and you play forward." Jason was up in a flash, and Quentin walked back to the bench.

Jamie was fuming. "Oh, shit," he said. "Malcolm's playing center? This game is over."

A few rows up, Jeff Colton was on his feet shouting, "You go, Malcolm. Show 'em what you can do!"

Paul changed his strategy to move the shooting mostly to the guards, freeing up Benny for outside shots and clearing a path for Frankie to take the ball in for layups. Malcolm did his best to play clean-up for the missed shots, but he wasn't always able to get the rebounds.

"Come on, Malcolm!" Jeff yelled. "Get in there and fight!" Malcolm tried to ignore his dad, but somehow Jeff's voice cut through all the other noise.

Two minutes into the fourth quarter, the Terrors were down by four points. The middle-schoolers, who had made themselves heard throughout the game, began a chant that grew louder and louder: "Quentin! Quentin! We want Quentin!"

James wanted to tell them to shut up, Jamie slammed the bleacher beneath him with his good foot, and Delia and Marcus didn't know whether to be frightened or glad. They wanted the students to like Quentin, but they weren't sure what kind of reaction the chant would cause. Paul ignored all of them. He had a plan, and he was sticking to it. He waited three more minutes. Then he turned to Quentin and said, "You ready, pal? Let's bring this game home."

Quentin nodded and ran to the scorers' table. A few seconds later, he was on the court. Jason went to the bench, and Malcolm moved back to forward. "Man, I'm glad to see you," he said to Quentin. Quentin smiled shyly, an expression that barely showed how happy the remark made him. Even without hearing from Paul, the team switched to running the "Quentin plays." Feeling more comfortable back at forward, Malcolm scored two baskets, and Benny hit an outside shot. Including Quentin's expected contributions, the score soon swung in favor of the Terrors. The students were on their feet again, this time shouting, "Go, Terrors! Go, Quentin!" Several of the Terrors' parents—Suzanne, Lydia, Meredith, Richard, and Marcus—were clapping too, but the others remained quiet. Paul and Frank were standing, their attention focused sharply on the game. Second by second, time ticked away. When the final buzzer sounded, the Terrors were two points ahead.

Cheers bounced off the high rafters and wooden walls in the gym. Frank slapped Paul on the back and said, "That's our sixth win, bud. We'll definitely be in the playoffs. We can win this division yet."

Paul shared his enthusiasm but was afraid to get too excited yet. "One game at a time," he said. "One game at a time," although his smile was broad as he congratulated the boys before they left for home. Benny joined him at the bleachers while he waited for Meredith to finish talking to Suzanne. He was beginning to get impatient when a man he didn't recognize approached him.

"Good game, Coach," the man said. "You've got a talented team, but you're playing one player too much."

"What are you talking about?" Paul looked to see if Benny was listening, which, of course, he was.

"Number twenty. You're letting him dominate."

Number twenty was Quentin, but Paul knew who the man was talking about before he said it. "Do I know you?" he asked.

"I'm just a basketball fan, trying to be helpful with a few tips. Give the other boys a chance. You'll find they're just as good if not better."

"We play as a team," Paul said, his throat tightening.

"Hi, everybody." Meredith had just come down from the bleachers and looked to Paul to introduce her to the man.

"This is my wife, Meredith," he said. "I'm afraid I don't know your name."

"That's okay," the man said. "I was just leaving." Then he turned and walked away.

Meredith frowned at Paul. "What was that about?"

"He thinks Dad lets Quentin play too much."

"Forget about it, Benny." Paul put his hand on his son's shoulder. "It's none of his concern." He meant what he said, but he also knew he would keep an eye out for the man at the next game.

On Sunday, Meredith was afraid Clarinda had stood her up. She rang her doorbell and knocked repeatedly on her door, but no one answered. The two of them hadn't spoken in the ten days since the trial, except for Meredith's brief call to ask if she could come over. Clarinda had said she'd be home at two o'clock Sunday afternoon, so that's when Meredith arrived. Had she forgotten? Or was she avoiding her? Meredith was looking through her purse for a piece of paper to leave a note under the door when a crack of light appeared next to the jamb. "Clarinda," she called, "it's Meredith." The door opened slowly to reveal Clarinda in a faded red sweatshirt and jeans. "May I come in?" Meredith asked.

"Sorry I didn't answer at first. I was asleep." Clarinda opened the door wider and waited for Meredith to enter. The apartment was clean and tidy, which immediately told Meredith that Lucy wasn't living there. A small single bed, squeezed into a recessed space in the living room that had probably been a shallow closet, the doors now removed, awaited her return. A frayed teddy bear held her place. Meredith didn't remember seeing the stuffed animal when she came to get a dress for Clarinda to wear to the trial. Maybe Clarinda had managed to buy it at a thrift store to welcome Lucy home. The thought made Meredith sigh.

Clarinda plopped down on a velour sofa, and Meredith sat beside her. "Have you been to the unemployment office?" she asked. Clarinda nodded. "Did they have any prospects for you?"

"Not now. Maybe later." Clarinda curled her legs under her and picked at her fingernails.

"How's your rent?"

"Paid to the end of the month."

"And then what?"

"I don't know."

"Have you talked to Lucy?"

"Twice. She's staying with a nice family, but she wants to come home."

"What does CPS say about that?"

"I have to prove I have a safe place for her to live and that I'm actively looking for a job. Social Services set me up with food stamps and some financial help, but it's only temporary. I also have to go to parenting classes twice a week." Clarinda hardly looked up from her fingernails as she spoke.

"How are the classes?" Getting information from Clarinda was harder than it had been before the trial, if that was possible.

"Okay. The people are nice. Nobody criticizes me, but then some of the women in the class beat their children. I've never done that."

Meredith decided it was time to quit trying to get Clarinda to talk and offer her some assurance instead. "Sounds like the most important thing you need to do now is find a job so you can pay the rent and have a place to bring Lucy home to. You can keep looking on your own while you wait to hear from the unemployment office. If you need a reference, use me. I'll vouch for your sincerity and your determination to get your life on track."

"You got any suggestions for places to look?" Clarinda raised her face with a skeptical expression.

"No, but I'll find some. For every three places you apply, I'll give you three more to try." *Oh Lord, what have I said?* Meredith was appalled at the words coming out of her mouth. As if she didn't have enough to do without finding potential employers for Clarinda. Why did she feel such responsibility for this girl?

"You'd do that for me?" Clarinda's skepticism softened.

"I'll try."

Driving home after the visit, Meredith realized why she wanted so badly to help Clarinda. All her life, the girl had rarely gotten a fair shake. The judge's ruling had been one time, but Meredith doubted there'd been many others. *Sort of like Quentin*, she thought. *The boy just wants to play basketball, and now he's the subject of a community feud, and none of it's his fault.*

At dinner that night, Marcus and Delia reminded their children that Mom was starting a new job the next day. "That means we all have to work hard tomorrow morning to get everybody out the door on time, including me," Delia explained with a laugh. "Since I have to be at the high school at seven, Dad will drop you all at school at eight."

"I don't want to go that early," Quentin moaned. "Homeroom's not until eight thirty."

"The girls have to be at school at eight, and I'm supposed to be at work by eight thirty," Marcus said. "You can take the school bus if you want to."

That was the last thing Quentin wanted to do. Crammed together with all those people he didn't know. "Why can't Rosalie and Camille ride the bus?" he whined.

"We live too close to the elementary school for them to have bus service," Delia said. "You know that. And it's too cold now for them to walk."

Quentin thought about his dilemma. "I'll ride my bike," he said. "It's not that far."

Marcus and Delia looked at each other. Neither of them was sure this was a good idea, but after all, the boy was thirteen years old. He could get himself to school.

"All right," Delia said, "but you better not be late."

12

P aul arrived at his law office on Monday, eager to get to work. He was still upset about the stranger's remarks at the game on Saturday, and he wanted to push the incident out of his mind, so he was looking forward to meeting with his first client. A friend of his wanted to transfer the deed to the family home to his adult son so he could, as he put it, ride off into the sunset with his true love. He had recently retired after forty years at the mill and bought a Winnebago so he and his wife could tour the United States. "I've always wanted to see the Grand Canyon," he said, "while I can still ride a donkey down to the Colorado River."

Paul was helping him with the deed and also with changes to his will. He was a joy to work with because he was so excited about his new life on the road. Just as Paul expected, he came into the office with a big smile on his face. "As soon as the weather's good, we'll be on our way."

"Then let's get this wrapped up," Paul said, handing the man a folder of papers. After twenty minutes of reading, discussing, and signing, they shook hands. "If you'll wait a few minutes, my secretary will make copies of everything for you." Paul took the papers into the next office and returned. "So how are you keeping busy these days?"

"I've got plenty to do," the man said. "We're selling all the furniture our son doesn't want and packing up most everything else to put in storage. The Winnebago's big, but it doesn't hold stuff like a three-bedroom house. And I'm saving a few afternoons a week to spend at the golf course with my buddies. I'm gonna miss them."

"They're going to miss you too," Paul said. "One less guy to tell gossip to."

"Yeah, we do like to talk. People say women are bad with gossip, but I think men are even worse. That reminds me of something they were talking about the other day. They say you got a new player on your basketball team this year. Said he's really good, and they don't understand why you don't play him more. What's that about?"

Paul shook his head. "Tell me something. How does everybody in town seem to know about my new player?" He slid his hand toward the pack of Winston cigarettes on his desk but fought back the urge to smoke.

"'Cause he's so good, I guess. And he's new. The basketball nuts in this town watch everything that's going on with basketball, even eighth graders."

"Did anybody tell you he's Black?"

"Yeah, they mentioned that. Said maybe that's why you don't play him more. They also said your team's winning games, but only by a few points, and they think you can do better. Got anything I can tell them?"

"Tell them I try to play all the boys as much as I can, and we're doing fine."

The secretary came in then with the copies, and the man turned to leave. "Thanks, Paul," he said.

"Happy trails," Paul replied.

Monday evening, the telephone calls started going out. "I think it's time the parents got together and talked about what's happening on the basketball team this year," James said. "You're invited to my house tomorrow night at seven thirty. The coaches won't be there. This is just for parents."

"I'm not going," Lydia said when she told Suzanne about the meeting. "It'll just be a bitching session, and I don't want to sit through that."

"Yes, you are going, and I'm going too," Suzanne said. "Somebody has to put these people in their place."

When Richard Campbell got the call, he was so annoyed he

almost hung up the phone, grateful that Laura hadn't been the one who answered. Of course, he'd have to tell her about the meeting. In fact, he was surprised that James hadn't told her about it already. And, of course, she'd insist on going and probably insist that he go with her.

Jeff Colton told James the meeting was a good idea and he would certainly be there.

While Elaine baked brownies to serve to their guests, she wondered if any good would come from the meeting. She thought Paul and Frank should be there, but James wanted the parents to feel free to speak their minds, and having the coaches there would inhibit them. She rarely argued with James, and in this situation, it wouldn't have made any difference, so she baked and cleaned and got ready for the showdown.

Richard and Laura were the first to arrive, with Laura already telling James what a good idea the meeting was. Lydia came next, very solemn and dreading every minute of what was about to come. Carson and Jason's parents were there, as well as the parents of all the other team members, except for Marcus and Delia and Paul and Meredith. Their absence felt like an uncomfortable void to some of the others, a sure sign that what they were doing was not totally aboveboard.

When Frank and Suzanne showed up, Elaine didn't know what to say, but Suzanne quickly filled in the empty space. "I know we weren't invited to your little soiree, but we need to be here. We mostly want to listen to what y'all have to say, but if any action needs to be taken, it'll have to come from Frank and Paul. Frank wanted to tell Paul to come too, but I think he can be spared listening to your complaints. And Frank and I will sit quietly and let y'all say what you want to say." With that, she swished into the room, garnering an angry glare from James and surprised stares from everyone else. True to her word, she led Frank to a bench away from the main conversation area that Elaine had created, with dining room chairs added to the sofa and living room chairs. Frank waved at Jeff and Richard and a few of the other dads. He was having a hard time staying quiet, but Suzanne had instructed him not to say anything until the others had spoken. Elaine scurried off to the kitchen and came back with the brownies, cups, and a pot of coffee.

James took a few sips of coffee before standing to start the meeting. "We're here to talk about changes in the basketball team this year and whether those changes are good for all the players. My personal feeling is that our newest player is overshadowing the others—and not in a constructive way."

"What do you mean 'not in a constructive way'?" Richard asked.

James cleared his throat. "The purpose of AAU basketball is to have all the players improve their skills and gain self-esteem because of it. That's not happening with our team this year."

"Why not?" asked Carson's father.

"I told you. Because Quentin Thomas is getting an unfair amount of playing time while others sit on the bench." James couldn't believe how obtuse some people could be.

"I agree," said Laura. "Adam hasn't gotten to play nearly as much as he did last year." Lydia had hoped not to have to say anything, but this was too much. She stared at James. "You didn't complain last year when Jamie was playing nearly all the time."

"Yeah, but this is different." Jeff wasn't surprised his ex-wife had to get her two cents in.

"How?" Jason's mother asked. Like most of the other parents, she'd been aware of the tension in the group since Quentin joined the team, and she wanted somebody to explain it to her.

Jeff's answer was quick. "Because Jamie earned his place on the team. The new kid helicoptered in and took over. Malcolm's felt the brunt of his arrival too."

"Oh, come on," Richard said. "Every single one of you would be thrilled if your son had Quentin's skills. And you'd be mad as hell if he didn't get to play most of the time."

"That's the goddamn truth." Frank jumped up from his bench in the corner. "I wonder what Marcus and Delia would think about this. Why didn't you invite them to this little party, just like you didn't invite Paul and me? Quentin needs somebody to stand up for him."

Since her husband had plunged into the fray, Suzanne was right behind him. "We'll stand up for him. What's he ever done to you, anyway? He's just a kid who wants to play basketball and happens to be really good at it."

"A lot of other kids on the team are good at it too, but nobody's going to know that. You're lucky Frankie's a guard, so he hasn't felt it much. But then, Frank's his coach, so he probably wouldn't feel it much, would he?" Laura felt good getting that off her chest.

"How dare you insinuate that I play favorites with my son." Frank's cheeks turned ashen, a color rarely seen on his ruddy complexion.

Richard was ready to defend his wife, even though he disagreed with her, and James had plenty to say on the subject of favoritism, but Lydia spoke first. "Do you know what I think? I think you're all jealous of Quentin, and I think it troubles you deeply that a Black boy is showing up your sons."

Nobody spoke for several seconds. Lydia's words seemed to suck the breath out of all of them. *I'm not racist* was running through each of their minds, and they were stunned that Lydia would say such a thing.

Elaine was horrified at the turn the meeting had taken. She hated conflict and would go miles out of her way to avoid it. Her biggest worry was what the townspeople would think if word got out that this team was having so much turmoil. She wanted the parents to go home and, in an almost reflexive action, began clearing cups and plates.

James finally breathed. He looked at Frank and then at Lydia. He couldn't decide which idea to attack first. "Let me tell you something," he said. "I don't care who's playing favorites, and I don't care who the person is who's being favored. But I do care that my son is being treated unfairly. The problem could be any of the boys on the team. It could be Frankie, but it's not. It's Quentin.

And I want to know if y'all agree with me. Frank, I didn't want you and Paul here tonight because I wanted us to come to some consensus before we approached you."

"Listen, James, nobody on this team is being treated unfairly." Richard clasped his hands together to keep from shaking a finger at James. "You're just mad because Jamie isn't high scorer any longer. But so what? The team is doing well."

"I get why James and some of the rest of us are not happy about what's going on." Jeff was talking in his most reasonable-sounding voice, the voice he used when he had to give patients bad news. "We're thinking of our kids' futures. High school starts next year, so if you think your kid could play college ball, you have to get serious about it now."

"Well, I resent what Lydia said." Laura was not trying to sound reasonable at all. "Here we are, trying to improve relations with the Black Christians who live closest to us, and you have the nerve to imply we resent Quentin because he's Black."

"Okay, everybody calm down," Suzanne said. "Regardless of your reasons, what do you want Frank and Paul to do to solve your so-called problem?"

"Play Quentin less," James said. "A lot less."

"Yes," said Jeff and Laura.

"Is that what you all want?" Frank asked.

A few echoed Jeff and Laura, and the dad of one of the substitutes said, "We'd be better off if he'd never joined the team."

"Remember that we weren't winning until he joined the team," Richard said.

"We just needed more time," James said.

"Let me see a show of hands. How many of you want us to keep Quentin on the bench?" Frank counted the hands that went up slowly.

"And who thinks we should keep doing what we're doing?" About the same number of hands were raised. Frank shrugged. "See, James. You weren't going to get a consensus."

"We might have if you and Suzanne hadn't shown up. At least you know for sure how we feel."

Elaine nearly dropped one of the cups she was carrying. "I think we've said about all that needs to be said on this subject."

"No. I'd like to know what you intend to do if we don't make any changes. You can always take your sons off the team." Frank's eyes narrowed as he stared at James.

"That would mean we're giving in, and we won't do that. We'll keep fighting for our sons' right to play."

"Maybe we'll just get new coaches." Jeff said this off-handedly as if he were suggesting a new practice time.

"Stop it!" Richard's voice was loud and clear. "Nobody's getting new coaches, and the coaches we have are going to run the team as they see fit."

"Easy for you to say. Your son will never play college ball." James was almost growling.

"Says who?" Frank took a few steps toward James. "I thought part of your argument was that lots of the boys are good players. They just don't get a chance to show it."

Now Richard was on his feet. "You don't have to fight my battles, Frank. But you have a point, and half the parents here could say the same thing about our first string and the fact that their sons don't get to play much behind those guys."

"Come on, Richard. We're going home." Laura stood and gave Richard a push toward the door.

"I'm going too." Lydia headed in the same direction.

Suddenly the other parents were gathering their coats and preparing to leave. "I don't know what you think you proved by this," Suzanne said to James as she walked past him.

"The parents got to insist that their sons be treated right," Jeff retorted.

"As if you had any idea how to treat a person right." Suzanne's gaze at Jeff was blistering. Lydia heard the remark and gave Suzanne an almost hidden smile. Good friends never forget.

"Hope to see all your sons at practice this week," Frank said as he left.

"There was a time when kids' basketball was fun," Elaine said when the last of her guests were gone. "I'm not sure it is anymore."

At practice the next day, Frank was thinking the same thing and dreading the time when practice would be over. He had asked Paul to stay late because he needed to talk to him. Paul had been inquisitive, but he hadn't pushed it. He knew whatever Frank had to say was important, so he arranged a ride home for Benny with Jeff, who was still attending a lot of the practices.

When the final scrimmage ended, Frank reminded Frankie that he was riding home with Jason's dad. Then he put the basketballs in their mesh bag and sat on the first bleacher, waiting for Paul to wind up his usual talks with the parents who were there. "What did James have to say today?" he asked when Paul finally sat next to him.

"He reminded me that Jamie went to the doctor and got the okay to play on Saturday, and I said that I could see Jamie's ankle was better and I would put him in the lineup."

"That's all he said?"

"Yeah."

"He should have told you about the meeting he had last night." Frank took a deep breath as concern wrinkled Paul's brow. "He invited all the parents of our players except you and me and Marcus. The only reason I was there was because Suzanne got wind of it and insisted that we go. You know Suzanne. Decorum and politeness never stand in her way." He smiled slightly, but Paul's expression never changed. If anything, it only got more dour. "You can guess why he did it. He wanted to complain about Quentin and hoped to get a lot of backers before he gave an ultimatum to you and me."

"What ultimatum? Are they gonna take their kids off the team?"

"It's more like take you and me off the team. Get new coaches."

Paul considered this possibility for a few seconds. "What if we won't go?"

"I don't know. It didn't get that far. I'd like to tell them all to go fuck themselves, but that's not the answer. Still, we have to do something."

"Do Marcus and Delia know about the meeting?"

"Probably not. And I sure hope Quentin never finds out about it." Frank saw Quentin as essential to winning games, and he didn't want him upset. He didn't want Marcus and Delia upset either, because he had a feeling that Delia would pull Quentin off the team in a heartbeat.

"I think they have a right to know," Paul said. "Maybe you and I should go see them."

"Not now. Let's see if we can't talk some sense into these idiot parents." Frank felt a spark of horror at Paul's suggestion.

"How in the hell are we gonna do that?"

"Let's turn the tables on them. Tell them they can either shape up or they won't be allowed to attend any games or practices. We'll kick them off the team."

Paul liked the idea, but he didn't think it would work, not as long as there were telephones and more secret meetings to be had. The same people would keep stirring up trouble. "I still think we should talk to Marcus and Delia. Maybe we should have a meeting of our own and invite *all* the parents this time. Have James and the others tell Marcus and Delia what they're upset about. If they had to say it to their faces, they might realize the harm they're causing."

"No. We need to end this. The Thomases don't need to get their feelings hurt. You and I are in charge of this team, and we have to take care of this."

"How? We can have closed practices, but we'll never keep them away from games."

"I don't know," Frank said, "but I'll think of something. Give me a few days."

"If you don't come up with something soon, I'm calling a meeting of all the parents and getting this problem out in the open."

Frank nodded. He had his work cut out for him.

After Frank left, Paul continued to sit in the gym. It was empty now, the vast space between the floor and ceiling silent except for the voices in his head. He understood why the coach of the high school team had started the first game here with a prayer. Paul felt the presence of deities too. He also felt the presence of evil. How could one thirteen-year-old boy cause so much hostility among adults? And not just the parents. James had told him about the man at the mill who said it wasn't fair that Quentin was getting to play more than Jamie. And the stranger at the last game who seemed almost threatening when he told Paul to play the other players more. Then there was the report that men at the golf course were saying he should play Quentin more. None of them had a son on the team. Why did they care?

Coaching basketball used to be fun when it was just him and his team. Now, it seemed to have grown into something bigger. Maybe the town and the townspeople were experiencing growing pains. Maybe he needed to grow so he could handle things better. He needed help, so he turned to the forces of good: *God, tell me what to do.*

Paul knew better than to expect immediate answers to his prayers. He sat on the hard bleacher with his head in his hands and waited for at least a sense of possibility. Late afternoon turned into night as he continued to sit. The towering windows that gave the gym its usual layers of otherworldly light were black. When he finally turned off the lights and plunged the gym into darkness, he had a good idea of what he must do.

13

Before the Westovers left for the Terrors' game the next Saturday, Meredith corralled Paul in the kitchen and made him sit at the oval table she refinished herself. He had told her about the parents' meeting. She sensed an anger in him that she almost never saw, making her fear he was going to say things he would regret. "Whatever you're thinking of saying, whatever you're thinking of doing," she told him, "don't do it at the game. The players will be there, and so will everybody who comes to watch. You can take care of this in private." If she had her druthers, she wouldn't be going to the game that day. Trying to find job leads for Clarinda was taking more time than she thought it would, so she'd hoped to carve out a few hours to spend on it Saturday afternoon. The game was in another town, so there'd be travel time involved, more than she wanted to spend. But now she was worried about Paul, and she probably should be worried about Frank. Frank had a hotter temper than Paul. And James was always a loose cannon.

"I'll control myself," Paul said. "Today is about the boys, but I don't promise anything for tomorrow."

So, all three Westovers set off for the game. As the miles rolled by, Benny was only vaguely aware of the unusual silence between his parents. He had his own thoughts to stew about. Ever since their argument at the last game, Jamie and Malcolm had ignored each other as much as possible, exchanging only glares and passes when they had to. Benny didn't see how they could possibly play together. At one point in practice, Jamie had thrown the ball so hard at Malcolm that he nearly knocked him over. There was also the question of how his dad was going to use Jamie and Quentin and if Jamie could keep his cool about that. Paul rarely discussed game plans with Benny. He figured his son only needed to be concerned about himself, not the other players. He wasn't aware that behind those large glasses, Benny studied everybody.

After thirty minutes on the interstate, the family arrived at a high school gymnasium much newer than the Tanner gym. "Looks like they've spruced it up a bit since we were here last year," Paul remarked. "But they'll never capture the feel of ours."

Benny wasn't sure what he was talking about. He thought it would be nice to have a new gym, one with bright colors like this one, but he shrugged off the thought when he saw Frankie across the court and went to join him. Suzanne was settling herself on the bleachers when Elaine and James came in with Jamie. Elaine deliberately steered James in another direction so it wouldn't be awkward when she didn't speak to Suzanne. She didn't know if she would ever speak to Suzanne again. How could anybody question the purpose of the Cultural Bridge program? And directly attack James like she did? She practically accused James of being a racist. And then the nerve of her bringing Frank to crash the meeting James organized. Elaine was sure Suzanne was the instigator of that intrusion. Didn't she know not to attend meetings she wasn't invited to? As far away from Suzanne as possible, Elaine and James sat next to Jeff Colton, who had never been a fan of Suzanne and was also miffed about the remark she'd made to him at the meeting.

Quentin arrived just as warm-ups were beginning. He dashed onto the court as Marcus and Delia led their daughters, Rosalie and Camille, to the bleachers. Believe it or not, nobody had told them about James's meeting. Richard originally thought he should tell them, but he was afraid it might do more harm than good, and Frank had managed to dissuade Paul from the idea, at least for now. Nevertheless, Delia felt an iciness among the parents that she hadn't felt before, and surprisingly, it didn't feel directed at her family, as any previous tension seemed to be. For the first time, the parents didn't all greet each other warmly as they usually did. Instead, they sat in huddles like soldiers waiting for orders. She was surprised when Suzanne came and sat next to her. She almost asked Suzanne if she felt the chill too, but was afraid she might seem weird, so she said nothing.

At game time, Paul told the team, "We don't have a home-court advantage here. You won't have your buddies yelling for you like last time"—everybody except Jamie and Quentin smiled—"but that's okay. We can win on our own and then brag about it when we get home. We're glad to have Jamie back with us, so I'm starting him at forward today, along with Quentin, Adam, Frankie, and Benny. Now, go get 'em, guys!"

That was one way to solve the problem of Jamie and Malcolm playing together, Benny thought, but he wasn't sure it was the best solution. Malcolm was disappointed, but more than that, he hoped his dad wouldn't get upset. As the starters took the court, he looked back at Jeff, who was frowning but quiet.

The first quarter went smoothly, with the Terrors gaining the lead early and holding on to it. Jamie and Quentin were an excellent combination. Jamie had the height and the arm to get quick, sharp passes into Quentin under the basket at just the right time. And occasionally, they'd switch, with Jamie under the basket and Quentin firing the passes. As much as Jamie hated setting up points for Quentin, he wanted to win, so he kept doing it. What he really wanted was for Paul to take Quentin out and let him do most of the scoring. He thought that might be happening when Malcolm approached the scorers' table but was disappointed when Malcolm sent Adam to the bench.

Laura was disappointed too. She poked Richard, who was reading *Time* magazine, in the ribs. "Paul's taking Adam out," she said. "He sure didn't get a chance to shine against both Quentin and Jamie."

"Can't you ever be happy?" Richard said. "Adam played the whole first quarter, and he did fine." After inserting a note card in the magazine to mark his place, he turned his attention to the game. Frankly, he hoped Quentin would outscore everybody else and grab all the rebounds just to show those snarky parents what a treasure he was to the team. And that was pretty much what Quentin was doing.

Jeff took notice when Malcolm went into the game. "Finally," he said to James, who nodded but never took his gaze off Jamie. A few seconds into Malcolm's playing time, Jamie decided to change things up. Instead of passing to Quentin, he faked his guard and went around him for a shot. The ball bounced off the rim and landed squarely in Malcolm's hands. Malcolm went back up immediately and swooshed the ball through the net. Jeff leaped to his feet, cheering. Quentin gave Jamie a puzzled look, and Jamie glared at Malcolm. That was the last thing he wanted to have happen. Paul was puzzled too, but he let it slide. The team had scored on the possession, and that was what mattered.

At halftime, Frank went to the men's room. He was chastising himself for drinking too much coffee when he saw that James was following him. He had expected to hear from James earlier in the week and was surprised when nothing happened. Now he recognized James's plan. Catch him when he wouldn't have a lot of time for rebuttal. When Frank came out of the men's room, James was waiting for him. "Got a minute?" James asked.

"Not really. I have to get back to the game."

"This won't take long. Don't ever come to my house uninvited again. That was a private meeting."

"A meeting that involved me and my basketball team. I had a right to be there."

"It's not your team, and no, you didn't."

"So I'm supposed to stand by and let you plan an insurrection?"

Several fans congregated around the concession stand jerked their heads toward Frank when they heard him say *insurrection*. It was a word they didn't often hear at the gym. Was there going to be a fight? Frank's tone made it sound that way. Who was revolting against whom? And why?

"Just don't go where you're not wanted. And watch out. There're going to be some changes made."

"I'm not worried." Frank looked at his watch. "And now I

have to get back to my team." He turned and walked toward the bleachers, where the players were gathered around Paul.

To begin the second half, Paul kept Jamie on the bench and sent in the other regular starters. "You're doing great," he said, "but we need to give that ankle a rest. I don't want you out of commission again." Jamie grunted. His ankle was beginning to ache, but he would never admit it.

"James isn't going to like that, and he's already riled up today," Frank said.

"Says who?" Paul asked.

"He ambushed me coming out of the men's room and let me have it for crashing his party. I'm a little worried about what he's going to do next."

"I promised Meredith I wouldn't say anything to him at the game, but tomorrow afternoon, he and I are going to have a sit-down, one-on-one discussion about what he's doing to the team."

"Does he know that?"

"Yep. He's coming to my house at five. Meredith's making me go to that Martin Luther King thing at the Methodist church at two, but I'll be home and ready for him by five."

"Do you want me to come?"

"I probably should have you there to keep me from punching him in the nose, but this needs to be between the two of us. I don't want him to feel bullied."

Before Frank could say, "Let me know if you change your mind," Benny came sliding toward them on the floor. He'd been making a fast break on a pass from Adam at the other end of the court, moving at breakneck speed, when an opposing guard tried to steal the ball, tripped him, and sent him, propelled by his own momentum, hurtling across the hardwood.

"Foul!" Paul yelled at the referee, who was already blowing his whistle.

The noise got Meredith's attention. Although she'd been trying to watch the game, her mind kept going back to Clarinda. She still thought retail was the best fit for her despite her experience at Belk. Either retail or restaurants. Both had shifts that could be flexible. The problem was there weren't that many restaurants in Tanner. Clarinda had been right about looking in Hickory for more opportunities. Another idea Meredith was toying with was setting Clarinda up as a cleaning lady. She remembered how clean and tidy her apartment had been when Meredith went to see her after the trial. She obviously knew how to keep a home in good order. And, if she was lucky, she could set her own hours. Meredith knew lots of women in Tanner who had others clean their homes. Granted, most of the cleaning ladies were Black, but some women would probably be thrilled to have a white woman clean their house. If she could only sell Clarinda on the idea. She was putting together a list of possible employers for Clarinda when Benny took the spill.

"My god," she said when she saw her son on the floor.

"He's okay," said Lydia, who was sitting next to her. "He'll be up in a second." And he was. Malcolm came over to give him a hand, and he was soon walking toward the foul line for his free throw. "We don't need any more injuries on this team," Lydia continued. "We have enough problems without that."

Meredith nodded, but she wasn't ready to talk about those problems. If she were, Lydia would be the person she'd talk to. If the parents demanded Paul step down as coach, it would kill him. He loved these boys, and she was sure he wouldn't go down without a fight, but just knowing they didn't want him would be a major blow. She remembered how she'd worried about parents' attitudes when the team lost the first three games. This was so much worse. She hoped Paul could finally settle things with James at their meeting the next day.

Sensing a need to change the subject, Lydia said, "That's an interesting list of names you're writing on your pad. Can I ask you what the list means?"

"Sure. It's a list of women who might be interested in hiring a friend of mine as a cleaning lady. She's a single mother who really needs a job, but her skills are limited. And she needs flexible hours, so I thought housecleaning might be a good fit for her right now."

"Okay. Tell me a little about her, and maybe I can help." Lydia was also thinking Elaine Parker might be able to help. She knew a lot of people through her job at the church. Plus, having Meredith and Elaine working together on a project might encourage them to help ease the rift between their husbands.

When Meredith told her Clarinda's story, Lydia was sure this was a good idea. She encouraged Meredith to contact Elaine the next day. Meredith didn't know if she could work with Elaine or not, but she wasn't going to tell Lydia that. She would think about it.

Benny was back in the game with no signs of being any worse for the tumble. Since halftime, the Terrors' lead had diminished and sometimes slipped away, but they always fought their way back. "We need both Quentin and Jamie in there," Frank said to Paul. "You saw what they did in the first half. They're great together."

Paul knew Frank was right, so as the fourth quarter started, he sent Jamie in for Adam. "Time's running out," he said to Jamie. "Let's wrap this up with a bang." Jamie took what he said to heart, and although he had nothing but scowls for Malcolm, he worked with Quentin and the others to end the game with a win.

One game closer to the playoffs. Paul was beaming when the players came off the bench. The other parents were beaming too, except Laura, who was angry that Adam played only half the game. She wanted to fuss at Paul about it, but Richard wouldn't let her, and she needed to get home to do last-minute preparations for the Martin Luther King celebration the next day. She had a lengthy checklist with only a few of the final items checked off.

Malcolm followed Lydia's suggestion and invited Quentin to come to his house after the game, so Quentin left with the Coltons. After Jeff watched his family depart, he seized Frank's attention to share information he thought would add to the coach's delight about the game. "Got some good news for you," he called. "I talked with a bunch of the guys in Kiwanis, and they all told me to encourage you to join. They think you'd be a good addition to the group. You can go to the meeting next month with me and make it official."

Frank stared at Jeff, his game-inspired smile melting from his face. He couldn't forget Jeff's threatening remark about replacing Paul and him as coaches and his disparaging words about Quentin. Frank didn't want to go anywhere with Jeff again, including Kiwanis, but he did still want to join the club. Ever since James's meeting, he'd been battling between his loyalty to Paul and the team and his political ambition. He needed another mentor, but he wasn't sure who it would be. Did he have the courage to approach George Simmons, one of his bosses at the mill who was at the meeting he attended? George was one of the men he was supposed to impress, but maybe he already had. In any case, he wasn't going to any meeting with Jeff. He didn't care if he never saw Jeff again. "Thanks for telling me," he said. "I'll have to look at my calendar about next month. Not sure if I can make the meeting or not."

"Don't wait too long. You have to strike while the iron is hot, and you only have a few months until the next town council election." Jeff's expression was questioning. "Call me when you know something." He buttoned his coat and walked toward the door.

Frank waited until Jeff had left the gym before putting on his own coat. "See you at practice on Monday," he said to Paul and then hustled to join Suzanne and Frankie waiting halfway across the gym.

Almost everyone had gone by then, so Paul was surprised to see James walking toward him. "About tomorrow night," he said. "I can't make it. Elaine's making me help clean up after the Martin Luther King thing or at least take the kids home and keep an eye on them so she can help clean up."

Paul wondered if he was telling the truth. He'd never been enthusiastic about meeting with Paul, and this was as good an excuse as any. "Okay. How about Tuesday night? We don't practice on Tuesdays."

"Can't do it. I have a late meeting at the mill that night."

"Thursday? Can you do Thursday?"

"Yes," James said dryly.

"See you then," Paul said. He hoped he could keep his courage intact that long.

14

Flowers delivered. Cooks from both churches confirmed that they were bringing their designated refreshments for the reception after the service. Choir directors ready with the musical selections. Sharon Robinson from Copeland and Elaine Parker from Tanner prepared to meet Justice Griffin when he arrived and make sure he had everything he needed before and during the service. Laura looked over her list one more time before she left for church. She'd considered skipping the regular morning service, but Elaine had been given that privilege since she and Sharon were taking Justice Griffin for a light lunch at Johnny's Restaurant, the best restaurant in Tanner. Someone, meaning Laura, had to be present in the morning to remind the congregation about the celebration and entice them to come. She'd persuaded their minister, Travis Staplewood, to give her a full five minutes at the lectern to speak her piece, and if she felt like talking longer, she would.

As it turned out, she managed to cram everything she wanted to say into the allotted time, after which Reverend Staplewood gave his own encouragement in support of the celebration. Laura smiled appreciatively at him and then stared at the congregation in a way she hoped said, "I know who you are, and if you don't show up this afternoon, you'll hear from me."

By the time people started arriving at the church around one forty-five, Laura had a good feeling that everything was going to go well. Elaine was not so sure. For one thing, it seemed to her that more people were arriving from Copeland than from Tanner. This did not look good for the First United Methodist Church. "We're outnumbered," she whispered to Richard, who was standing with Laura and her to welcome the guests.

"Yeah, so far," Richard said. "Does that bother you?"

"It embarrasses me. And makes me feel a little insecure."

"What if you were the only white person here?"

Elaine gave him an incredulous stare.

"That's the situation African Americans face a lot of the time," he said. "I've been to faculty meetings at the college where Clarence Whitaker was the only Black person there. He's not the only Black professor we have, but he's the only Black professor in the history department. You should try visiting the AME church sometime. It'd be good for you."

Elaine couldn't imagine going to the all-Black church alone. She was sure James wouldn't go with her. She chased the idea out of her head. For now, she had to be a good hostess at her own church. The first person she recognized from Copeland was Sharon Robinson, smiling as usual and wearing a very chic, broad-brimmed, red hat. Soon she saw Erlene and Alfred Duncan and a few others from the organizational meeting. It made her feel good to be able to exchange warm pleasantries with these people whom she very likely could have gone her entire life without meeting, although they lived in the next town. Another thing she noticed as she greeted people was that Suzanne and Frank weren't there. Not that she really expected Suzanne to come, but she said she'd see if she could get Frank to come. Elaine doubted she'd even mentioned the service to Frank.

Lydia arrived with Malcolm. Jeff had debated with himself about whether he had to go or not. He finally decided it would be good for Malcolm to see him there, and his attendance could only do good things for his reputation in Tanner.

Marcus and Delia had had a much longer debate about attending. "We still haven't gone to a single service at the AME church," Marcus said, "and you swore you'd never go to church with Laura Campbell again. So why should we go? Let's wait and go to the regular service at the AME church next Sunday. We can start to make our own friends, and we won't have to deal with anybody from the basketball team. I couldn't bear it if Laura starts telling the people from Copeland what good friends of hers we are."

"Going to the celebration has nothing to do with us or with anybody else," Delia said. "It has to do with the Reverend Martin Luther King, Jr., who's one of the greatest men of our times. Maybe of any time. We've never been to a celebration of his birthday with white people. I want our children to know that white people recognize his greatness too."

How could Marcus say no to that? "I wish you'd told me you felt that way a few weeks ago. At least we could have gone to the church in Copeland and made a few friends by now."

Delia gave him an impish smile. "Since when have you been afraid to go to a place where you hardly knew anybody? That's the story of our lives, isn't it? And you might be surprised. Some of the people you know at the mill may be there. Plus, I like some of the parents from the basketball team. Suzanne made a point of sitting with me at the last game."

"Okay, you win." Marcus figured Delia was likely to take the children and go without him, so he may as well go along. Also, he'd heard Glenn Griffin was speaking. Never having seen Glenn in person, he was curious about a Black man on the North Carolina Supreme Court. All five Thomases—Marcus, Delia, Quentin, Rosalie, and Camille—took their seats in the fifth pew of the sanctuary ten minutes before the service began.

Paul and Meredith came with Benny. Meredith meant what she said about making the celebration nondenominational, which was what the planners wanted all along. When it was time to start, Laura and Richard joined Adam and Annabelle on the pew where Adam was reading a Marvel comic book. "Put that away," Laura demanded. She'd already made him leave his knit cap at home, so he felt exposed and was hiding behind the comic, but he did what he was told.

Elaine found James where he was sitting with Jamie and Gloria, who was three years older than Jamie. James had refused to greet people with Elaine by saying he had to stay with the kids to make sure Gloria didn't bolt. A world-wise eleventh grader, she was not happy to be at church.

Choirs from both churches filled the choir loft and spilled out behind the lectern and pulpit. A snare drum and an electric guitar with amplifier were set up with music stands in front of the chancel rail. As the two ministers and Justice Griffin entered the sanctuary, the choirs and the congregation rose, and two musicians from Copeland seated themselves behind the instruments. The opening hymn, "Joyful, Joyful, We Adore Thee," drawn from Beethoven's ninth symphony, nearly raised the roof of the First United Methodist Church of Tanner. The people from Tanner looked around in amazement. Even Gloria wore an expression of delighted surprise. When the final vibrations faded away, Travis Staplewood stepped forward to give the official welcome to the event and praise Dr. King. Alexander Jennings, pastor at the African Methodist Episcopal Church, spoke next, offering an official response and the opening prayer. Their remarks were followed by the first anthem, which was every bit as stirring and joyful as the opening hymn.

When the idea for the joint choirs was first raised, both choir directors had their doubts about the success of the combination since the choirs had such different styles. They were thrilled, however, that the voices blended together beautifully, and the congregation's response was an undeniable acclamation of their achievement. When Pastor Jennings rose to speak again, his first words were, "I believe we're in the presence of angels, for I've surely heard voices from heaven today," and the AME members responded, "Amen."

"Where are the angels?" Camille Thomas asked Delia, who replied, "Everywhere. You just have to know how to look." So Camille spent the rest of the service staring at people to see if she could tell which ones were angels.

Reverend Staplewood spoke again after Pastor Jennings. Both men talked about the gifts of Dr. King and the challenge of continuing his fight for equality. Their remarks were followed by the second anthem, which, while not as rousing as the first musical selections, still inspired a feeling of affirmation and light. For everyone except Alfred Duncan, that is. "I thought they were gonna do "Lift Every Voice and Sing," he stage-whispered to Erlene.

"It's not over yet," Erlene said as she patted his hand.

And finally it was time for Justice Glenn to speak. A handsome man in his early fifties, he had an air of grandeur yet humility about him. He spoke warmly about the time he met Dr. King. "I got a chance to shake his hand, and that has been one of the high points in my life," he said. He talked about the many positive steps toward equality that North Carolina and the nation had taken, including his own appointment to the state supreme court. "Don't give up," he said. "If we make two steps backward, let's find a way to make three steps forward together."

As he returned to his seat, the congregation applauded and shouted, "Amen!" Even some of the people from Tanner joined in saying "Amen" this time. Lydia was quiet but didn't restrain Malcolm, who was caught up in the moment.

When the clapping subsided, the choirs rose to signal the singing of the final hymn. "Oh, boy," Alfred said when he recognized the first notes of "Lift Every Voice and Sing."

"Told you so," Erlene said.

And once again the church's antique glass windows seem to swell with emotion and joy. In the resounding silence that followed the hymn, Reverend Staplewood pronounced the benediction and invited everyone to the reception in the fellowship hall. Most of the congregation crowded through the two staircases that led to the lower level. Richard smiled at the mixed-race group moving as one body. He was eager to see if they separated when they reached the reception. Sure enough, after they passed the refreshment table, they broke into small groups, mostly characterized by color. Richard left Laura to tend to her hosting duties and steered Adam and Annabelle toward a group from Copeland that included a few young people about their age.

James, who was also a hostess widower, saw what happened and brought Jamie over to say hello. He was in full command mode now, so he didn't stay long to chat before he and Jamie moved on to another group of people, mostly from Tanner. Jeff was there with Paul and Meredith, but James still didn't stay long. Eventually he would find his spot in the room and wait for people to come to him. Gloria abandoned him as soon as she saw some of her friends, and Jamie stayed behind with Benny when his dad left the group from Tanner.

Justice Griffin was surrounded by people from both churches. Everybody wanted to talk with him. Lydia was in the group, hoping to get a chance to ask him more about progress against racism in North Carolina. At the moment, he was talking about his experiences in the North Carolina Senate before he became a justice. When he paused, Elaine, who had abandoned her hostess duties in order to spend time with him, said, "Justice Griffin, you are so articulate."

Embarrassed by the remark, Lydia moved away from the group. She didn't want to hear the justice's reply, although she knew whatever he said would be the right thing to say.

15

Knowing Elaine had as much as she could handle on Sunday, Meredith waited until Monday to call her about Clarinda. She thought long and hard about whether she could work with Elaine on anything but finally decided Clarinda was worth it. The first thing Elaine said after answering the call was, "What did you think of the celebration yesterday?"

"I enjoyed it," Meredith said. "You and Laura and the people from Copeland did a great job putting it together. Justice Griffin's remarks were perfect for the occasion. I got to speak with him briefly after the service, and he was just as interesting unscripted."

"I know. Doesn't he speak really well?"

"Of course he does. He's a Supreme Court justice."

Elaine sensed a rebuke in Meredith's comment but wasn't exactly sure why. "I'm just glad so many people showed up and everything went so well. I tried to call Laura this morning to congratulate her on her part in putting it all together, but she didn't answer. I think she's probably taken to her bed this morning to get a much-deserved rest. Too bad the rest of us had to go to work." Elaine laughed. "Did you get a chance to talk with any of the AME members?"

"I did," Meredith said. "I talked with several of them. Sharon Robinson seemed to be making an effort to talk with everyone from Tanner. She strikes me as a woman who can get things done. I also met another woman who's a lawyer like me. We had a lot in common, although she works for a firm and I work for the government. I hope your church will keep doing things with them. Maybe I'll suggest something similar to our church, although it may be a harder sell there. I'm sure Sharon could suggest another church for us to partner with."

She took a breath, and when Elaine didn't immediately say anything, she changed the conversation to tell Clarinda's story. She was as honest as she could be without casting Clarinda in too bad a light, but she had to reveal that she'd appeared in family court. The point of the telling was to emphasize that a job would be an invaluable first step in getting her life back on track and regaining custody of her daughter. "So, I was hoping," she concluded, "that you might be willing to talk with some of the women in the church to see if anyone needs a cleaning lady. Or, it just occurred to me, maybe a babysitter. That would be particularly good if Clarinda could take her daughter with her or keep the other child in her home." Meredith was surprised she hadn't thought of that before.

"Will you be a reference for this young woman?" Elaine asked. The plan sounded a little shaky to her.

"I will," Meredith replied.

"Okay. I'll ask around about the cleaning lady position. The childcare part seems more iffy to me, especially if this woman abandoned her own child."

"She didn't abandon her. She was sick and couldn't get home to her. But never mind. If you can find someone interested in hiring a cleaning lady, that would be great."

"I'll try," Elaine said, "and I'm really glad you came yesterday. I'll let you know if I find anyone."

During lunch period at Tanner Middle School on Tuesday, Malcolm asked Quentin to come home with him again. It wasn't something he'd planned on doing, at least not this soon, although he'd enjoyed shooting baskets with Quentin on Saturday. But when he saw Quentin looking around the cafeteria with an anxious expression on his face, trying to find someone to sit with, Malcolm waved him over to sit next to him, and as they talked, the invitation spilled out.

"I'll have to ask my mom," Quentin said, reminding Malcolm

that he hadn't asked his mother either, but she wouldn't mind. She liked Quentin.

"You can call her from my house," Malcolm said, which was just what Quentin did, and Malcolm did too. After getting the okay from both moms, they set about finding something to eat. What they didn't tell their moms was that since Quentin had ridden his bicycle to school, he doubled Malcolm all the way home, a practice he was strictly forbidden to do. But nobody had gotten hurt, so what difference did it make?

Around five thirty, Delia drove into the Coltons' driveway. "I could have let Quentin ride his bike home, but from your house to ours is a long ride, and I figured I could get the bike in the trunk of my car," she told Lydia at the front door. "I hope so, anyway."

"Come on in," Lydia said, motioning to her as she held the door open. Lydia's living room wasn't large, but it had a commanding stone fireplace where, every now and then, she built a fire, mostly on holidays. Although the house was still a rental, it had more space than the townhouse where she and Malcolm had lived with Jeff when they moved to Tanner and was just around the corner from the townhouse. Even though she liked this part of town, Lydia wished she could have moved closer to the schools, but none of the houses near the schools were for rent, and she couldn't make herself commit to buying a house in Tanner. Renting was cheaper, anyway. "Can I get you something to drink? The boys got cold playing basketball outside, so they're back in Malcolm's room. We could visit for a little while if you'd like."

"I'd like to visit, but nothing to drink, thank you."

"Then have a seat." Lydia gestured toward the flowered couch that doubled as a bed when her family came to visit.

Delia was grateful to have this time with Lydia. Of all the mothers of boys on the team, Lydia seemed the most sincere. At least Delia never doubted she was telling the truth. "Thanks for inviting me in," Delia said as she settled on the couch. "I want to tell you how much I appreciate Malcolm inviting Quentin to your house. Quentin's friendly, but he hasn't made many friends here—actually, not any. I was delighted when Malcolm invited him over, and he was too, although he'd never say it in so many words. But I could hear it in his voice when he called this afternoon."

"Malcolm enjoyed having Quentin come over. The invitation this afternoon was totally spontaneous. I didn't know anything about it until he called me after school."

Delia smiled. "I'm glad to hear that. I worry about Quentin and this basketball team." She searched Lydia's face for any kind of shock or disapproval before continuing. "Some of the parents have so much resentment toward Quentin, or so it seems. And that scares me. I wanted to take him off the team a few weeks ago, give the boys and parents a chance to get to know him as a person instead of a basketball player, but Marcus wouldn't hear of it. He said if we let him quit the team, we're setting an example for him to run from uncomfortable situations all his life. I guess Marcus is right. But I'm still worried."

"Don't let the bully parents scare you. They're loud, and they're rude, but they're not dangerous. At least, I don't think so." Lydia slid closer to Delia and patted her hand. Although she knew the parents' behavior had to be unsettling to the Thomases, she never realized they were frightened.

"Sometimes appearances can be deceiving," Delia said. "Several nights ago, we got a nasty phone call from somebody. Thank goodness Marcus answered the phone. It could have been Quentin or even one of the girls. Do you suppose the caller would have said those awful things to them?"

Lydia squeezed Delia's hand. "Oh, mercy. What did they say? Was it a man or a woman?"

Tears dampened Delia's eyes. "Marcus said it was a man. And, of course, he wouldn't give his name. Marcus didn't recognize the voice." Her lips trembled. "He said we didn't belong in Tanner, that we should go back to where we came from. I don't know if he meant Greensboro or Africa. We've gotten remarks about Africa before."

"Did you call the police?"

"No. Marcus said he wasn't threatening us. He was just somebody blowing off steam. Whether he was angry about the basketball team or just at us in general, who knows? Or maybe the world in general. If it happens again, Marcus said he'd call the police."

Lydia was sad for the Thomases and sad for her town. She couldn't believe somebody in Tanner would make a call like that. Delia was right about appearances. Racism and resentment ran deep, and sometimes no matter how hard a person tried to hide them, they reared their ugly heads. "I'm going to talk to the team parents to see if anyone knows anything about it."

"No, don't do that," Delia said. "We'd rather no one knows about it yet. Like Marcus said, it was probably just somebody blowing off steam. Besides, there's trouble enough among the team parents already. They were so distant from each other at the last game, and for the first time, their contempt didn't seem aimed at us. Do you know what's going on?"

When Delia wiped her eyes with her fingers, Lydia got up to get her a tissue. Glad for a few minutes to pull her thoughts together before answering Delia's question, she went for the box in the bathroom instead of the kitchen. How much did Delia need to know? Were details just going to scare her more?

"You're right about the tension," she said when she returned. "I guess it's because the boys are getting older, and some of the parents really want their sons to shine in high school. Maybe they think they can get a college scholarship. Who knows? But they've become competitive about spots on the team and playing time. Please don't take Quentin off the team. He's a nice young man, and I hope he and Malcolm continue to be friends."

"Would this have happened if Quentin hadn't joined the team?" Delia's face was calmer now. She appreciated Lydia's efforts to tell her what was going on and yet spare her feelings by not getting to what Delia considered to be the heart of the matter.

"I don't know. Maybe the parents who act that way would have turned on the players we've had since the beginning, or any new player who's as good as Quentin could have caused the problem."

"I mean, is it because he's Black?"

And there it was. Lydia drew a quick breath. "I honestly don't know. Maybe. Maybe not. They'll get over it. They'll have to."

Delia wanted to believe her, but she wasn't sure she could take another two months of hard feelings and the fear creeping around her mind. "At least Quentin has Malcolm," she said.

"And you have me," Lydia said. "Call me anytime."

"It's getting on toward suppertime. I guess I'd better gather up Quentin and head for home. I have no idea what I'm going to fix for my family to eat. Getting back into the groove of working all day and still getting supper on the table is harder than I thought it would be." Delia smiled sadly. "But I like my job. And I'll be right there when Quentin gets to high school next year. Not that he'll like that, but I will."

16

Quentin was looking forward to seeing Malcolm at school the next day. Maybe they could sit together at lunch. And then they had basketball practice later that afternoon. It was going to be a good day, he thought as he pedaled off that morning. He did sit with Malcolm at lunch, along with Frankie and Benny. At practice, Paul and Frank congratulated the boys again for their win on Saturday.

"If we can keep our record above fifty percent, we'll land a spot in the playoffs," Paul reminded them. "And I think we have a good chance of doing that. I've been working on a new rotation plan and a few new plays to go with the new rotation. It all hinges on trying players at new spots and seeing what other skills you have."

The boys looked at him with anticipation and apprehension. *I hope he doesn't make me play center again*, Malcolm thought.

I hope he doesn't do anything to make them all hate me more, Quentin thought.

He better let me play center, Jamie thought.

I hope he knows what he's doing, Frank thought.

"Here's what I'm thinking," Paul said. "We're going to try letting our usual forwards play guard occasionally and our guards play forward. Forwards and centers will change out more often too. For our first scrimmage, I want Jamie at center, Quentin and Frankie at forward, and Malcolm and Adam at guard. Malcolm, you be point guard for now. I know you can call the plays."

Frank was still skeptical as play began. There were mistakes at first, but he was surprised at how well the boys knew the plays for another position. Malcolm would never be the point guard that Frankie was, but he was doing a credible job. Adam made a good shooting guard because he already had an outside shot. Frankie was a better ball handler than he was a shooter, and his height was better suited for outside play, but he was doing okay. Jamie and Quentin were obviously interchangeable at forward and center, so there was nothing to be learned there. Soon Paul switched them all around again and moved them from one scrimmage team to another. As he watched the plays unfold, Frank began to realize the genius of Paul's plan.

If he took the players out of their usual roles occasionally, he could substitute more often and maybe shake them from their attachment to a single position. That way, he could vary their playing times more and, he hoped, keep them and their parents from thinking they owned a particular place. The change might cut down on the bickering and jealousy and, if he was lucky, develop more well-rounded players.

"How'd you come up with this idea?" Frank asked Paul toward the end of practice.

"Coaching magazine," Paul said. "I figured it couldn't hurt unless it costs us a lot of games. And maybe we'll confuse people who have no business interfering with our team about who's playing when, where, or how much."

Frank laughed. "You sly devil."

"Good job today, fellows," Paul called as the boys gathered their coats off the bleachers. "I knew you could do it."

"I still don't know how you do it," Malcolm said to Frankie when they headed for the door, but they were both laughing, so maybe Paul was on the right track.

Outside, clouds had moved in and covered the moon and stars. A chill breeze was blowing, rattling the withered brown leaves that clung stubbornly to the trees. The boys climbed into the cars of their waiting parents. "Do you need a ride home, Quentin?" Frank called when he saw Quentin take his bicycle from the bike rack.

"No, sir. I can ride my bike. It's not far, and I have a headlight."

Frank shook his head and wondered if he should make arrangements with Marcus to take Quentin to practice with Frankie and him.

Quentin threw his leg across the bicycle bar and began pedaling out of the parking lot. Car taillights marked a series of red splotches that he followed to the road, where they soon disappeared into the darkness. Quentin tightened his jacket collar against the breeze. After the parents' cars left, very little traffic appeared to keep him company. He hunched over his handlebars and pedaled faster, trying to keep warm and get home sooner. One car passed him and was soon out of sight. For a while, he was alone again, humming a wordless tune in his head. The sound of a second car, louder than the first, approached him from behind. Instinctively, he tried to move closer to the road's shoulder. The sound grew even louder, followed by a blow that felt like a cannonball tore through him. Then nothing. The car that hit him kept going as if nothing had happened. The breeze picked up and drove some of the dead leaves into a dance above the fallen bicycle. Quentin lay unconscious, a stone's throw away at the edge of the football practice field.

James was in a grumpy mood as he drove Jamie home. "What was Coach doing moving y'all around to positions you don't play?" he asked his son. "At least he didn't make you play guard. Now that would have been a waste of talent under the basket."

"He didn't say why. Just that he thought it would be good for us. He moved Quentin to guard at one point. I'd probably have been next." Jamie shrugged. If Coach had made him play guard, he'd have shown him the best damn guard he'd ever seen.

"He better not do it in a game." A few minutes of silence passed. "Listen, I'm going to drop you off at home. I want to make a liquor store run, and you don't have to go. I won't be gone long. Mom's probably there if she hasn't already left to pick up Gloria. She told me this morning she had to pick her up at a friend's house or something like that." James stopped the car in front of their house. "You have a key, don't you?"

Jamie nodded. He'd had his own house key since he was eleven.

After leaving dinner on the stove and giving Annabelle strict instructions not to answer the door for anyone, Laura left home before Richard and Adam returned from practice. Tonight was book club night, and she didn't want to be late. She had a lot to say about the book they were going to discuss. ... *And Ladies of the Club* by Helen Hooven Santmyer was historical fiction, and she tried to tell herself the attitudes of the characters were representative of the late eighteenth and early nineteenth centuries in the United States, but she still couldn't stand that they were so sexist and racist. "The author uses the book for what are obviously her own personal views," she told Richard. "And she rarely gives much ink to any other views. She skips over those people."

Meredith was also headed out to book club, but all she left for Paul and Benny were instructions to go to Johnny's Restaurant for dinner. She hadn't finished reading the book—who could blame her? It was more than a thousand pages long—but she hadn't been to book club in months, so she ought to put in an appearance. She also liked the symmetry of discussing it at book club when it was about women in a book club. And the author hadn't published it until she was in her eighties. She deserved some respect. With Meredith's love for studying people, she found the characters in the book interesting, each of them so different from the others. She wanted to know what happened to them later in life. As she watched the dark road roll under her car, she promised herself that she would finish reading the book.

Jeff left the hospital a little before seven o'clock. One of his older patients who'd been with him since his return to Tanner had been there a few days with double pneumonia. Jeff was nearly ready to release him, but for now, he wanted him near a respirator just in case. Soon he would send him home with antibiotics and an oxygen tank. At least he hoped it would be soon. He was frustrated that the pneumonia was taking so long to improve.

Out on the highway, Suzanne picked up Edskiburgers at the

take-out window of Ed's Drive-in. She'd spent all afternoon on the telephone selling magazines and newspapers in her job as a tele-marketer and didn't feel like cooking dinner. She loved talking to people on the phone, which was why she was so good at her job. She'd moved up from selling vacuum cleaners to printed material, a product she considered to be much more refined, but all that con-vincing and cajoling could sometimes wear her out. Besides, she loved Edskiburgers with the onions and spices cooked in with the meat, and she and Frank had sometimes double dated with Ed and his wife when they were all in high school. She felt good about sup-porting his drive-in.

Around seven thirty, Delia began to worry. Quentin should be home. Practice wouldn't have run this late. She was sure every other mother, just like her, had dinner waiting on the table, and the coaches knew that. She called Lydia, who told her practice had ended about an hour ago and she had seen Quentin ride off on his bicycle. Now Delia panicked. "Marcus!" she yelled. "We have to go find Quentin!"

"Why?" Marcus asked from his easy chair.

"Practice ended a long time ago, and he's still not home."

"I'll go," Marcus said. "You stay here with the girls."

"I can't just sit here and do nothing." Horrible scenarios rushed through Delia's mind.

"He probably stopped off somewhere. I'll find him. You stay here in case he comes home. I'll find a way to call you in fifteen minutes in case he's here." Marcus ran for the car and began driving toward the gym. He hoped he knew the route Quentin would take.

Margery Russell was driving home from work when she saw the bicycle by the side of the road. She'd had to work overtime at the mill and was tired and hungry, so she almost didn't stop, but something about the bicycle didn't look right. The rear wheel was sticking up above the ground, not like it would have been if some-one had just dropped it there. Margery slowed down. She was a cautious woman. She looked for details and reviewed her work, which was why she often stayed late at her job. She also tried to avoid trouble and rarely inserted herself into questionable situations. She stopped her car and looked for other cars on the road, but there weren't any. She opened the door and stood next to the bicycle.

In the tall grass between the road and the practice field lay a body, barely visible in the darkness. Margery let out a startled yelp. This couldn't be happening to her. Her first instinct was to get back into the car. Instead, she walked slowly toward the body. It was lying on its stomach, so she could barely see the face. It was a boy, a teenage boy. Was he dead? How did they do that on television? Put their fingertips against his neck to feel for a pulse? She reached for him reluctantly until she noticed his back was rising and falling. Not much, but enough to suggest he was alive. This time, she did get back into the car and drove to the nearest house. Soon the police and an ambulance were on their way. Margery drove back to the boy and waited in her car until the police arrived. She had to make sure nothing happened to him lying in the cold grass all alone.

Marcus took the most direct route to the gym but saw no signs of Quentin. *Good god, son*, he thought. *Which way did you go?* He drove around in front of the high school and down a different side street and was approaching the gym from another direction when he saw flashing lights next to the practice field. "No, no, no!" he screamed into the windshield. Paramedics were unloading a stretcher from the ambulance as he parked behind the police car. He reached Quentin before the paramedics did. "That's my son!" he yelled as the police tried to hold him back. From a distance, he watched Quentin being prepared for transport to the hospital. "Quentin!" he called as the stretcher went past him.

"Follow them to the hospital," a police officer said. "They'll let you know what's going on there."

At the hospital, volunteers steered Marcus to the emergency waiting area, promising a doctor would be out soon. He immediately used the pay phone to call Delia, who rushed to the hospital with Rosalie and Camille in tow. They ran into the emergency room just before Quentin's doctor arrived. "The X-rays show a broken femur and cracked pelvis," the doctor said.

Delia felt suddenly cold. "Will he be all right?" she asked.

"He should be after surgery and a lot of physical therapy."

"Can we see him?" Marcus asked.

"Yes. He's awake now. Fortunately, we can't find any signs of brain injury. There's a mild concussion but no traumatic injury."

Marcus, Delia, and the girls followed the doctor to a curtained-off section of the emergency room. Quentin lay in a bed, his eyes half closed. Delia rushed to hug him, but a nurse told her to stand back. "His leg isn't set yet, so it's better not to move him. They'll be taking him to surgery soon." Delia settled for a kiss on his cheek.

At the feel of her lips, Quentin opened his eyes. "Mom," he mumbled.

"I'm here, darling," Delia said.

"I am too," Marcus said, his voice gruff.

Rosalie and Camille were too stunned to say anything. They'd never seen their brother look so pitiful before.

"We gave him a sedative to keep him more comfortable until he goes into surgery," the nurse said. "He may not be very responsive."

Delia didn't care. She just had to see that he was alive. Marcus patted his hand, which caused his eyelids to flutter again. "You're going to be all right, son," Marcus said.

Delia sat in the only chair in the area. Marcus leaned against the wall, and the girls sat on the floor. Quentin's chest rose and fell slowly. Occasionally, his face contorted, revealing the medication hadn't completely suppressed the pain. A sheet covering the lower half of his body hid the damaged parts of him. Delia wanted to see his leg, that sweet little leg she had bathed and caressed when he was a baby, but nurses kept coming in and out, and Delia was afraid to touch him. Instead, she talked to him softly. In almost a croon, she told him of good times to come and reminded him his birthday wasn't far away.

Delia and the girls had hurried out of the house so quickly that none of them thought to bring anything to entertain Rosalie and Camille during the long wait, and they grew restless on the floor. Rosalie began to whine first, complaining that the floor was too hard and she was bored. Then Camille took up the chant, a shriller echo to her sister's words, until Marcus gave them a look that drove them into silence. They tried hard to be quiet, but the effort eventually became more than their nervous systems could take. Camille poked Rosalie, and Rosalie poked her back, and soon they were scuffling like puppies. Marcus grabbed Rosalie's hand and jerked her to her feet. His eyes blazed. "You're going back out to the waiting room until you can learn to behave," he said.

Camille began to cry just as a nurse and two orderlies came to wheel Quentin away. "Surgery?" Delia asked.

"No," the nurse said. "We're going back to imaging. The doctor wants another CT scan to be sure there's no damage to any of the organs in the pelvic region."

Delia took a deep breath, and Camille cried louder. When Quentin was gone, Marcus pushed the girls toward the waiting room, and Delia followed. Away from the strange smells and beeping machines, Camille calmed down. "It's going to be a long night," Marcus said. "Why don't you take the girls home and give them some supper?"

"I can't leave," Delia said. "Quentin needs me."

"He'll be going to surgery soon," Marcus said. "You can't do anything for him then. I'll be here. I'll be here all night. You take care of the girls and come back in the morning."

The thought of leaving Quentin alone in the hospital made Delia flinch. She couldn't imagine not being there if anything happened. But her girls were tired and hungry. If they were in Greensboro, she could call a friend to come get them and let them sleep over at her house, but Delia didn't know anybody here well enough to ask for that kind of favor, and Rosalie and Camille didn't know any adults well enough to feel comfortable with them all night. She really didn't have a choice. "All right," she said as her throat began to tighten. "But you call me at least every hour and let me know what's going on. Tell Quentin where I am and that I'll be back as soon as I can."

Marcus hugged her close, sharing her pain and fear. "At least every hour," he said. "If that's not enough, call the hospital main line and ask them to put you through to the nurses' station in the emergency room. I'll be here." Then he hugged each of his daughters and walked back toward Quentin's bed to begin the long vigil.

Delia thanked God that the girls were quiet once they got into the car. Her eyes burned and her muscles ached as she fought to maintain a brave face for them on the drive home. When they got there, the spaghetti sauce and pasta were still on the stove where she'd left them. The salad was in the refrigerator. She turned on two burners to warm up the food and sent Rosalie and Camille to wash their hands.

"Is Quentin gonna die?" Camille asked as she sucked up strands of spaghetti.

"No. Of course not," Delia said. "He just broke his leg. I imagine he'll be in a cast for some time, but he will get well."

"How'd he break it?" Rosalie asked. "Did he fall off his bicycle?"

"We don't know for sure. We hope he can tell us what happened when he wakes up from surgery. Since we found him beside the road, he may have been hit by a car."

Camille's eyes grew large. "Why'd the car hit him?"

"If that's what happened, I'm sure it was an accident. It was dark out, and the driver probably didn't see him."

"Who's the driver?" Rosalie asked.

"We don't know. Like I said, there may or may not have been a car or a driver."

"Where'd he go?" Camille still had a wide-eyed stare.

Rosalie frowned. "Looks like he would've stopped to help Quentin."

Delia couldn't have agreed more, but she didn't want to discuss it with her daughters, certainly not without more information.

As she was washing the dishes, the telephone rang. "Delia, this is Lydia. Did Quentin come home? I tried to call you earlier, but there was no answer."

Delia felt tears rising again, but she managed to tell Lydia what happened.

"Jesus Christ!" Lydia couldn't have been more shocked. Things like that didn't happen in Tanner. "Who did it?"

There was that question again. Delia was so worried about Quentin that she had hardly thought about the driver, but now she needed to know. "I have no idea," she said. "The police didn't say. I think whoever did it was long gone by the time they got there. Maybe Marcus knows more now. I should get off the phone. He's at the hospital and promised to call me soon."

"I'm so sorry," Lydia said. "Let me know if there's any news." After the call ended, she agonized over what she should do next. If she told certain people, the news would be all over town by morning. Yet maybe people needed to know so they could offer help. Maybe somebody had been in the area and knew what had happened. Eventually, she decided to wait until she knew more. She didn't need a lot of people calling her to ask probing questions.

Delia put her daughters to bed and waited by the phone. She'd been home longer than an hour. Why hadn't Marcus called? Twice she picked up the phone to call the hospital, and twice she put it down. If he had any news, he would call. Finally, after midnight, the phone rang. "He's out of surgery," Marcus said in a tired voice. "Everything went well. He should wake up from the anesthesia soon. You get some sleep. I won't call again until morning unless there's an emergency."

Sleep? Delia thought. *I doubt I'll ever sleep again.*

17

At six thirty, Delia called the high school to tell them she wouldn't be in that day. She explained that Quentin had been injured and she needed to be at the hospital. Mercifully, the secretary didn't ask many questions once she learned he would recover. Marcus called to report that Quentin had woken up for a few minutes and then gone back to sleep. "I'm coming home now," he said. "I'll get the girls off to school so you can come see Quentin. Then I'll get a few hours of sleep and go to the office for a while."

Delia had never dressed so quickly in her life. As soon as Marcus walked in the door, she was off. Quentin's eyes were closed when she arrived. He lay in bed, his right leg slightly elevated under another crisp white sheet. She almost started crying when she saw him, but curiosity helped her hold it together. Since he appeared to be asleep and no medical personnel were in the room, she gently lifted the sheet to peek at his leg. The hip and upper thigh were swollen with small incisions along the side. A stack of pillows under his knee and calf raised the leg to about a forty-five-degree angle. Delia couldn't help thinking of the diagrams in her class's geometry book. She touched the leg lightly and lowered the sheet.

When she looked up, Quentin's eyes were open. She leaned over to hug his shoulders and kiss his cheek.

"It's okay, Mom," he said. "Something just came out of nowhere and knocked me for a loop."

"Are you in pain?" Delia asked.

His sad smile grew a little brighter. "Oh, no. They've got me on lots of happy juice."

"What happened, sweetheart? Did a car hit you?"

"I don't know. One minute, I was riding along. Then there was this powerful blow to my back, and the next thing I remember is waking up in the hospital."

"You didn't see what it was? If it was a car or a truck?"

"No, Mom. They came at me from behind."

Delia was relieved to hear a bit of teenage scorn in his voice. He sounded almost like himself. "So, what did the surgeon do to your leg?"

A nurse who had just entered the room spoke. "Let me see if I can find a resident to explain the procedure to you."

She left, and a tall young man with pale skin and soft gray eyes came into the room. He said hello to Delia but directed his conversation to Quentin. "You're a lucky young man," he said.

"I don't feel lucky," Quentin murmured.

"It was only a single break, and we were able to align the bone with what's called intramedullary nailing," the doctor continued. "That means we went in near your hip joint and put a metal rod into your bone."

Delia felt a wave of nausea, but Quentin said, "Cool."

"I explained everything to your dad before we did it, so we had his okay."

"What about his pelvis? Isn't it broken too? What about that?" Delia needed to know everything.

"His pelvis wasn't broken. There's a crack in one of the smaller rings, but it should heal on its own. His leg will keep him immobile enough to hold those bones in place." The doctor turned back to Quentin. "You'll be in the hospital for several days, and then we'll send you home, most likely in a wheelchair. A physical therapist will teach you exercises while you're here to keep you from losing muscle strength while you're sitting or lying around." He smiled. "It'll be a good time to catch up on all the books you haven't read and the TV shows you haven't seen. But you'll need to keep up the exercises so you can be back on your feet soon."

"When can I play basketball?"

"Not for several months, I'm afraid." The doctor patted Quentin on the shoulder. "But you'll get there, I promise."

Quentin sat in silence. Just when he was making friends on the team, this had to happen. They'd probably forget all about him if he were off the team, which he obviously was. "Will the hospital let Rambler come see me?" he asked.

"No. They don't let any dogs, except service dogs, come in here," Delia said. "You'll be going home soon. You can see him then."

Quentin closed his eyes and eventually went back to sleep.

The day dragged by as doctors and nurses came in and out of the room, sometimes waking Quentin, sometimes not. When he was awake, Delia tried to find something he would like on the room's TV, but daytime programming was not designed for thirteen-year-old boys. Around two o'clock, she told him his sisters would be coming home from school soon, so she needed to be there, but she would gather up his *Mad* magazines and bring them back to the hospital for him.

The cold air was a welcome relief from the stuffy hospital atmosphere. Delia sat in her car, gasping mouthfuls of it until a barrier inside her broke, and she began to cry, something she had hardly done since Marcus's first phone call. She didn't know why she'd been so stoic. Maybe she'd been in shock, and none of it was real to her. Spending hours with Quentin, his leg swollen and elevated above the bed, his face mostly sullen, had made it very real. She didn't know how long she sat there while sobs rolled through her body, but when it was over, she felt a strong need to visit a house of prayer. She just didn't know which one to go to. She'd enjoyed the Martin Luther King, Jr. Day celebration at the Methodist church, but she had no desire to go there on her own. It would always make her think of Laura Campbell. She could go to the Baptist church—that's where Meredith and Paul went, she thought. She wanted a place where she felt comfortable. Then she remembered how gracious Sharon Robinson had been to her at the MLK service. Maybe she could go to her church. It wasn't that far away, and she had time to do it if she didn't stay long.

Slanted shafts of January afternoon sun offered the only light in the church's sanctuary, but it was enough for Delia to find her way to one of the front pews. She took a seat and studied the painting of Jesus praying in the Garden of Gethsemane that covered almost the entire wall behind the pulpit. She loved the painting, and today she felt much of the anguish that Jesus must have been feeling. Why did God let this awful thing happen to Quentin? How would she have the strength to help him get through it? As she prayed for guidance, she felt a hand come to rest on her back. Later, she would be embarrassed to admit that, for a second, she thought maybe God had come to help her. But the voice she heard was a woman's voice. "Mrs. Thomas? Welcome to our church."

Sharon Robinson stood behind her, a soft smile on her face. "I'm glad you're here. Can I help you with anything?"

Delia was afraid she would cry again, but she didn't. Instead, she told the older woman what happened to Quentin. "I just needed a quiet place to pray," she said. "I didn't know where else to go."

"Of course you did. And you came to the right place. Would you like to talk to Pastor Jennings? He may be in his office. I know he'd be willing to talk with you."

The offer was appealing, but Delia didn't have time. "I have to go home now," she said. "My daughters will be getting back from school very soon."

"Are you gonna need help looking after the girls while Quentin is in the hospital?"

"I don't know. I haven't planned that far in advance. I guess so. Probably." Delia's thoughts were scrambled.

"I'm sure some of the ladies here would be happy to help. I'll put out the word."

After Delia had gone, Sharon gathered the flower urns and put them by the back door for the florist to pick up. Then she went to the secretary's office to use the telephone. She would call her friends in Copeland, but first she called Elaine Parker. Elaine had been a lot easier to work with than Laura Campbell in organizing the Cultural Bridge group. There was something about Laura that Sharon didn't like, but she wanted to be sure the women from Tanner knew about Quentin.

"First United Methodist Church," Elaine said after only one ring.

Sharon gave her all the facts she knew about Quentin's injury. Elaine was quiet for a minute before saying, "That's horrible. I can't believe it," with a tremble in her voice.

Sharon imagined the shock on her face. "I thought you would want to know. I'm going to organize some of our ladies to offer child care for the Thomas girls while Mr. and Mrs. Thomas are at the hospital, and I'm sure they could use some food and whatever else y'all can provide. I saw Mrs. Thomas this afternoon. She seemed quite upset. I'm sure having your child get hit like that is a lot to handle. Thank God it wasn't any worse than it was."

"Yes," Elaine said. "Thank God."

After taking a little time to compose herself, Elaine called Meredith to ask her to organize the team parents to do something. After all, Meredith was the head coach's wife, and Elaine was doing her a favor by trying to find a job for that woman who had abandoned her child. "I can't possibly do this myself," she told her. "Laura will probably help you. And maybe Lydia."

"Of course," Meredith said, her throat dry and her heart pounding. That could have been Benny out there. She had every intention of calling Laura and Lydia right away, but she was summoned to a meeting with the public defender's policy unit, so as it turned out, Paul was the first person she told about Quentin's injury when she got home that night.

"What the fuck," Paul said. "We have to get in touch with Marcus and Delia. We have to make sure Quentin's all right. I can't imagine what they're going through right now. How could this happen? Where was he when he got hit?"

"Elaine didn't say. I'd guess he was on the road by the football field. There aren't many streetlights down there. Surely the driver didn't see him." Meredith took off her coat and hung it in the closet.

Paul grunted as wild thoughts zigzagged through his brain. "I hope it was an accident. But why didn't the driver stop?" He'd begun to pace across the living room floor.

"You don't think somebody would do this on purpose, do you? Maybe the driver didn't realize he'd hit a person. I've heard stories of drivers running over people and thinking it was an animal or a bump in the road."

Paul continued to pace. "Two months ago, I'd have said of course nobody would hit him on purpose, but after all that's happened, I don't know anymore. I've seen sides of people I never knew existed."

"What sides of people?" Benny stood in the doorway to the dining room, although nobody had seen him.

"Come in and sit down," Meredith said. "We need to tell you about a terrible accident that happened last night."

When Elaine told James about Quentin, her troubled state was more than he thought the event warranted, but if she was that upset, other parents might be also, so surely Paul wouldn't expect him to come to their meeting tonight. Although he didn't know what Paul wanted to say to him, he was certain it couldn't be good. With Quentin sidelined for the rest of the season, as James assumed he would be, there shouldn't be any more problems, so there shouldn't be a need for any more meetings, either. James breathed a sigh of relief.

Before Meredith contacted Lydia to ask her to help with the Thomases, Lydia had already decided the team parents needed to organize some kind of effort. Together, the two women decided a meals program was a good place to start. "Delia's already struggling to get dinner on the table because of her new job," Lydia said. "With Quentin in the hospital, she won't have any time to cook."

"Oh, dear Jesus," Laura said when Meredith told her what had happened. "You think God watches over all children, and then something like this happens. We need to have a prayer vigil. We can do it at my house tomorrow night."

"That's great if you want to arrange that," Meredith said. "Lydia and I are working to set up a meal schedule to provide dinners to the family for a while. I was hoping you'd help with that. Elaine told me that the ladies from the AME church in Copeland have offered childcare for the Thomas girls so Marcus and Delia can spend more time at the hospital, so we thought food was the best way we can help."

"How does Elaine know about the AME ladies?"

"Apparently, Sharon Robinson was the one who told Elaine about the accident."

"How did Sharon Robinson know?" *And why did she call Elaine?* Feeling slighted, Laura tried to put the puzzle pieces together. "Oh well," she huffed. "God works in mysterious ways."

Frank didn't learn about the accident until basketball practice the next afternoon. Paul was so concerned about getting in touch with Marcus and Delia that he forgot to call Frank. When Meredith was calling team mothers about arranging meals, Suzanne's line was busy, and then it got too late to call, so she didn't talk to Suzanne until the next morning after Frank had left for work. So, Frank learned what had happened at the same time most of the boys did. The news made him so angry that he had to walk away from the team to make sure he didn't say something he would regret. Of all the unfair, untimely accidents he could think of, this took the cake. It was unfair on so many levels. It was, of course, unfair to Quentin, who was just a kid trying to make it in a new town. It was unfair to his parents, who were trying to do the same thing. And it was unfair to the team, who were on the verge of building a winning season and earning a place in the post-season playoffs.

The rage he felt made him want to hurt someone. He wanted to find the driver of that car or truck or whatever and knock him into the next century. He stood at the far side of the gym and hit his fist against the wall until Paul sent the boys to practice free throws and came to get him. "Who was driving the car?" Frank asked with a bit of a snarl.

"I don't think they know," Paul said. "At least, not yet."

At that very moment, a Tanner police officer was at the hospital asking Quentin the same thing. "Do you have any memory of the accident?"

Quentin tried to shift his position in the bed, but the pain it caused made him stop. "No," he answered. He was annoyed because people kept asking him this question, and he always gave the same answer. "Whatever it was came up from behind. I heard it, but I never saw it. It hit me, and then I don't remember anything until I woke up in the hospital."

"What did it sound like?"

"Like a car or a truck or whatever."

"Quentin, don't be rude. He's only trying to help." Marcus, who had come to the hospital from work, put his hand on Quentin's shoulder.

"What else can I say? It sounded like something with a motor. It was louder than the car that passed me a few minutes before, so maybe it was going faster. I don't know. Maybe it just needed a muffler."

"That's good," the police officer said. "Anything like that you can remember may help us find the driver. Were there a lot of cars on the road with you before you were hit?"

"I don't know." Quentin frowned and laid his arm across his eyes.

"He's tired," Marcus said. "I'll keep talking to him, and if he remembers anything else, I'll call you. Let me walk out with you."

The officer nodded, and the two men started down the hall. "Did you find any evidence on the bicycle?" Marcus asked. "You always hear about paint transfer on television. Is that possible?"

"As far as we can tell, the car didn't hit the bicycle. It hit your son. The seat is twisted from banging against the ground, but other than that, there're no dents or scrapes. We think the car must have been traveling at forty-five or fifty miles an hour, which is way over the speed limit for that road, and clipped your son with the side-view mirror. That's why we think it was a car and not a truck or some other vehicle. On a truck or van or any other tall vehicle, the side mirror would have been too high to hit his back. Might have hit his head. Might have missed him altogether. But a car mirror would be just about right."

"Was it an accident?"

"Probably. If the driver wanted to hit your son, he would have hit him directly with the car, not clipped him with the mirror. Quentin said he didn't remember how many other cars were on the road with him when he was hit. Do you know of anyone who might've been driving on that road at the same time? Didn't you say he was coming from basketball practice?"

Marcus flinched. "Parents of other players might have picked up their sons and been driving the same road then, but they would never hit Quentin. Never." He rubbed his hand over the close-cut hair on the back of his head.

"I'm looking for witnesses. If these parents were on the same road, I need to know what other cars they saw. We might get lucky if somebody remembers even a partial license plate number."

"I can give you their names and phone numbers. Maybe somebody saw something, but I'd be surprised. It was good and dark by then, and I think they'd have said something about it by now."

"It's a long shot, but you never know." The officer hesitated before opening the door to the parking lot. "Mr. Thomas," he asked, "is there a reason anybody would want to hurt your son?"

"I don't know. A few people have been less than welcoming to us. About a week ago, we got a harassing phone call. I have no idea who it was." Marcus had some suspicions, but he would never name them.

"Why didn't you call the police?"

"Because I didn't think anything would come of it. If it continued to happen, I would have, I guess."

"Do you know anybody you think might have hit your son?"

"No," Marcus said. And he meant it.

The first parent the police officer was able to reach on the telephone was Paul Westover. Paul was in his office pondering the exact wording for a client's will when the call came. "I'm ashamed to say I saw him get on his bicycle, but then I pulled away in my car and got so far ahead of him, I couldn't see him anymore. The only cars I remember seeing were the cars of the other parents, and I'm sure it wasn't one of them."

Frank said almost the same thing, except he mentioned he planned to tell Marcus he would bring Quentin home on nights when Marcus couldn't make practice. "Guess I was a little late with that idea," he said.

"Sorry, I can't help you," James Parker said. "I don't drive home that way. I go in the other direction."

"I remember a white van," Richard Campbell said. "Made me think of a dry cleaner's delivery van, but there weren't any markings on it that I could see, and I didn't notice the license plate."

By the time the officer called Lydia, she had gone over in her mind the events of that night a hundred times. She could see Quentin riding away on his bike. She remembered passing him on the road by the football field. She saw his headlight fading into the distance. And then nothing. She and the other parents couldn't have been too far ahead of him, could they? And yet they missed the whole thing. If only she'd had enough sense to follow him home. She could have done that. But she had nothing to tell the police officer. Not even a car speeding past her farther up the road. Nothing out of the ordinary.

The officer thumped his fingers against the paper with his notes. Even the van sighting led nowhere. The rearview mirror was too high to hit Quentin.

18

Saturday's basketball game was a home game, for which everybody on the team was grateful. No one was in the mood to do any traveling. Meredith told Paul he should postpone the game because the players were still in a state of shock. Paul countered by saying that would make matters worse. It would draw attention to the incident and put the Thomases in the spotlight, making them more uncomfortable than they already were.

"Do you think they care about spotlights right now?" Meredith demanded.

"I don't know, but I'm not taking any chances. They deserve all the consideration we can give them. To me, that means keeping things as normal and low-key as possible."

So, the Westovers and most of the others made their way to the old gymnasium on Saturday. Approaching the structure, Lydia thought it looked gloomier than usual, even though only a few clouds rolled across the sky. Inside, the atmosphere was rowdy in a subdued sort of way. Lydia wondered if the feeling was really all that different or if her perceptions were a reflection of what was in her own head. Her frame of mind wasn't helped any when Jeff came and sat beside her. She hadn't seen or heard from him since the Martin Luther King celebration, and then only at a distance. That suited her fine. She wondered what he wanted with her now.

"How's Malcolm," he asked. "You and I haven't talked in a few weeks. Is there anything I should know about? He seems fine at my house."

Lydia couldn't believe what she was hearing. Did he really not know? She hadn't wanted to call him, but surely somebody had.

"Except for Quentin getting hit by a car, there's nothing new." Jeff's voice was curious but calm. "When did that happen?"

"Wednesday night after practice."

"Is he all right?"

"Mild concussion, broken leg, and cracked pelvis. The driver didn't stop. Just kept going. No clues yet about who it was." Even though it wasn't Jeff's fault that nobody told him, Lydia was annoyed with him for not knowing. He always seemed to be on the fringes of what was happening in Malcolm's life.

"I take it he's out of basketball for the rest of the season?" Maybe there was a hint of hopefulness in Jeff's voice, but he tried to suppress it.

"Well, yeah. He has to work on walking first." Lydia was being overly dramatic, but she didn't care.

Jeff ignored her sarcasm. Quentin's absence would relieve the tension on the team. Malcolm would get to play more, and maybe Frank would quit being so cool to Jeff. He needed Frank on his side in town politics. He hoped Quentin would be all right, but the boy was young and strong. He'd bounce back. Jeff made a mental note to approach Frank about the Kiwanis Club again in a week or so after things had cooled down.

Paul gathered the players around him and gave them a pep talk about winning this one for Quentin. "When he comes home from the hospital, we'll go see him, and it would be great to tell him we dedicated this game to him and won it. Go get 'em, Terrors." The starting lineup looked like it had for most of last year. Jamie, Malcolm, Adam, Benny, and Frankie in their usual positions.

"No new strategy, Coach?" Frank asked.

"No need for it," Paul said with a sigh. "But I'll switch 'em around a little bit when I start subbing in the second quarter to keep them from realizing what my real motive was for making them play different positions at practice."

Jamie took control of the starting jump ball and slapped it over to Frankie, who dribbled down the court, then sent a quick pass to

Malcolm, who lobbed it into the basket. "Now that's what I'm talking about!" shouted Jeff. Lydia cringed at his outburst, but she was happy to see Malcolm smile.

The opposing team returned the points, sending the Terrors back down the court to run a new play. "You know what to do," Jamie said to Frankie as he passed him on the court. "Just like old times."

"It's not old times," Frankie muttered. "We've got a hole in our team," but when he didn't see any signs from Paul, he did what he knew Jamie wanted him to do. He called a play that fed Jamie the ball under the basket. And Jamie didn't disappoint.

"Now we're pumping!" James yelled.

Richard looked at him with disdain. Something didn't feel right about cheering with Quentin lying in a hospital bed. He knew that was ridiculous. The other boys deserved to play and be cheered, but even the bleachers felt empty without Marcus and Delia there. How quickly the family had established their place on the team, at least to Richard's way of thinking. He watched Laura's excitement as Adam got off a good shot. He was happy for Adam too, but he couldn't shake the image of Quentin in the hospital or, even worse, the image of Quentin lying by the side of the road. Why didn't the driver stop? He turned to Laura and asked, "Do you suppose it's possible the driver deliberately clipped Quentin with his side mirror instead of hitting him directly to make it look more like an accident?"

Laura was annoyed at the distraction from the game. "If he worked that hard to make it look like an accident, then why didn't he stick around and explain that's what it was? Say he was sorry and all that? Seems like he would've fared a lot better selling it that way than he will when the police catch him and he has a hit-and-run to deal with."

"If they catch him. At this point, I'm sure he has no intention of getting caught. Maybe he just clipped Quentin because he didn't want to hurt him badly, just put him out of commission for a while."

"Or maybe it was an honest accident, and the driver was too

scared to stop. Quit trying to do the police's work for them and pay attention to the game. Adam's playing really well."

Richard tried to focus on the game, but it didn't seem important compared to what happened to Quentin. It caught his attention later, however, when Paul moved Adam to guard and put Benny at forward. Then he took Jamie out of the game, moved Malcolm to center, and sent in Jason at forward. Richard realized Paul had something up his sleeve, but he wasn't sure what.

The first play with the new lineup ended in zip when Benny missed his shot and Malcolm lost the rebound. The opposing team moved ahead by two points and then four and then six. Paul called a time-out. "Try some give-and-go," he said to the boys. "And keep your eyes on the ball. We need snappy passes and solid rebounds." The players did up their game, closing their point deficit to two. Paul sent Jamie back into the game at forward for Adam, moved Benny to point guard, took out Frankie, and sent in Carson at the other guard position.

"What on earth is he doing?" Laura hissed. When nobody answered her question, she set her chin firmly in her right palm and grimaced at the game. Paul kept the same lineup until halftime, which saw the Terrors down by four points.

As the teams gathered around their respective coaches, Laura walked down a few bleachers to talk to Meredith. "Did Paul tell you about his plan to make the boys play different positions?" she asked.

"Not that I remember," Meredith said, "but I'm sure he has a reason for what he's doing. By the way, your prayer vigil last night was nice."

Organized quickly on Friday, the vigil had been surprisingly well attended. Several of the team parents came, including Delia and Marcus, who also brought their daughters. Richard and Adam sat near the back of the room, and a few other players could be seen in the group. Laura had contacted Sharon Robinson to invite people from the Copeland church and also to remind her that Laura was a leader in the Tanner church, not just Elaine. Then she called people from the Tanner church, many of whom showed up. Altogether, about thirty people crowded into Laura's living room, filling all the chairs she had assembled, with some attendees making themselves comfortable on the floor. Nobody could say Laura Campbell threw a prayer vigil and nobody came.

On every table in the room candles flickered, creating a subdued and reverent ambiance. A small collage of photos of Quentin that Laura had taken during basketball games sat on the coffee table that had been shoved against a wall to make room for chairs. "That's creepy," Suzanne whispered to Lydia as they walked in. "Makes me think he's dead."

"Hush," Lydia said. "Everybody knows he's not dead."

Laura welcomed the group and then asked Marcus to give them an update on Quentin's condition. Delia sat with her head bowed as Marcus explained about the surgery and the doctor's prognosis. "We hope to bring him home from the hospital next week," he said. "For now, he'd appreciate phone calls and cards, and when he's home, he'd love for some of you to visit."

"I'll send Frankie over," Suzanne whispered. "He'll cheer him up."

"Malcolm will want to go too," Lydia said.

After thanking Marcus for his comments, Laura said, "I want to open our vigil with words from the Bible, Romans 12:12. 'Rejoice in hope, be patient in tribulation, be constant in prayer.'" She paused for the reading to sink in. "Now we will have five minutes of silence to prepare our hearts and minds to reach out to the Lord."

The group sat quietly with a minimum of coughs and rustlings, mostly from the younger members. Then Laura began to pray aloud, asking God's blessing on Quentin. When she had finished, she asked for others to lead the group in prayer. Sharon Robinson rose and offered a heartfelt plea for Quentin's recovery. She was followed by another woman from the AME church. Then, a moment or so of silence before Meredith Westover asked for mercy for Quentin and also strength for his family and friends so they could be of the most help. When she sat down, Paul squeezed her hand in appreciation. Any kind of public speaking made him nervous.

Several more prayers were offered before silence overtook the group once again. When Laura was sure no one else wanted to speak, she said, "We'll have five minutes of silent prayer so everyone can say what's in their heart about Quentin." The time crept by slowly. Richard formed a few thoughts asking for Quentin's healing, but most of his thoughts concerned the hit-and-run driver and how badly he wanted him found. Paul's silent prayers were pretty much the same. *Help us find that son-of-a-bitch and make him pay for what he did.*

Eventually everyone's prayers were brought to a close by Laura. "I hope you all have been able to voice your concerns and also to listen, because that's how we gain wisdom. I'll close our meeting with more verses from the Bible, this time from Psalms. 'He sent out his word and healed them; he rescued them from the grave. Let them give thanks to the Lord for his unfailing love and his wonderful deeds for mankind.'"

As people began to gather their belongings in preparation to leave, Marcus stood and said, "Thank you to all of you for your concern for Quentin and our family. We appreciate the friendship many of you have shown us in the few months we've been in Tanner."

"But many of you haven't," Richard said under his breath, causing Elaine, who had come to the meeting without James or Jamie, to look at him over her shoulder, her frown showing more sadness than anger.

Lydia left Laura's house with Suzanne, who was quieter than usual, at least for a while. Before they separated to go to their cars, she blurted out, "I don't get the point of prayer vigils. Just because a bunch of us were praying for Quentin, does that mean God is more likely to help him get well? What about all the sick and injured people who don't have friends to pray for them? Does God ignore them? Think about it."

Lydia sighed. "I think the point of prayer vigils is to motivate the people praying to figure out what they can do to help people in need and their families. I was glad Meredith mentioned the Thomases in her prayer. I can't imagine how much they're hurting right now. I wouldn't be surprised if they left town."

When Meredith mentioned the vigil to Laura at the ballgame, she wondered if Laura had any thoughts about moving the energy of the vigil group forward but realized she probably didn't when Laura said, "Yes, I felt a weight lifted off my chest during the meeting. God is holding Quentin in his hands, which is a good thing because if Paul keeps coaching like this, we're going to need him back sooner than we thought."

"If you have pointers for Paul, go tell him," Meredith said as she marveled how Laura could have such opposing opinions of Quentin. This was the first time she had ever admitted he was an asset to the team.

"I will," Laura said and went back to her seat.

"What's your plan now?" Frank asked Paul as the second half of the game began.

"Play to win." He put the starters in their usual positions and called the plays himself, but it wasn't enough. Although the lead went back and forth a few times, the opposing team pulled ahead in the fourth quarter and stayed there. The Terrors lost by ten points. Paul made a few comments about mistakes the team had made and then told them to shake it off for now and come back on Monday ready to win the next game.

"We could have used that game," Frank said after the boys went to join their parents. "I think we're still safe, though. Right now we're seven and four with four games left to play. We only have to win one of them to put us above the fifty-percent mark and into the playoffs. We can do that."

"Sure we can," Paul said, but without much conviction.

Earlier in the day, Sharon Robinson had arrived at Marcus and

Delia's house to spend time with Rosalie and Camille while their parents went to the hospital to see Quentin and do some grocery shopping. Delia prepared the girls by reminding them that they had met Mrs. Robinson at the Martin Luther King, Jr. Day celebration.

"I know," Rosalie said. "She was the one with the big hat."

"And the big smile," Camille added.

Sharon was wearing another big smile when she greeted the Thomases and gave each a hug. "Now, y'all go on and give some love to Quentin and do what you have to do today. We will be fine," she said. "I brought along some cards and some coloring books. I'm going to teach them how to play gin rummy."

"Y'all be good now," Delia said to her daughters before she and Marcus headed out the door. When they reached the hospital, they were surprised to see the same police officer as before standing in the lobby. "Oh, no," Delia said. "This can't be good." Was he going to tell them Quentin was worse? Somehow, Delia's addled mind connected the two.

"I called you a little while ago, but the babysitter said you were on your way to the hospital, so I decided to meet you here," the officer said as he motioned them over to a couch in the waiting room. "My news isn't good."

Delia drew a quick breath.

"I talked to all the parents who were at practice that night, and nobody saw anything unusual. I'm sorry."

Delia relaxed. That was bad, but she was afraid of worse.

"That means we still have almost nothing to go on," the officer continued. "We'll keep investigating, but I'm not optimistic. About ninety percent of these cases never get solved, and frankly, we don't have the manpower to keep working on it a lot longer. I know you want to know who did this to your son, but it also means there's no one liable for your medical expenses. Have you notified your insurance company? If you have coverage for uninsured motorists, that might take care of it."

Delia and Marcus looked at each other. "I think we have that," Marcus said.

"Well, look into it. And it might be worth your while to hire a lawyer to deal with the insurance company." He paused. "Again, I'm sorry. I'll stay in touch and let you know anything new we learn." He paused once more. "You know, I can't stop thinking about that phone call you got. I think you said it was a man. Did you recognize anything about his voice? Accent? Loudness? Words he used?"

Marcus shook his head. There hadn't been anything distinctive about the caller's voice. He originally assumed it was somebody he knew, because why would a stranger call him? But he knew better than that. Meanness was often easier if it was directed at somebody you didn't actually know.

After the officer left, Marcus gave Delia a hug that he hoped was reassuring. "They'll find the driver," he said. "Have faith."

"You heard the man. Only ten percent of hit-and-run cases ever get solved. And with nobody responsible, we'll end up with huge medical bills." A tight ball of fear landed in Delia's stomach.

"It'll be all right. I know we have uninsured motorist insurance, and we have health insurance that will probably take care of it."

"Not if you lose your job at the mill," Delia said.

"Now you're getting way ahead of yourself. Even if Mr. Henry dies, it'll take a long time before they make any changes at the mill. Quentin'll be back on the basketball court long before the mill gets sold, if it ever gets sold. Now let's go see our boy." He pushed Delia toward the elevator and hoped he was right.

19

As a manager, James was one of the first to receive the phone call at the mill. After that, the news spread like an alarming virus. Frank got the call not long after James, and Marcus not long after that. Henry Galloway was dead. The revered patriarch of the Galloway family and Foxrow Mills had a heart attack at eleven thirty Sunday night.

By noon on Monday, nearly everybody at the mill knew. "What happens to the mill now?" was the most frequent response to the sad news. After all, Henry was ninety years old and had been failing physically for years. Surely the Board of Directors had plans for his succession, but who would it be? Henry's son, Wallace, had died decades earlier, and his daughter, Alice, had walked away from any managerial interest in the mill as soon as she got married. That left Nancy and her brother, Tom, who, like his aunt, wanted nothing to do with managing the mill.

By afternoon, news of Henry's death had spread through the businesses and professional people of Tanner. Paul heard it from one of his clients, and Richard heard from another professor at the college. Elaine learned about it when Henry's daughter-in-law, Caroline, contacted the church to make funeral arrangements for Sunday. Lydia learned the news from Nancy, who called her in tears Monday morning. She drove out to the farm during lunch.

When Lydia arrived at the genteel old farmhouse, Nancy had stopped crying but looked as though she could burst into tears at any minute. Caroline was surrounded by her friends in the living room, so Lydia and Nancy sat in the kitchen with Marie and Pansy, who was scurrying around to keep plenty of tea and coffee ready for the many guests who would be stopping by to offer their condolences. Lydia hadn't seen any other family members in the house, so she asked Nancy, "Has Alice been by?"

"She was here last night, but not today," Nancy answered.

"What about Tom?"

Nancy looked more upset, so Marie said, "He's flying in from Connecticut tonight."

"Him and Mr. Henry never got along too well, so he'll likely leave after the funeral," Pansy added, causing Marie to frown at her.

Lydia had gotten to know Tom the first year she lived in Tanner, and she wasn't surprised as most of the townspeople were when he left Tanner and went to work for General Electric. She hadn't seen him in years.

Before Lydia could say anything else, Caroline appeared in the doorway. "Nancy, darling," she said, "the ladies would like to talk with you. Do you think you can do that?"

Nancy nodded at her mother, although Lydia wasn't at all sure she was ready to face the well-meaning ladies of Tanner. When Nancy stood, Lydia hugged her and walked with her toward Caroline. "I'm so sorry about Mr. Henry," she said to Caroline, who offered a soft "Thank you" before she left with Nancy.

"If there's anything I can do to help y'all, especially Nancy, please let me know," Lydia said to Marie and Pansy. When she passed the door to the living room on her way out, Nancy seemed all right, and since the women were talking so much, she hardly had to say a word.

The top of Elaine's desk in the church office looked like her mind felt. Total disorganization. So much going on, and now Henry had died. Last week had been filled with so many shocks, and her emotions ricocheted through sadness, disappointment, and fear. It was as if a black cape hung over her world and refused to be removed. Overseeing a funeral might be the thing that would break her. She took a few sips of her coffee before she reached for the telephone answering machine. She could check the recorded messages and avoid the funeral a little longer. Church members rarely called over the weekend. They saved their complaints for later in the week when she was busiest.

To her surprise, there was a message from Meredith. "Sorry to bother you today, but I know last week was a whirlwind, and this week's starting off just as bad, so I want to remind you about Clarinda. She really wants to get her daughter back. Also, if I don't take care of my personal business early in the week, I'm likely to get caught up in a court case and never get back to it. Let me know if you get any leads, and I'll handle it from there."

The rest of the cassette tape was blank, as Elaine expected it to be. Clarinda? Elaine had to think for a few minutes to remember who that was. Oh, yes. That girl that Meredith was trying to find a job for. As if Elaine didn't have enough to do. *Okay,* she told herself. *This can be your good deed for today.* At the moment, her savings account of good deeds was running low, so she needed to make a deposit. With a big sigh, she put a piece of paper into the typewriter and began writing an announcement for the church's weekly newsletter about Clarinda's availability for work. She'd also put a notice in the Sunday bulletin that weekend. She thought about including Meredith's telephone number for replies, but decided that since Meredith wasn't a member of the church, she might get in trouble for that. She directed interested persons to call the church office instead.

Delia went back to work that morning. Marcus begged her to take another day off and stay with Quentin at the hospital. "I can't," she said. "I need to work while he's in the hospital because I'll have to take time off when he comes home. I'll have to take care of him then." She was actually more worried than she let on about how much care he would need at home and who was going to do it. She knew there were visiting nurses who made home calls but that would mean more money, depending on what their insurance would and would not cover. She could take more time off, but not indefinitely. She'd been working at the school for only two weeks, and she'd already taken two days off. She didn't want to lose her job before she'd really started.

The father of every player on the Terrors team showed up for practice that afternoon. "They're scared," Frank said to Paul. "After what happened to Quentin, they want to make sure their kids get home in one piece."

"So now something's more important to them than playing time," Paul said with a scowl.

"I think so. Or maybe they want to see what you're going to do with the team without Quentin. Saturday didn't go so well." Frank scratched his head. "Maybe it's a little of both."

"They'd better stay off my back," said Paul, remembering that James never came to meet with him. "I will coach however I want to, and their kids will not get hurt on their way home, because number one, they're not on bicycles, and number two, nobody has a grudge against them."

Frank drew a quick breath. "You actually believe somebody deliberately hit Quentin?"

"I think it's possible. The whole thing seems too perfect to have been an accident. Quentin wasn't killed, thank God. He was hurt just bad enough to take him out of basketball, at least for the season and maybe longer."

"I don't believe it," Frank said. "Things like that don't happen here."

"I didn't used to think so, either. I've learned a lot this year. I just hope the police can figure it out." Paul sighed. "Let's get this practice going." He walked toward the boys shooting foul shots on the court. Frank followed him, his mind a jumble of conflicting thoughts.

Most of the fathers had gathered in small groups spread across the bleachers. Not wanting to admit their reasons for being there, they tried to act as if their presence was a normal occurrence.

"The boys and coaches need our support," Jeff said to Richard Campbell. "They've been through a terrible shock."

Where was your support at that awful meeting at James's house? Richard thought, but he said, "They always need our support."

"Support can come in different ways," Jeff said. "They need to know we'll do everything we can to help them win games and reach their full potential as players."

"What in hell are you talking about?" Richard asked. "What do you think we ought to be doing?" To him, "reach their full potential" sounded like a broad, shining generality that was probably masking questionable ideas.

"Lots of things, like coming to practice the way we are today. And attending games."

Richard couldn't resist any longer. "And holding meetings behind the coaches' backs?"

"No, of course not. That wasn't my meeting."

Richard shook his head. "Then you aren't out to get rid of Paul and Frank any longer? Wonder what changed your mind."

"I was never out to get rid of Paul and Frank. I just wanted all the boys to be treated fairly."

"Could have fooled me. And you have no idea about the irony in what you just said."

Hearing the heat rise in the voices near him, James moved closer to find out what was going on. Out on the court, the boys began running defensive drills with Paul yelling, "Ball, ball, deny, deny, talk, talk, hands, hands!" As the boys repeated, "Ball, ball, deny, deny," and their shoes squeaked across the floor, the din grew louder. Rather than try to speak above the noise, Richard and Jeff fell silent, but the friction between them continued through their blazing glares.

When Paul blew his whistle and the clamor died down, James said, "What's got y'all so hot under the collar?"

"I don't know," Jeff said. "I simply remarked that the team needs our support more than ever."

"Yeah," Richard said. "I'll tell you what kind of support we should have offered weeks ago. When we saw Quentin was riding his bicycle to practice, one of us should have stepped up to give the kid a lift. How hard would it have been? Then he'd be out there where he should be, practicing with the others."

"Don't blame what happened on us," James said. "His parents should have taken better care of him. It's their fault he isn't out on the court right now."

"It's nobody's fault except the person who hit him," Jeff said.

Richard spoke slowly and evenly. "And all the people who think basketball is so goddamned important."

Quentin wasn't thinking about basketball at that moment. He was thinking that he should call a nurse to help him go to the bathroom. Damn, how he hated that. He didn't want a woman watching him pee. Why didn't they have any men nurses? The physical therapist who came for the first time that day had him stand with a walker, but they wouldn't let him walk anywhere by himself. Explain that. They said it was because of the pain medication he was taking. He was willing to give up the pain pills if they let him go to the bathroom by himself and especially if they let him go home. He wanted to see Rambler. And he wanted to eat his mom's cooking. The food at the hospital tasted like vomit.

To end the practice, Paul had the boys run stop-and-turn sprints plus shoot a foul shot when they reached each end of the court. The drill had been Frank's suggestion early in the season, and Paul used it at every practice so the boys would be ready when that all-important foul shot came at the end of a game. When they were all panting and sweating, he called them off the court and motioned to the dads to come get them.

"Good practice," he said as each one passed by him. Then he watched as they and their fathers left the gym two by two. After telling Benny and Frankie to gather up the balls and turn off the lights, he and Frank stood at the door and watched everyone get into their cars. "I've never left a kid after practice or a game unless I knew he had a ride home," Paul said. "Now I know that's not enough."

Clarinda crossed and uncrossed her legs again as she sat in a narrow plastic chair in the anteroom of Child Protective Services. Why did these chairs have to be so uncomfortable? Probably because they knew the people who waited here were so desperate about their children that they would sit on a rock if they had to and for as long as they had to. She ran her hands over her corduroy skirt, smoothing out imaginary wrinkles. No wrinkle could have survived in this skirt after the many times she ironed it, just like she did every Tuesday afternoon before meeting with her case worker. If the meeting went well, she'd be allowed to visit Lucy afterward, so it had to go well, including everything from her appearance to her attitude. Immediately before she entered the case worker's office, she put on her practiced humble smile, the one that had always worked to her advantage in the past.

She liked her case worker, who was named Peggy, even though the woman was not interested in small talk and always went straight to the purpose of the meeting. "How's your job search going?" were the first words out of her mouth.

"I'm trying," Clarinda said. "I see the unemployment office once a week, but they never have anything for me. They're more interested in people who've been laid off. I applied at nearly every store in town, but they say they don't have anything."

"How about restaurants?"

"Nothing." Clarinda couldn't keep her practiced smile from drooping.

"Are you just looking for waitress positions? They have other positions."

"If you mean like busboys and dishwashers, they're all guys. That's why they're called bus*boys*." Clarinda regretted the sarcasm as soon as it flew out of her mouth, but was Peggy crazy? Had she ever heard of a woman in a restaurant kitchen unless she was a chef? Then she remembered Meredith's idea. "My lawyer thinks I can be a cleaning lady or a babysitter. She's trying to help me find a job like that."

Peggy's left eye blinked. The tic had annoyed Clarinda at first, but now it was just part of their routine. Peggy never said anything about it. "What do you think about those types of jobs?" she asked now.

"I'll take any job I can get if it means I get Lucy back. I'm usually good with children, so I think I'd be a good babysitter."

Peggy's eye blinked again. Why would anybody put the idea of being a babysitter into Clarinda's head?

Clarinda sensed her doubt and exclaimed, "My lawyer is helping me find leads for jobs like that. I think she'll come through."

"I hope she does. What will you do about the rent next month if you don't find something by then?"

"I'll beg the landlord to give me some extra time. He can be nice when he wants to."

They talked a little longer about Clarinda's progress in the parenting classes, and when Peggy was satisfied Clarinda was really trying, she led her down the hall to the playroom where Lucy was waiting.

Marcus and Delia spent Tuesday night working to make their house ready for Quentin's homecoming on Thursday. The doctor's announcement that he was ready to leave the hospital had surprised them both. He wasn't ready to leave. He was still so helpless. He could walk a short distance with a walker, but other than that, he stayed in bed. He would need equipment, like a toilet seat with side bars and a shoe loop to lift his leg. And their biggest problem was Quentin's second-floor bedroom. He'd have to sleep in their first-floor bedroom for who knew how long. Learning to go up and down steps would take a while.

"I hope Quentin's doctors aren't making a mistake," Delia said as she carried his stack of *Mad* magazines down to the new bedroom. She also had Rambler's bed, although she knew he wouldn't leave Quentin's side at night or during the day. The dog knew something was up because he kept running from bedroom to bedroom along with Delia and Marcus. Suzanne had kindly offered to lend them Frankie's Atari console to help entertain Quentin. Frankie had agreed only when Delia promised he could come play on it with Quentin whenever he wanted to.

Marcus had moved Quentin's TV down to the new bedroom and was squatting behind it to hook up the Atari. "Delia, honey, the doctors know what they're doing. They've done all they can do for him in the hospital, and he'll be so much happier at home."

"But what if he needs something we can't do for him?"

"We'll figure it out. And the physical therapist is going to start coming on Friday. We can ask her for suggestions. And there's going to be an occupational therapist starting next week. He'll be fine."

Delia grabbed a handful of hangers holding dresses out of her closet and headed upstairs. "I won't be needing these for a while," she said ruefully. "I told the principal I'll have to stay with Quentin for as long as he needs me. I just hope I have a job to go back to."

"We can hire somebody to stay with him." Marcus stood up and grunted. His knees felt older than the rest of him. "There're visiting nurses and home health aides. All kinds of people we can call on."

"But that costs money." Delia draped the dresses over her arm.

"We'll figure it out," Marcus said. "Now where's that smile? Our boy's coming home. And he's going to be fine. We should be celebrating."

Delia managed to give him a smile. The strong Black woman. That's who she was and who she would continue to be, no matter what.

Quentin had no trouble smiling when he learned he was going home. "Schweet!" he shouted when the doctor gave him the news. He'd have jumped for joy if he could have, but he settled for banging his walker against the floor.

"Easy now," the doctor said. "Don't break that walker. You're going to need it. Thursday morning. Unless something unexpected happens, that's when I'll be signing your release papers. Does that sound good to you?"

"Totally awesome." Quentin reached for the walker again but stopped himself. He couldn't risk annoying the doctor. "Thank you, thank you, thank you," he said instead.

"Okay. Tomorrow the physical therapist will spend more time with you. We'll keep a close watch on your vital signs to make sure you're ready to go on Thursday and decide whether you need pain medication to take at home. I'm guessing you don't. What's your pain level today?"

"I'm good," Quentin said. If he asked for more pain meds, they might restrict what he could do at home. Not a chance he wanted to take.

"Have a good day, and I'll see you tomorrow." The doctor turned to go, leaving behind a still-smiling Quentin.

Marcus took off from work early on Wednesday to collect the equipment Quentin would need at home. He'd put in an order with Ralph Peterson's pharmacy days earlier, so all he had to do was pick it up. "Good luck to Quentin," Ralph said as he helped load the stuff into Marcus's car. "I'm so sorry about his accident. Any leads yet on who hit him?"

Marcus shook his head. "Not yet. And the more time goes by, the less likely they are to find him."

"You know," Ralph said, "I bet it was some kid. Driving too fast and then scared out of his wits when it happened. Certainly too scared to tell anybody."

"Maybe. But I think by now a kid would be so scared of what would happen if he's found out that he'd confess to his parents just for the relief of getting it off his chest."

"I don't know. Fear does funny things to a kid. To anybody. I'll keep my ears open. If I hear anything, I'll let you know." He slammed the trunk of the car with a satisfying thud.

"Thanks," Marcus said. He'd take any gossip he could get if it led to the bastard who hit Quentin.

20

Thursday morning, Marcus and Delia stood patiently by Quentin's hospital bed. "When's he coming?" Quentin asked for the umpteenth time.

"He's seeing other patients. He'll be here as soon as he can," Marcus said.

"I can't wait all day." Quentin had been awake since six o'clock, and now it was ten.

"Yes, you can," Delia said. She gave Quentin what she hoped was a comforting look, although she was getting a little irritated with the doctor too. She and Marcus had been there since eight.

Finally, the doctor exploded through the door with a nurse behind him. "You ready to go home?" he asked Quentin.

"Have been," Quentin said, causing Delia's comforting expression to turn into a glare.

The doctor looked over his chart, nodded, and said, "Then let's go. Get out of here. Mrs. Watkins," he gestured toward the nurse, "will give you your discharge orders, and I'll see you in two weeks." He saluted Quentin and then was gone.

Delia opened the small suitcase she'd packed that morning and handed the clothes in it to Quentin. The clothes he'd been wearing the night of the accident had been cut off him, even his corduroy jacket. "Thanks," he said. Then he looked at the three adults in the room. "Can you give a guy some privacy?"

They stepped out into the hall and closed the door not quite all the way behind them. "I'm right here if you need help," Mrs. Watkins said.

Quentin slid out of his hospital gown and threw it onto the

chair next to his bed. Without bending his injured leg, he leaned over, pulled his pants over his feet, and gently wiggled them up to his waist. Getting the garment under his bottom sent sparks down his leg, but he did it. Delia had wisely bought a pair of extra-large sweatpants to accommodate his swollen leg. The shirt and sweater were a breeze to put on, but then he looked at his bare feet and realized it would take some maneuvering to get his socks on. Not to mention his shoes. "I need help," he called, hating the words as they came out of his mouth. He didn't want to be dependent on anybody.

The adults returned, and while Delia dressed him in his shoes and socks (*Just like a baby*, he thought), Mrs. Watkins reviewed the discharge orders with him.

And then he was headed home. The sky was so blue. Just a pale winter blue, but so much brighter than it had looked from inside the hospital. He sat in the back of the car, his legs stretched out across the seat. Every bounce of the car was ten knives sticking in his leg and hip. Despite his protests, the doctor had given him a prescription for pain medication. His parents might have to get it filled after all.

At home, Marcus helped him into the wheelchair and pushed him into the house through the garage, where there were no steps to contend with. Rambler met them at the door, barking and trying to jump into Quentin's lap until Delia took a firm hold of his collar. When Quentin was settled in his parents' bed, she let the dog crawl in next to him and lavish him with licks.

"If you're up for it," she said to Quentin, "Frankie and Benny want to visit you this afternoon. Do you feel like seeing them?"

Quentin was wearier than he expected after the trip home, but he would never turn away Frankie and Benny. It was the first time any of his teammates except Malcolm had wanted to spend time with him outside of basketball. "Sure," he said before closing his eyes.

He meant to rest for only a few minutes, but at three thirty, Delia woke him to tell him Frankie and Benny were there. He rubbed his eyes and carefully pushed himself to a sitting position.

The boys drifted quietly through the door, watching him as if they were afraid he might break.

"Long time, no see," Frankie said. "How're you feeling?"

"Like somebody hit me with a car."

Frankie was stumped about what to say next until Benny laughed. "It's a joke, dumbo. Don't you get it? He feels like somebody hit him with a car because somebody did hit him with a car."

Quentin wasn't sure he'd meant it as a joke, but because Benny laughed and Frankie smiled, he laughed too.

Delia waited in the kitchen with the boys' moms. Meredith had come from court and wore one of her numerous gray skirted suits. "Would you like us to stay," she asked, "or are you busy?"

"I don't give a shit if you're busy or not," Suzanne said. "I think you need a break for some relaxation time with friends." She scooted into a seat at Delia's kitchen table and removed a bottle of Cabernet from her large straw purse. "Now, if you can provide us with three glasses, I am prepared with a corkscrew." She popped the corkscrew out of the purse screw side up and looked at Delia expectantly.

Delia sized up the situation and realized there was no way to get out of it, even if she wanted to. Meredith came to the same conclusion and said, "Can I help you with the glasses?" Delia passed her three wine glasses from the cabinet and collected cloth napkins from the linen drawer.

Suzanne expertly twisted the screwdriver into the bottle's cork, pushed down the handles, and jerked the cork out with a satisfying swish. "Ah," she said as she sniffed the Cabernet. "A very good year, even if it was a recent one." Then she filled the glasses and raised hers. "Here's to Delia, who's been through so much already, and there's plenty more to come. Being a caretaker can be a real pain in the ass."

Neither Meredith nor Delia expected that particular toast, but Meredith raised her glass and took a sip. "How about we wish Quentin a quick recovery?" Delia said.

"There's plenty of time for that, and he's getting plenty of attention," Suzanne said. "We're concerned about you. I know the women from the AME church have helped out with the girls, and the good ladies from First United Methodist have been bringing food, but that won't last forever. You and Marcus are the ones who'll have to keep going and going like the Energizer bunny." She took another sip of wine. "Now sit down and let's share some gossip."

"Oh?" Meredith said as she and Delia took seats at the table. "What do you know?"

Suzanne leaned back in her chair. She was wearing one of her favorite geometric design blouses, complete with shoulder pads. It was one of her favorites because the turquoise color in the design matched her eyes. At the moment, those eyes twinkled with mischief. "Well," she said. "Frank says he thinks Jeff Colton's planning to run for town council president at the next election."

"How does he know that?" Meredith hoped he was mistaken.

"Just a feeling he has. Jeff's been on the council for years now, so he probably thinks it's his turn to be president. And he keeps pressuring Frank to run for council member. It's like he's building what he thinks will be his supporters on the council. The irony about that is Frank would never support him for anything."

"Why not?" Delia asked. She knew nothing about Tanner politics and very little about Jeff Colton.

"Because he's a total douchebag," Suzanne said.

"Don't say that. He's Malcolm's father," Meredith snapped.

"He was also Lydia's husband, and that's how I know what a jerk he is. And don't forget he was in favor of replacing Paul and Frank as coaches of the basketball team."

"He wanted to replace the coaches?" This was news to Delia. "Why?"

"He was just upset with them," Meredith said, swallowing her anger with Suzanne for bringing up the subject. "It's no big deal. Nothing ever came of it."

"I think it was a big deal. And I don't trust Jeff. I wouldn't put it past him to have been the creep who hit Quentin." Suzanne reached for the bottle of Cabernet and refilled the glasses all around.

Delia was more confused than ever. "Why would he hit Quentin? Ralph Peterson told Marcus he thought it was probably a teenager who made a mistake and was too terrified to tell anybody about it. That's what I believe. I can't stand to think anybody would deliberately hurt Quentin."

"Believe what you want, but Jeff Colton is sneakier than you think. He'd do anything to get what he wants."

"Can we talk about something else?" Meredith said. "I don't know how we got on this subject. I thought we were going to brighten Delia's day. Does anybody know any good news? How's your new job, Delia?"

"The first two weeks were great. The students are ninth and tenth graders, so about the same age as our boys. They've been feeling me out, but they're mostly polite about it. I still have them a little off balance since they don't know what I might do. I think I can build a good relationship with them if I can keep the job."

"Keep the job?" Suzanne frowned. "Why wouldn't you keep the job?"

"Like I said, I've only been there two weeks, and now I'm having to take time off to care for Quentin. I don't know how long I can keep that up and keep the job. I need to go back, but I can't leave Quentin alone. Marcus has his job, of course. So I need somebody else. I can't keep imposing on my friends." Friends? It was the first time Delia had used the word to describe the women of Tanner or Copeland. Were they her friends?

"The problem is most of us have jobs too," Suzanne said. "Except Laura Campbell. She's a professional volunteer. Maybe she could volunteer to take care of Quentin. Surely that would fall within her Christian duties."

"No," Delia said. "No more volunteers." *Especially not Laura Campbell.* "I'd hire a person for at least a few days if I knew one who wouldn't be too expensive. I just need her here to get Quentin what he needs and call Marcus or me if there're any real problems."

"Maybe I can help you with that." Meredith patted Delia's

hand. "I know a young woman who's looking for a job herself and might be perfect to spend time with Quentin. I can't say much about her until I talk it over with her, but I'll bet she can be the solution to your problem."

"That would be heaven-sent," Delia said.

"Let's drink to that." Suzanne reached for the wine bottle again, but Delia and Meredith shook their heads.

"I'd better go check on Quentin," Delia said. "I don't want him to overdo it on his first day home." She went into the bedroom and returned with Benny and Frankie. "Thank you both for coming," she said to them. "Come again soon."

"We'll be back," Frankie said. "Maybe we can play Atari then."

"Maybe so," Meredith said, "but now we all need to get out of the way and let Delia spend some time with Quentin. Come on, Benny." She motioned to her son and waved goodbye to the others. Suzanne and Frankie were not far behind.

That evening, Meredith told Paul what Suzanne had said about Jeff. "President of town council, I can see," he said, "but hitting Quentin? I don't know."

"None of the team parents could have hit Quentin," Meredith said. "I don't know what she's thinking about."

"Well, it's not out of the realm of possibility." Paul pulled a cigarette from his pack of Winstons and lit it. He was trying to quit, but any stressful thoughts sent him reaching. "You know how much some of them resented Quentin. But Jeff's too calm and calculating to have done it. There is somebody else, though, who might be guilty. James. He's a hothead. He could never have planned to do something so cruel, but if the opportunity presented itself, yeah, he might not be able to stop himself."

"But wasn't he at practice that night, and didn't he have Jamie in the car with him when he left? He wouldn't do that with Jamie in the car."

"Maybe he dropped Jamie off and went somewhere else. I

don't know, Meredith. I'm just saying anything's possible." The smoke from Paul's cigarette curled up through the light from the lamp next to his chair. He resolved that this would be his last year coaching the team.

Paul's resolution loomed in his mind as the Terrors took the court for their next game. Coming off the loss the week before, the players were both determined and uneasy. They had little faith in their ability to win like they had before, but they weren't about to let that show. They wanted to at least look like they were still confident in themselves, even if their confidence about their world had been badly shaken. Quentin's injury had first scared them because they didn't know what was going to happen to their teammate. As they were reassured that Quentin would recover, each of them developed a gnawing fear that something bad could happen to him. They all rode bicycles. They walked along the sides of roads, not always paying attention to the traffic. They could be lying in a hospital bed or worse. That fear was too painful, so they focused on their doubts about playing basketball. They had to win this game.

Paul sensed their uncertainty, even if he didn't fully understand its depth. He wanted to hug them all, but they'd never let him, so he had to just get them through the rest of the season as best he could. And since it was his last season, he'd play them to win regardless of what the parents or anybody else thought.

The opposing team had an excellent record—only two losses. A few of the players were taller than Jamie, but most of them matched the Terrors in height. The Terrors got off to a good start, picking up a quick six-point lead, thanks to a surprise three-pointer by Benny, but Jamie was having trouble keeping a lid on the center, who had at least two inches on him. So far, the center had scored all of the other team's points, and Jamie hadn't gotten close enough to drop any. With the lane covered so well, the Terrors had to hope for outside shots, but Benny's hand didn't stay hot for long. He missed the next two shots he put up, and Malcolm and Adam didn't do much better. The score was soon tied, and then the Terrors fell behind.

Paul called a time-out to slow their opponents' momentum. "Try to drive the lane and see if you can draw some fouls from that center," he said to Frankie and Benny. "Adam and Malcolm, that means y'all have to pull your guards out of the way. Even if the drive doesn't work, maybe you'll distract the center enough to free up Jamie. Send him a quick pass so he can score."

"What about the guys guarding us?" Frankie asked.

"Give 'em a good fake. You know how to do that. Come on, guys. You can do this." Paul gave them each a high five as they trotted back onto the court.

In the bleachers, the parents were restless. James couldn't stand the fact that Jamie was being shut down. "Go up strong, Jamie!" he yelled. "He's not that much bigger than you are!" Although Elaine normally tolerated James's outbursts, today his demands crawled all over her. She hoped Jamie couldn't hear him. Avoiding the glances of the other parents, she crept away from him and sat down next to Meredith.

Maybe Jamie hadn't heard James, but Meredith definitely had. She stared at him, remembering what Paul had said about him and Quentin. Surely this man would never hurt a child, but in the heat of the moment? She wished she'd asked Paul if anything out of the ordinary had happened at practice that afternoon, anything that could have set James off more than usual. Elaine's sudden presence interrupted her thoughts. "Don't mind me," Elaine said. "I just want to watch the game from a different perspective."

"Sure," Meredith said, glad to be distracted. "I need to talk to you, anyway. Have you been able to spread the word about Clarinda at the church? And if you have, have you gotten any responses?"

"I put a notice in the church newsletter and in the bulletin for tomorrow. So far, I haven't heard anything, but the newsletter just went out, and nobody's seen the bulletin yet. It may take some time."

"Okay. Thanks. And I've had another idea. See what you think about this. Delia and Marcus need a person to stay with Quentin until he goes back to school. They both have jobs, and I know Delia's worried about taking time off since she just started at the high school a few weeks ago. I'm thinking Clarinda could stay with Quentin for a while. Maybe by the time he goes back to school, she'll find something else." Meredith was glad the idea didn't sound totally crazy when she said it out loud.

Elaine nodded. "I suppose it could work if you think she's responsible enough to do that. I don't know her, so I can't say. What does Delia think?"

"I haven't asked her yet. I wanted to run the idea by somebody else first."

Elaine was surprised that Meredith had picked her to ask for an opinion. Probably it was because Elaine already knew Meredith was looking for work for this girl. And she was doing Meredith a favor by giving her space in the church publications. "Then I say you ask Delia. Might solve a couple of problems, at least temporarily." She hoped the conversation was over. She didn't like talking about Quentin.

James continued to yell at Jamie even though Paul's plan worked a couple of times and Jamie got to drop a few baskets, but then the other center caught on to what they were doing and managed to keep an eye on Jamie as well as thwart Benny and Frankie. The Terrors struggled to catch up. Malcolm was having a particularly hard time hitting the basket, which caused Laura to call out, "Give the ball to Adam! He can make those shots!" Richard tugged at her arm and told her to pipe down, but as usual, she ignored him.

It's a good thing Jeff's not here, Lydia thought. *He'd lay into Laura or yell at Malcolm and probably do both.*

At game's end, the Terrors were down by eight points. "Another heartbreaker," Frank said to Paul. "But maybe we never had a chance against these guys. Our boys are trying, but it's like they're in a fog. Maybe they were just intimidated."

"Or maybe their minds are somewhere else," Paul said.

After riding home from the game with Paul and Benny, Meredith went to see the Thomases. She could have called Delia, but her idea was important enough that she thought she should talk to Delia and Marcus in person. Delia answered the door and invited her into the living room, where Marcus and Quentin were watching the North Carolina–Wake Forest basketball game on TV. Quentin sat on the couch propped up with lots of pillows, both legs stretched out on the cushions next to him. "I'm glad to have you all together," Meredith said as she sat in the easy chair next to the couch, but I can wait until halftime to talk about what I came to ask you."

"We can talk now," Marcus said. "There's only about a minute left in the half." He turned off the TV. "What can we help you with?"

"I hope I can help you," Meredith said, "and maybe you can help a friend of mine." She explained Clarinda's circumstances as kindly as she could. "Clarinda needs a job," she said, "and I think you need somebody to stay with Quentin starting on Monday. I know Clarinda would do a good job. She's highly motivated, and I think she and Quentin would get along well. She'd be happy to fix your lunch and bring you whatever you need."

"I don't need help," Quentin said. "I can take care of myself. I can walk with my walker and get food out of the refrigerator if I want to. If I have a problem, I'll call Dad or Mom."

"What if we're not available right then?" Delia asked. "You need a person here with you. Is Clarinda reliable? Can we trust her?"

"Absolutely. And she'll charge a lot less than a visiting nurse or a home health aide. Plus, she's young, Quentin. Probably has some of the same interests you do. Probably even enjoys playing Atari."

"Can she meet with us tomorrow?" Marcus asked.

"Yes, I'll bring her over," Meredith said.

21

The First United Methodist Church overflowed with mourners at Henry Galloway's funeral the next day. When Paul arrived, at least fifty people were standing on the white brick steps leading up to the front door. Paul's first thought was to turn around and go home. He wasn't sure why he was there. He didn't know Henry, and he didn't work at the mill. He simply felt an obligation to pay respects to the family who had done so much for Tanner. Meredith didn't share his sense of duty. She often thought Henry took advantage of the townspeople largely because he could. Even those who didn't work for him, like Paul, could feel his power if they did something he didn't like. She was sure at least half the town would show up, so Henry didn't need her presence. She would rather use the time to visit Clarinda. Checking up on the girl wasn't her responsibility, but she worried about her fragility. Clarinda needed support if she was going to get her daughter back.

Knowing the church would be crowded, Marcus and Delia arrived early and secured seats a few rows behind the section reserved for family. Despite reassurance from coworkers, Marcus still worried about his job security. Even if the company wasn't sold, there would be changes in management, and his boss could be transferred. Losing your mentor and champion at a company could be a death knell for your job. He'd seen it happen at Cone Mills, and it could happen to him. Delia was worried too. Not that she would mind moving back to Greensboro, but she knew how much this job meant to Marcus, and with her new job, she finally had something in this town she was excited about. She guessed it was good that she and Marcus came to the funeral—Marcus had said it was a command performance—because attendance would demonstrate their loyalty to the company and the Galloway family. Marcus also pointed out that all of the vice presidents and other senior managers at Foxrow Mills were there, at least all of the ones he knew. Before the service began, Delia couldn't help noticing that most of the mourners were white, with only a few Black people, mostly men, scattered among the congregation. She hoped they were all from Foxrow. The more Black managers, the better for Marcus.

Frank twitched in his seat so much that Suzanne told him to cut it out. He looked like he had poison ivy. He hadn't realized he'd been squirming, but he was uncomfortable knowing that so many of the Foxrow top brass were sitting all around him. He'd worked his way up the corporate ladder slowly, so although he was proud of his achievements, as had been so clear to him at the Kiwanis meeting, he still wasn't confident about how to act in the presence of so much corporate authority. He looked down at his gray suit, white shirt, and navy blue tie and hoped he was dressed appropriately. He couldn't count on Suzanne to help him in that department. She was wearing a scoop-neck dress with a multicolored print that looked like a watercolor painting. When he questioned her choice of attire, she said Henry would rather see a pretty woman in a pretty dress than some vampire garb.

Elaine spent a long time deciding what she should wear. She'd be filling a couple of roles at the funeral, and she wanted her appearance to be perfect. First, as secretary of the church, she'd be representing church leaders and staff. Then, as James's wife, she'd be representing the family of a Foxrow manager. James always wore the right clothes for every occasion, and he expected her to do the same. She was confident her black wool dress with a single strand of pearls was the right choice, so she felt comfortable when she arrived at the church. James led her down the aisle with his usual self-assured stride and a somber expression replacing his customary smile in large groups of people. Elaine nodded to a few of the church members she saw but maintained the solemnity the occasion required. She and James arrived too late to sit near the front of the church. Instead, they slid into one of the back pews next to Jeff Colton. Jeff had no ties to the mill, but he was savvy enough to know that if he had political ambitions in Tanner, he needed to put in an appearance at this funeral.

Lydia sat toward the middle of the sanctuary with Suzanne and Frank. They had squeezed together to make room for her at the end of their pew. Since she was next to the aisle, she had a clear view of the Galloway family as the funeral director led them to their seats in the front rows. Henry's daughter, Alice Otis, and her husband, Ralph, came first. Alice was only sixty-seven years old, but her skin had a leathery quality to it, probably because she spent a lot of time riding horses. Today her wrinkles seemed carved even deeper into her face. She and Henry had never seen eye to eye, but losing your father is difficult no matter what. Nancy and Caroline came behind Ralph and her. Nancy had been holding up well until they entered the church. All the sad-looking people, flowers, and pipe-organ dirges made her lose control, causing tears to stream silently down her face. Caroline kept an arm around her shoulders and whispered to her from time to time.

After them was Nancy's brother, Tom. Tom had lived on the farm and worked at the mill until about ten years ago when he announced to his grandfather that he was leaving. All hell broke loose, but he left anyway. During the short time that he and Lydia were both in Tanner, they had worked together to find out what really happened in the suspicious death of Henry's brother a half-century before. At the time, Lydia thought Tom was the only family member who appreciated what Nancy was capable of, so they became allies in that too. He had a reputation as a playboy, and he didn't find Lydia unattractive, but she was married at the time, so their friendship remained just a friendship. Then, before she knew it, he was gone. Nancy said he had a lot of girlfriends where he lived in Connecticut, but she never mentioned marriage, and Lydia wasn't about to ask. She didn't want Caroline to think she was pining after him. He hadn't changed much, she noticed, maybe a little heavier. She hoped he was happier than he was when she knew him. Tom was followed by Alice's son and daughter and their families and several more people Lydia didn't recognize. Probably distant relatives who, of course, were going to show up for Henry's funeral.

Henry's body lay in a mahogany casket in front of the chancel rail, surrounded by a truckload of flowers. As the minister climbed the stairs to the pulpit, Lydia wondered if all the people waiting outside had been able to find seats. Staff from the funeral home had been setting up folding chairs when she arrived, but she doubted there was room for enough. Thoughts of fire codes flitted briefly through her mind, and she realized it would have been a good idea to sit closer to an exit. She hoped Henry had been on good enough terms with God that no lightning would come crashing toward the steeple.

Her own relationship with Henry had been less than cordial. He greatly resented her efforts to investigate his brother's death and dragging Tom into it. The last time she had been in a room with him, he left with no goodbyes and no mention of ever seeing her again. The only reason she came to the funeral was to support Nancy. She hoped she would get a chance to talk with her after the service. Surely Caroline would spare her from having to greet all the mourners, but maybe Lydia could get a few minutes with her.

While the minister made his way through the sermon and the eulogy for Henry, Lydia's mind kept drifting to Nancy. How lonely she'd been when Lydia first met her. How eager she'd been to have Lydia as a friend. Gradually, Lydia's thoughts expanded to include Quentin. She thought she'd seen that same look of eagerness on his face. What was he eager for? To win basketball games? No, he was doing that already. Lydia suspected he was eager to have the boys on the basketball team like him. She would remind Malcolm that inviting him to their house to shoot baskets was a good idea.

After the service, the funeral director led the family to the vestibule where those who wanted to could wait to speak to mourners. Since they were sitting near the back of the church, James and

Elaine, along with Jeff, were among the first people to reach the family. They spoke with Alice and Tom before James and Jeff wandered off to find mill and town executives to chat up. Elaine considered talking with Suzanne as she and Frank emerged from the sanctuary, but after the remarks Suzanne had made about Cultural Bridge, she decided to look for someone else. How could that woman be so judgmental?

Lydia entered the vestibule looking for Nancy, who she immediately saw was not with her brother and aunt. Skirting the crowd around Alice and Tom, she slipped down the stairs to the fellowship hall and found Nancy and Caroline sitting in a corner by themselves. Nancy wasn't crying, but she looked distraught. Lydia kissed her on the cheek, which caused her face to brighten a bit. "Would you like me to stay with you for a while so your mother can go back upstairs?" Lydia asked.

Nancy nodded. Caroline was leery of leaving Nancy with Lydia. She wasn't sure Lydia always had Nancy's best interests at heart, but she also felt guilty about leaving Tom and Alice to deal with the crowd, so she gave Nancy a hug and left.

In the vestibule, Marcus and Delia waited their turn to speak to the Galloways. Marcus was particularly curious about Tom, whom he'd heard stories about but never met. Tom was the maverick grandson who may have been the reason Henry took the company public. The initial public offering had been announced only two years after he left. Marcus wondered how he could be so bold or maybe so stupid as to walk away from a controlling position with Foxrow Mills. He didn't look stupid with his deep blue eyes and strawberry blond hair. When Delia saw him, she could imagine the twinkle that was probably in his eyes on other occasions.

"I'm so sorry about Mr. Henry," Marcus said as he shook Tom's hand. "I've only been with the mill for several months, but I've learned to respect the company, and I'm confident a lot of that is because of Mr. Henry."

Tom looked at him intently before asking, "What's your name, and where do you work at the mill?" After Marcus told him, he said, "I'm glad you're here. If there's ever anything I can do to help you, let me know. Folks don't like me much around here, but I still have some clout."

Marcus thanked him and waited for Delia to offer her condolences. On the way to their car, he asked her, "What do you think he meant by 'anything I can do to help you'?"

"Who knows?" Delia said. "So much about this town is misleading or ambiguous."

"And sometimes people say exactly what they think."

Late in the afternoon on Wednesday, Lydia drove to Foxrow to see Nancy. She was still worried about her friend, and when she'd called earlier in the day, Nancy encouraged her to come, so she headed out right after work. The temperature had fallen significantly all day, reminding the people of Tanner that winter was reaching its peak. So far, they'd had no snow, but that was about to change. Even though the cloud cover was sparse, Lydia could smell it in the air. She thought she might have seen a few flakes as she climbed the worn stairs to the wide porch and double front doors. She turned the buzzer and was surprised when Tom answered it. Pansy had said he'd probably leave right after the funeral. "Come in," he said. "Nancy'll be glad to see you."

"Thanks. How nice that you're still here. I know your family appreciates your support." Lydia followed him down the wide center hall, bedecked on both sides with colorful flower arrangements the size of boxwood bushes.

"Appreciation might not be what they're feeling for me right now. But I'm going to be here at least several more days." He gestured toward the tiny den tucked behind the master bedroom, where Nancy sat with a book.

"Lydia!" she exclaimed, her face the most radiant it had been since her grandfather died. Nancy considered Lydia to be her very best friend. She liked her even more than the people she worked with, and she liked them a lot.

The aroma from the flowers followed Lydia into the den. "Such a nice scent," she said as she gave Nancy a hello hug. "No wonder you like to sit here. Have you been doing a lot of reading the past couple of days?"

"Yes. Mama won't let me go back to work, but I think I'm better off there than here." Nancy had started at the lingerie factory doing hand stitching on ladies' nightgowns and helping with packaging, but in the twelve years she had worked there, she'd learned to use a sewing machine and to run the single-needle embroidery machine. Her new skills made her proud and did wonders for her self-esteem.

"Why are you better off there?" Lydia asked.

"Because I'm bored here, and I miss my friends."

Lydia nodded knowingly. The two women talked about Nancy's work and the books she was reading. They were also big movie fans and continued to talk about a movie they saw just before Christmas—*The NeverEnding Story*. Nancy particularly liked the dog Falkor in the movie, and Lydia liked the concept of the Nothing. Lydia was careful not to mention Henry. Since they had talked about him at the church after the funeral, she didn't see any need to talk about him again, and she didn't want to spoil Nancy's cheerful mood.

After an hour, Caroline appeared at the door to summon Nancy to get ready for dinner. Nancy obediently said her goodbyes and left Lydia to show herself out, but as she was putting on her coat, Tom came into the den, a glass of scotch in his hand. "Don't rush off," he said. "Let's talk for a few minutes. Would you like a drink?"

"No, thank you. Don't you have to get ready for dinner?"

Tom smirked. "Dinner's not for another thirty minutes. That's just Mom's not-so-subtle way of telling you it's time to leave. I want to tell you why I'm staying longer than I planned."

Lydia put her coat back on the sofa in front of the ceiling-high bookcases and waited.

"It's like this," Tom said as he sat on the sofa and motioned for her to sit next to him. "Foxrow board members are making noises about selling the company. Prospective buyers have been circling for more than a year now because it's a very profitable business. Some of the larger textile corporations would love to add it to their empires." He smiled like the owner of a prize pig at the county fair. "It could never have happened before Grandpa died because no one would ever cross him that way, and he was the majority shareholder. Now his shares will be divided between Nancy and me. Nancy will have a legal advocate to make decisions about her shares, but Mom expects the advocate will go along with whatever she tells her to do. The wild card is me. Nobody knows what I'll do. If I vote to sell, then that's enough shares to close the deal."

"You won't sell, will you? The mill's been in your family for nearly a century. It's who y'all are."

"Depends on the offer. Only one's come in so far, but I'm sure there'll be others."

Lydia was disgusted that any self-respecting corporation would put in a bid to buy a company only days after the patriarch's funeral. "What does your mother think? And Alice?"

"Mom rues the day Grandpa decided to take the company public. She told him it was a mistake then, but he wanted fresh capital coming in. Alice owns a fair number of shares, but not enough to be the deciding vote. She took most of her stake in the mill in cash years ago and did her own investing. Guess she didn't have much faith in Grandpa or my dad, and she's done well for herself. She'll probably vote to sell, but it still won't be enough."

"What will happen to your family if you sell the mill? You're the pillars of Tanner. I can't imagine the town without you."

"Mom and Nancy and Alice will stay. They're too rooted here to go anywhere else. I'll go back to Connecticut, and things will go on like they always have."

"Why are you telling me this?"

"Because I know you can keep a secret. After all the work we did together to figure out how Uncle Howard died, I trust you. We're alike in a lot of ways. Also, I'd like to see you again before I leave, and it's best to start with a clean slate between us. No hidden agendas. Maybe dinner this weekend?"

Lydia couldn't help laughing inside at the reaction Caroline would have when she learned Tom was taking her to dinner. "That would be lovely. I could use a little levity right now. Things are tense with Malcolm's basketball team, and some of the parents are showing sides of themselves I guess I knew were there but didn't expect to come out like this."

"What's going on?" Tom would never have expected turmoil on a kids' basketball team in Tanner.

"You must be the only person in town who hasn't heard about the new player on the eighth-grade AAU basketball team. I get questions about it from people I would have guessed cared nothing about sports at any level."

"Is it serious?"

"It is. Our new player was hit by a car on his way home from practice a couple of weeks ago. It landed him in the hospital, and the driver disappeared. I'll tell you more about it at dinner, and you can tell me more about what you think is going to happen to the mill. I'm sure Caroline is at the dinner table frowning because you haven't shown up yet. Call me when you know the details about this weekend." Lydia reached for her coat, and Tom stood to help her put it on. As he walked her to the door, she was thinking that things were certainly taking a turn for the worse in Tanner. Maybe it really was time for her to leave.

The next Cultural Bridge meeting took place Thursday night at the church in Tanner. Laura had carefully selected the room for the meeting. They could have met in one of the Sunday school rooms, but Laura wanted the ambiance to be just right, so she reserved the ladies' parlor, a carpeted room with plush furniture and an adjoining kitchenette that was usually used by brides before their weddings. She and Elaine were pleased to see that everyone who attended the

January meeting was present, including Sharon Robinson and the two couples from Copeland. The original two couples from Tanner were also present, plus the choir director, Norma, and her husband, Brad. "I had such a good time at the Martin Luther King celebration that I want to be part of whatever the group does next," Norma said.

"Before we start the meeting," Sharon said, "please give us an update on Quentin Thomas. I haven't talked to Delia since he came home, and I hope he's doing well. He's the boy who was hit by a car on his way home from basketball practice a few weeks ago," she explained to the others from Copeland, most of whom already knew what she was talking about.

"As far as I know, he's doing just fine," Laura said.

"Thanks to one of the basketball team parents, Marcus and Delia were able to hire a young woman to stay with him during the day until he goes back to school," Elaine added. "I offered to help them find someone from the church, but this young woman needed the job, so I hope the arrangement works out."

"Have the police had any luck finding the driver of the car?" Sharon asked. "A true hit-and-run with no evidence of the car," she explained to the Copeland folks.

"That dude is long gone," Alfred Duncan said in a loud whisper, eliciting a frown from his wife, Erlene. "Or if he's not, he's somebody you'd never expect. Somebody that you all know. Somebody from Tanner that's laying low."

"Hush up, Alfred," Erlene said. "You don't know anything about this."

"But that's the way it always is. The devil among us. We think evil comes from outside, but it doesn't. It's usually brewing right here at home. I'll bet you the driver knows that kid."

"If that's the case, sometimes the sinner needs as much help as the person sinned against. We should be praying for both of them," Sharon said.

"Amen," said one of the men from Copeland.

"Amen," echoed Laura. "Now let's move on to committee

business. First, give ourselves a round of applause for the Martin Luther King celebration. Thanks to all of us, it was a moving and uplifting affair." Everyone clapped.

"But it was just a beginning," Elaine said. "We need to decide on our next project."

"Let's have a bake sale," Alfred suggested, "and bake extra pies and cookies for us."

"Assuming we sell everything and don't save any for ourselves, what would we do with the money we raise?" Elaine asked.

"Raising money sounds so cold to me," Candace Washington from Copeland said. "I want to do something that brings us not only in touch with each other but with other people in our towns, people who need some help."

"Like who?" Candace's husband, Darnell, asked.

"I don't know. Poor people, sick people, elderly people."

Sharon sat up straighter in the soft wingback chair she had settled into. "You know," she said, "our congregation has a lot of elderly members who could most likely use some help."

"Too bad we're in the dead of winter, or we could do yard work," Brad said.

"There'll be snow to shovel soon," said Alfred with a grimace.

"There's plenty to do in the winter," Sharon said. "Pick up groceries. Pick up medicine. Drive people to doctor's appointments."

"Tanner has a nursing home now," Laura said. "When the new hospital was built, they turned the old one into a nursing home. I'll bet some people there would like a little company occasionally."

"We should organize in teams." Julia Harris from Tanner was getting into the spirit of the idea. "One person from Tanner and one person from Copeland should visit our shut-ins and other elderly people and see what they need."

"Okay," said Elaine, "we all have homework to do. Come to the next meeting with a list of elderly people in your town and services they need. Otherwise, we'll find out when we go to visit them. And see if you can recruit more church members for our group. The more people we have for this, the better."

In the back of her mind, Laura remembered Richard saying something about how they should do a service project. She didn't want him to think the new endeavor was his idea since he wouldn't go to the planning meetings, so she'd be sure to stress the idea came from a facetious remark that Alfred made. After everyone else had left the meeting, she and Elaine stayed behind to tidy the room. "Who'd have thought we'd come up with a good project because Alfred wanted us to bake cookies for him?" she said with a laugh.

Elaine shrugged. "I have a feeling Alfred is smarter than he lets on."

"What did you think about what he said about the driver who hit Quentin?"

"The driver doesn't know Quentin. If he did, he'd have stopped to help." Elaine plumped the pillows on the sofa and took her purse from a side table in preparation to leave.

"I'm not sure," Laura said. "I also wonder why everybody thinks the driver was a man. It could have been a woman. Maybe even Meredith."

Startled by the remark, Elaine dropped her purse back onto the table.

"Think about it." Laura took a few steps toward her. "Meredith is a lawyer. An aggressive lawyer. She pushed that woman she defended in court on the Thomases. Do you think they really wanted a woman who abandoned her own child taking care of their child? Of course not. But Meredith gets what she wants. She wanted Quentin out of the way so Paul would have an easier time coaching the team."

"You're delusional," Elaine said. "Whoever that driver was, he hit Quentin by accident. Nobody would deliberately hurt a child."

"Believe what you want, but I agree Alfred is smarter than he lets on. And I think he's on the right track here. We just have to get the culprit to confess."

"Now I know you're delusional. Nobody is going to confess. Accept it. We'll probably never know who hit Quentin. Now I need to go home." Elaine picked up her purse again and this time walked straight out the door.

Laura huffed a few times before deciding to tell Lydia her theory about Meredith. Lydia would see the wisdom of it. On the drive home, she mulled over possibilities about Meredith until she was convinced Meredith had to be the culprit. She was so convinced she couldn't wait to call Lydia. She had to tell somebody right away, and that somebody was, of course, Richard, who was reading a book in the living room when she got home.

"It occurred to me tonight," she said as she sat on the ottoman where Richard's feet were propped, "that everybody assumes the person who hit Quentin was a man, but it could just as easily have been a woman,"

Richard nodded.

"And it could have been Meredith. She would do something like that to make coaching the team easier for Paul."

Richard put down the book and grabbed his wife's hands. "Listen to me, Laura. You can't go around saying things like that. You have no evidence that Meredith did anything. It's just a harebrained idea you dreamed up."

"But it makes sense."

"No, it doesn't. And I'll tell you another thing. If you keep pushing the possibility that the driver was a woman, people are going to suspect you."

She jerked her hands free in horror. "Why me? I have no reason to hurt Quentin."

"Sure you do. As much as anybody else. You made it quite clear at the games that you didn't like it when Quentin got to play instead of Adam. You told James you thought that hideous meeting he had was a good idea, and you said at the meeting that Quentin was getting to play too much. You've made your opinion on the subject pretty well known, so why wouldn't people think you wanted Quentin off the team?"

Laura sucked in a few deep breaths. "But who could ever think I'd hurt him? Do you think I did it?"

"No, I don't. I know you too well. But I can see how other people might think that."

"Then other people are crazy! I don't deserve that!" Laura flailed her hands in a gesture of despair.

Richard pushed her hands back down into her lap. "Please just keep your thoughts to yourself," he said, even though he knew that was impossible for her to do.

Tom arrived promptly at six thirty to take Lydia to dinner Saturday night. When Lydia knew him twelve years ago, he drove a silver Corvette that everybody in town recognized. Now he was driving a dark blue Honda Accord, which surprised her until she remembered he'd flown into Charlotte from Connecticut, and it was likely a rental car. "I thought we'd drive over to Hickory," he said as he held the car door open for her. "An old friend suggested a place called Mama's Garden."

"I'm surprised you still have friends in Tanner."

"I have a few. And this one was always a great arbiter of food. He taught me the superiority of onion rings over french fries when we were twelve, and he hasn't steered me wrong since."

"I don't doubt this friend knows his restaurants, but I'd rather not drive to Hickory. Malcolm's home alone, so I shouldn't stay out too late. He's kind of sad. They lost their basketball game today, and he's still upset about what happened to his teammate."

"Okay. So where would you suggest?"

"Let's go to Johnny's."

Tom laughed. "Johnny's? Is that still around? Not exactly a mecca of fine dining, but if that's what you want, that's what you shall have." He turned the Accord in the direction of the old restaurant that had started out as a diner and through the years grown into a hometown favorite with a broad menu and two separate dining rooms.

"I think you'll be surprised when we get there," Lydia said.

And he was. He certainly didn't remember Johnny's being so refined. The white tablecloths and navy blue window curtains added a feel of elegance to the place. "Looks like Tanner's coming up in the world," he said.

"Do you mean that, or are you poking fun at us?"

"I mean it." Tom tried to look hurt that she would even suggest sarcasm.

"Are you sorry you left? Do you think you might reconsider and move back?"

Tom shook his head. "No. Things are going to change around here."

A waitress came and gave them menus. After she left, Tom looked around the dining room, and satisfied there was nobody in earshot, he lowered his voice to say, "Another offer for the mill came in yesterday."

"Was it better than the first one?"

Tom frowned and made a gesture like he was pushing air down to the table. "Not so loud. I don't want to cause a panic in Tanner, but yes, it was a little better." He turned his attention to the menu.

"So, what's going to happen?" Lydia whispered.

"Is the barbecue here Texas-style or Eastern Carolina-style?"

Lydia sighed. "Kind of a mixture, but more vinegary than tomatoey. Now tell me what's going to happen with the mill."

"I don't know. It'll take a while to make a decision, and we need to find out what the shareholders think. The board wants to hold out for more money, which is a good idea. Now that I know nothing drastic is going to happen soon, I need to go back to work." Tom looked at the pages of the menu again. "They don't serve booze here, do they?"

Lydia laughed. "Not in Tanner."

"But I thought the laws in North Carolina were changing."

"They are, but Johnny knows if he serves alcohol of any kind, half the people in Tanner won't darken his door."

Tom shook his head. "We should have had a drink before we came. I guess we may as well order." When the waitress returned, they both ordered steaks, although Tom muttered, "It won't be the same without a good red wine."

Despite the lack of wine, Tom had to admit the steaks were delicious. "Tell me about the deal with the basketball team," he said as he was finishing his meal. "You said one of the boys got hit by a car and nobody knows who was driving. That's terrible."

"The trouble started even before that." Lydia told him most of the details surrounding the conflicts among the parents of the players while doing her best not to blame any particular people for the difficulties. "Now it's reached the point where a few parents suspect other parents of deliberately hurting Quentin. That can't be true."

Tom thought about what she said while he pulled a cigarette from a pack in his pocket and lit it. "Since I don't have a kid, I can't understand exactly how y'all feel about this, but I can give you an opinion from an outside observer who doesn't live here anymore. Tell the parents to quit complaining and accusing, or you'll kick their kid off the team. That ought to shut them up."

Lydia was horrified at the suggestion. "That's not fair to the boys!"

"Trust me. It'll never happen. They'll either shut up or find another team to put their sons on."

"There aren't any other AAU teams for this age group in the area. We're lucky we have this one."

"Then if they want their kids to play, they better quit complaining." Tom took a long drag from his cigarette and held it. To him, managing parents and kids was just like managing employees. Tell them what you want them to do, and if they don't do it, give them a persuasive consequence. Lydia had heard a similar tactic before, but it put the onus on the parents, not the boys. There had to be a reasonable way out of this.

"Do you want dessert, or are you ready to go?" Tom asked.

"No dessert." What she wanted was to change the conversation. She was so tired of dead ends everywhere she looked for answers to help the team. "How much longer will you be in town?"

"Just until Tuesday." He signaled the waitress for the check and gave her his credit card.

"Do you think your mother and Nancy will be all right?"

Now it was Tom's turn to laugh. "My mother will be in hog heaven without Grandpa to answer to. She'll tell the board exactly what she thinks about selling the mill, which is a rip-roaring no, and then she'll start pressuring me, which is another reason I need to get out of town."

"Will you be back anytime soon?" Lydia was surprised that she cared whether he came back or not.

"I'll see how things go, but I imagine I'll come more often now than I used to."

When he'd signed the credit card receipt, he helped Lydia put on her coat. They were both silent on the drive home, but when they reached Lydia's house, Tom said, "How about if I come in for a drink since Johnny's was totally dry?"

"Not tonight. I really need to spend some time with Malcolm."

"Then I'll have to take a rain check," he said. He unfastened his seatbelt and leaned across the gap between the seats to take her face in his hands. She instinctively unfastened her seatbelt and moved closer to him. He slid his hands down to her back and held her as tightly as he could, given the separate seats. His embrace was warm, and his lips insistent. He had wanted to do that twelve years ago, but she was married then, and he didn't think she'd be interested, or at least not willing. After a short time, he gently pulled away. "I'll tell you what," he said with a smile. "Next time, we have to go inside. I'm not limber enough anymore to play front-seat lip hockey. Leave that to the kids. I need a couch."

22

Sunday afternoon, Lydia took Malcolm over to Frankie's house to shoot baskets or whatever eighth-grade boys did to while away an afternoon. Since the Terrors had lost their third basketball game in a row, the players were all down in the dumps. Suzanne thought they didn't need to be alone on Sunday, so she invited Malcolm over to keep Frankie busy while she tried to figure out a way to cheer up Frank. She would have shooed him off to get in a few frames with his bowling pals, but the bowling alley was closed on Sundays. Now he was drinking a beer and flipping channels trying to find a pro basketball game to watch, but all he could find was golf. Suzanne wondered how Paul and Benny were handling the loss. Maybe she should call Meredith to see what was going on at their house. Maybe she should see if Frankie and Malcolm wanted Benny to join them.

After dropping off Malcolm, Lydia drove out to Foxrow to check on Nancy. She hoped Caroline would let her go back to work on Monday. In Lydia's opinion, Nancy didn't need to be sitting home alone. She had been doing so well before she lost her grandfather, and even though the old man hadn't been particularly nice to her, she felt his absence.

Bulging gray clouds hung in the sky, offering a hint of snow as Lydia climbed the familiar worn steps to the wraparound porch. This time Pansy answered the buzzer and invited her to wait in the massive center hall while she went to look for Nancy. "Never know where that girl might be," she muttered.

That day, Nancy was easy to find. She lay stretched out on the couch in the living room, watching an old movie on television. Lydia was glad to see she looked less melancholy than she had at their most recent visit. As always, she was glad to see Lydia.

"What'cha watching?" Lydia asked.

"Something with Jimmy Stewart. It's about an invisible rabbit." Nancy swung her legs around and sat up on the couch. Her fine red hair had some curl in it, a sure sign she'd used a curling iron.

"Oh, sure. *Harvey*. I've seen that."

"Do you believe Harvey is real?"

Lydia shrugged. "I don't think it matters whether he's real or not. If the James Stewart character believes he's real, then he's affecting the character's life, and that's all that matters."

"Like a ghost," Nancy said. "Grandpa's ghost is still here. I can't see him, but I know when he's around because Mama is upset."

"What do you mean she's upset?"

"She fusses at Pansy and Marie. And sometimes she fusses at somebody on the phone."

"Does she fuss at you?"

"No. I just try to stay out of her way."

Lydia wondered what was going on with Caroline. Maybe Nancy was right about Henry's ghost hanging around. She'd bet her eyetooth, though, that there was more to it than that. The question was whether or not she should tell Tom. If Caroline's mood was affecting Nancy, maybe she should.

Frank was still troubled about the Terrors on Tuesday, the night the Kiwanis Club held their next meeting. Jeff had called a couple of times that week to encourage him to go, but Frank had insisted that he wasn't sure if he'd be able to make it, so he'd plan to go alone if he could go. He still wanted to join the club, but he wanted to stay as far away from Jeff as possible. A few days earlier, Suzanne had told him she suspected Jeff was the driver of the car that hit Quentin. At first, Frank thought the idea was nuts, but the more he considered it, he wasn't so sure. Jeff hadn't been at practice that night, which was unusual. Most of the time, he showed up to keep an eye on Paul and Frank. Also, Lydia had told Suzanne that when she mentioned Quentin's injury to Jeff at the next basketball game, he acted as if he knew nothing about it, which was surprising since almost everybody was talking about it. "Give me a break," Suzanne had said to Frank. "There's no way he couldn't have known about it, not if he'd talked to his son at all."

Frank arrived at the meeting alone like he'd planned. George Simmons, the VP of Frank's division at the mill, was sitting next to an empty seat. Did he dare go sit beside him? George had been friendly at the previous meeting. Frank hadn't seen him at work since then, but he likely wouldn't have. They moved in very different circles. *Let our regrets be for things we did and not for things we didn't do*, Frank repeated to himself. It was a mantra Suzanne had taught him, and so far, it had served him well. He sat down next to George.

"Hey, Frank," George said with a slap on the back. "Glad to see you at another meeting. I was just talking to Alvin Henderson." He gestured toward the man on his other side. "Do you know Alvin? He's head of the mill's sales department." Frank did not know Alvin. He knew who he was, but he'd never met him. George introduced Frank, and the two men exchanged pleasantries. "Frank's in my division," George said. "A good man and a hard worker."

The compliment caused Frank's back and shoulders to straighten involuntarily. He hoped he could think of something intelligent to say. Before he had to say anything, however, George continued, "Al and I were just talking about the future of the mill now that Mr. Henry's gone. What's the word down in the planning department? Are the people you work with worried? Are you worried?"

Frank sat up even straighter. Did they really want to know what he thought? He felt like an insider, for sure. "Of course, we're all worried about what'll happen to the mill if it's sold. Rumors are flying, but nobody knows what's going to happen. A few folks have said they have feelers out for other jobs. I've worked here twenty-three years, so I'm staying till the bitter end if that's what it comes down to. Is there any news about a sale?"

"No, it's way too soon. We just don't want everybody running scared. The next time somebody says something to you about it, tell them it's too soon. If the board wants to sell, they'll have to take a vote of the shareholders first. If the shareholders approve, it'll still take months and maybe years to close the deal. You could really help us by making sure that message gets out." George nodded for emphasis.

At that moment, one of the local dentists, whom Frank recognized but didn't actually know, walked over to talk to George and Alvin. Assuming his conversation was ended, Frank looked around the room for other men he knew at least a little. He spotted several and was considering going to talk to one when Jeff Colton walked through the door. Wearing his usual confident smile, Jeff made his way up the center aisle, speaking and shaking hands with nearly everybody he passed. *For Christ's sake,* Frank thought, *he's already campaigning to be council president.* Frank wondered how the council would feel about him if they knew he was a hit-and-run driver. *If* he was a hit-and-run driver. Frank felt an urge to hide behind the men sitting in front of him and was glad there was no vacant seat next to him.

The following evening, James took his usual seat halfway up the bleachers at basketball practice. He was frustrated about the Terrors' streak of losses and determined to figure out some advice to give the coaches. He had been a star player in high school, even though he didn't talk about it very much, so he should have some kind of insight to offer before the season went down the tubes. Because he was concentrating so hard on every drill and play, he was more than a little annoyed when Jason's father, Sam, sat down next to him. "Team's really been struggling, haven't they?" Sam said. "It's too bad about what happened to Quentin. We need him."

James turned slowly to look at him. His frustration had reached a low boil. "That kid?" he asked. "That kid did this team more harm than good. We were building our players to be the best they could be until he came along and screwed up Paul's thinking. Do you think having him on the team was good for Jason? How many games did Jason get to play in after he came? Has Jason learned to be a better player this season? Have any of our players gotten any better? No. It was all about Quentin. And look at the mess we're in now that he's gone. I wish the guy who hit him had done it a lot sooner."

Before Sam could say anything, Richard Campbell, who was sitting in front of James, stood up, turned around, and landed a blow directly to the left side of James's face. James sprawled back against the bleacher behind him, and as he was struggling to stand, Frank, who had seen what happened, sprinted up from the court and grabbed James's left arm. Sam grabbed his right arm, and together they held him down where he sat.

Richard backed a few steps away. "What is wrong with you?" he said. "This is a child you're talking about. A living, breathing human being, and you're wishing he had gotten hurt sooner. I bet you wish he'd been hurt worse too." By this point, all activity had stopped on the court, and everyone was looking at Richard. "You know what?" he said. "I bet you're the one who hit him. You couldn't stand that he was taking all the attention away from Jamie."

"That's enough!" Paul yelled as he made his way up the bleachers.

"I'm leaving," Richard said. "I can't stand to be around these people anymore. Come on, Adam. Let's go."

"You coward!" James yelled. "You know I'm right. Every one of you has thought the same thing. You're just too afraid to say it."

"Get out of here, Richard," Paul said. "This practice is over. We're all going home."

Frank and Sam held on to James until Richard and Adam left the gym. His left cheek was blazing red, and his left eye was beginning to swell. "Do you want me to take you to the emergency room?" Paul asked.

"Hell no."

"Then at least let me drive you and Jamie home. Frank'll follow us in your car, and then I'll drive him back down here to get his. You need to get ice on that eye as quick as you can."

James grunted and broke free from Frank and Sam, who had loosened their grips. He followed Paul toward the door with Jamie a few steps behind, eyes round as basketballs.

Elaine had supper ready in the oven when James and Jamie burst through the front door. "What on earth?" she said when she saw James's face. "What happened to you?" She rushed to put her arms around him. He tolerated her embrace for less than a minute before pulling away.

"That crazy Richard Campbell hit me!"

"Why?" Elaine couldn't imagine professorial Richard Campbell hitting anybody.

"Jamie, go upstairs and wash your hands for dinner. And stay up there until I tell you to come down," James said. Jamie dropped his coat on the couch and did what he was told. "Who knows why he did it?" his father continued when he had left the room. "I said I thought Quentin had done the team more harm than good. Everybody knows that, but nobody else will say it. As soon as I said it, that son-of-a-bitch zonked me right in the face."

"What did you do then?" Elaine knew her husband's temper.

"Nothing. I didn't do a damn thing. He was the one yelling at me." James's entire face was turning as red as his left cheek, and his eye was nearly closed to a slit.

"Sit down. I'll get you some ice. Maybe we should take you to the emergency room."

"I'm not going to any emergency room. I already told Paul that." James dropped into his easy chair.

Elaine ran into the kitchen for ice. "Why did you say that about Quentin?" she asked when she returned and was trying to stretch an ice bag as far as she could to cover James's cheek and eye.

"Gimme that," he said, taking the bag from her hand. He tilted his head back and plopped the bag directly on his eye. "Because it's true and because that crybaby Sam McBride was whining about how much the team needs Quentin. He doesn't realize that the other boys, including his own kid, could be better players now if it weren't for Quentin."

Elaine sat on the edge of the couch. "I doubt that. Quentin was inspiring to them. They wanted to be as good as he was."

"They resented him and the favoritism the coaches showed him." James took his hand off the ice pack. The chill was irritating his eye on top of the pain from the blow.

"*You* resented him and the favoritism the coaches showed him." Elaine couldn't believe she said that. She almost never confronted anybody, especially not her husband.

"Everybody resented him!"

The front door opened suddenly. Jamie's sister, Gloria, started talking as soon as she was halfway inside. "I hope I'm not late for dinner. Jennifer's mom," and then she stopped and stared at her parents. "Daddy! What happened to your face?"

"He's all right," Elaine said. "Please go upstairs. Jamie's up there, and he'll tell you what happened. Dinner's going to be late." Gloria moved slowly toward the stairs, still keeping a wary eye on her parents. James and Elaine were silent until her footsteps faded away.

"It doesn't matter what I said. Richard had no right to hit me." James removed the ice pack from his eye. It was swollen shut now, puffy and slightly blue. "And you know what else? That dickhead said I was the driver who hit Quentin. Where does he get off saying that? He has no evidence, no proof. I think I'll file assault charges against him. Show how little he knows about it. But I'll tell you this. One of those parents knows more about it than they're letting on. Some of them were at that practice. They drove home when he did. One of them had to have seen something or done something. But they're keeping their mouth shut. I'm going to see every one of them and put on the pressure personally. Men and women. I'll prove it wasn't me. And maybe when I find out who did it, I'll shake his hand."

Tears began to run down Elaine's cheeks. "Don't do that," she said.

James's cheek was nearly as puffy as his eye. "Why not?"

"Because they didn't do it, and they don't know who did."

"How are you so sure?"

Elaine hung her head as sobs made their way up her body. "Because it was me," she whispered.

"I don't believe you." James's voice caught in his throat. "You couldn't have. How in God's name could it have been you?"

"It was an accident. A horrible, tragic accident." She wiped her eyes with the backs of her hands. "I didn't mean to do it."

"You're hallucinating. It's some bad dream you had."

"No, James. It's real."

"Why didn't you say anything?"

"How could I? I hit a person and didn't even stop. I was so scared. I don't know where my brain was. I saw the bicycle flip over in the rearview mirror, but I never saw the person. I swear I never saw the person." She was crying again. "Something in me kept my foot on the gas pedal. I don't know why. I drove past two stop signs before I finally stopped. I pulled off onto a side road and sat there, frozen."

Her nose was beginning to run. James reached for a box of tissues he thought was on the bookcase, although he could only see out of his right eye. "How long did you sit there?" he asked.

"Until I heard sirens. I drove back toward the school and saw the red lights flashing."

Footsteps sounded on the stairs. "Go back to your room!" James yelled. "Then what happened?"

"I guess I really panicked. All I could think about was getting Gloria and going home."

"Gloria?"

"That's why I was out. I was picking up Gloria at Jennifer's house. She told me they were doing a history project together, but I thought she was lying and they were really hanging out with some boys at Tubby's." When James gave her a blank stare, she explained,

"You know. That little grocery store where they sell beer and don't always check IDs." James nodded. "Anyway, I wanted to get there early and catch them still at Tubby's. I was hurrying, and I guess I was distracted. I don't know. Quentin came out of nowhere."

"What I still don't get is why you didn't tell me." The pain in James's face exploded into his brain. None of this made sense.

"By the time I pulled myself together enough to go get Gloria, I realized the only way I could keep it all together and not destroy our family was for no one to know it was me. I prayed that the person hadn't seen the car and that I didn't leave any evidence behind."

"But why?"

"I didn't want to go to prison, James. I figured that if the police were already there, they'd get the person to the hospital and everything would be all right."

"What about after you found out it was Quentin?"

"That made it worse. I didn't want to go to prison, and I was afraid our friends would think you put me up to it and blame you."

"Oh, fuck!" James jumped to his feet and started pacing the living room.

"Dad?" Jamie's tentative question wafted down from the second floor.

"It's nothing," James growled. "Dinner will be ready soon." He stared hard at Elaine. "So, what do we do now?"

"I think I should turn myself in. I can't live with this any longer."

"No! We've come this far. We're not turning back. The police are about to give up on the case. Most of these cases never get solved. Quentin is going to be all right. Everything will be all right if this never goes beyond us."

Elaine went into the bathroom to wash her face and get ready to serve dinner. She looked at herself in the mirror and thought, *Quentin's family deserves to know the truth.*

23

On most days, Quentin and Clarinda kept the Atari buzzing. "Do you know how to play?" he'd asked the first day she came to care for him. As far as he was concerned, the idea of this skinny white girl taking care of him was ridiculous. He was taller than she was. What was she supposed to do if he fell?

"No. But I can learn."

Okay, Quentin thought. *She might be good for something.* He set about teaching her to play video games, and soon she could beat him—at least once in a while. Between games, she fixed his lunch, stood outside the door when he went to the bathroom (which he hated), brought down books and other things he wanted from his room upstairs, and let the therapists into the house when they arrived. Also, once a week, one of his teachers came by to bring him assignments and help him with any problems he was having. For the first few days, Delia called every chance she got, but eventually she began to feel comfortable with Clarinda there.

Quentin was harder to win over. But he was basically a kind person who eventually let down his guard and let Clarinda in. She'd had very few dealings with thirteen-year-old boys, although she was little more than a year away from being a teenager herself. Growing up with drug-addicted parents, however, had given her a thick skin and a defensive attitude that served her well in this situation. When they weren't playing Atari, they watched television, usually any program Quentin found interesting, which wasn't easy since daytime programming was aimed at stay-at-home mothers. Quiz shows were mildly entertaining, with *Family Feud* being their favorite. Sometimes when there was nothing they wanted to watch, and Quentin was too tired to play Atari, Clarinda would read to him, often from the sports pages of the newspaper. The day of the altercation between James and Richard, she was finishing an article about NC State basketball coach Jim Valvano when Quentin asked, "How much longer do I have to stay home?"

Clarinda shrugged. "I don't know. Your parents know more about that than I do."

"They don't tell me anything. You must know how long they hired you for."

"They didn't give me a specific date."

"So I could be here forever." The hopelessness in his voice seemed to well up from his toes.

"Nothing lasts forever." Clarinda sighed. "I used to think the one thing in life I could be sure of was my little girl. Then I got sick, made some mistakes, and I don't have her anymore."

"What happened?" Quentin had never heard of anybody having their child taken away. Clarinda must have done something horrible.

"It's a complicated story, and it doesn't matter. What matters is I'm not going to let this last forever. I'm doing whatever it takes to get my daughter back. She's only five years old. She needs her mother. Your leg will heal. I don't know when, but probably sooner than you think. Your job is to do what the doctor tells you to."

"Who told you what you have to do to get your daughter back?"

"Child Protective Services. I'll never forget that name. Seems like they watch everything I do. They know I'm here with you. That's part of the deal. I have to have a job to get Lucy back, and right now, you're my job."

"Sorry if you lose your job, but I want to go back to school. Well, not really. Not this school. I just want to get out of here. I feel like I'm trapped in a cage. My life can't get any worse."

"Then do what you're told."

Quentin lay back on the bed. "That's what everybody says. Doesn't seem to do much good," he muttered. "Things just keep getting worse."

Richard dreaded telling Laura that he'd hit James. He didn't regret doing it, but after all the scolding he'd given her about voicing her feelings and having no self-restraint, it was hard to admit his own outburst. He considered not telling her, but she'd find out. Elaine would probably be on the phone that night, calling to tell Laura to do something about her husband because he was out of control. And Adam knew what had happened. He saw the whole thing. Richard couldn't tell him not to tell his mother. Trying to explain it to him in the car after practice was hard enough.

"I shouldn't have hit Jamie's dad," he began. "I always tell you not to settle an argument with your fists, and what I did was wrong. It's just that he said some things he shouldn't have said, things that aren't true. He's been saying them for weeks, and I couldn't take it anymore. I wanted him to stop, and I lost my temper. I'm sorry that you saw it."

"What'd he say, Dad?"

"I don't want to repeat it. I just want you to know that what I did was wrong, and I hope you'll behave better than that."

Adam was quiet the rest of the ride. At home, he went to his room without speaking to Laura. "What's wrong with him?" she asked.

"I let him down. I'm not the hero he wants me to be."

"Oh my god. What'd you do?"

Hoping she would understand the vitriol of James's accusations and the fire they set off in him, Richard told her what happened. "I'm not sorry I did it," he said at the end. "I'm just sorry Adam saw me do it."

"Adam and everybody else at that practice. Do they know why you did it?"

"I'm sure James told his side of the story to anybody who would listen. He's lucky Sam and Frank held him down so he couldn't hit me back. This way, he comes off looking pretty good."

"Oh my god," Laura said again. "Did you hurt him bad?"

"Look at me. I'm not big enough to hurt anybody bad. I'm

lucky Sam and Frank kept him off me. He's a big guy. I just hope he doesn't bring charges against me. He's got a lot of witnesses to back him up."

"We can't let him do that. I'll call Elaine and tell her you're sorry, and you'll apologize to James if that's what he wants."

"I'm not sorry, and I won't apologize. I hope he learns to keep his vicious opinions to himself."

"So, what do we do now?"

"We wait."

"We can't do that." Laura dropped into a chair and hit her forehead several times with the heel of her hand. Her take-charge philosophy of life was roiling inside her. She would talk to Elaine and maybe James, whether Richard liked it or not.

The next day, Laura decided it would be better to visit Elaine at the church than to call her. Thursdays were very busy at the church office, so Elaine might not take time to talk to her on the telephone, but if she were standing in front of her, Elaine wouldn't be rude enough to ignore her. Plus, face-to-face conversations were more persuasive. "I'm here to apologize for Richard," she said when Elaine looked up from her typewriter. "I don't know what happened to him. He never loses control like that. I think he was overtired. He's been working long hours lately. Please tell James he's very sorry and it will never happen again."

"I'll tell him," Elaine said. "And don't worry. He's not going to press charges."

"Elaine," Travis called from his office, "I finished my message for the bulletin."

"Coming," Elaine replied as she stood up from her desk. "I'm sorry, Laura, but I have a lot of work to do. Don't worry about James. Nothing's going to happen."

Laura smiled as she left the church. Once again, she had matters under control.

When Lydia returned home from work that afternoon, a large cardboard box waited on her doorstep. Puzzled about its origin, she whisked it inside to the kitchen and seized her utility scissors. Snip, snip, and the box was open. Immediately, the aroma of roses burst out. Twelve of the long-stemmed variety were tied with a crimson ribbon to match the color of their petals. *What the hell is this?* Lydia thought as she snatched the card from between the stems.

"Happy Valentine's Day. I hope to see you again before too long. Fondly, Tom" was written on the card. With so much going on in her life, Lydia had forgotten all about Valentine's Day. She rushed to the telephone to call Tom.

"Thank you!" she exclaimed when he answered. "You're so thoughtful. I'm afraid I didn't even send you a card."

"You're welcome." Tom chuckled. "I figured the flowers would be a surprise. Hope I didn't overstep any boundaries."

"No. Not at all. I'm just sorry I'm such a blockhead. I do wish you a happy Valentine's Day. It's just that the situation with the basketball team keeps getting worse, and that's all that's been on my mind. Last night, one of the dads punched another dad for saying mean things about Quentin, the boy who got hit by a car."

"I never knew Tanner could be so violent. What's happening to y'all down there?"

"I have no idea. It's like something evil came up out of the ground and is spreading like sewer water. The stink is becoming unbearable."

"Is there anything I can do to help?"

Come back to Tanner, Lydia wanted to say, but that probably wouldn't help. "Keep sending flowers," she said instead. "They'll help me keep my sanity."

Richard stayed home from the game the next Saturday. James did too. Now that he knew the truth about Quentin's injury, he wanted the whole matter forgotten. Showing up at the game with a shiner would cause a lot of questions in the minds of people who knew exactly why Richard hit him. If only he had kept his mouth shut after it happened, but he'd been determined to prove Richard had no reason to attack him. Now, any mention of Quentin would spark conversations about the car incident. James's absence, however, sparked questions on its own. It was the first game he had missed all season.

"He's not feeling well," Elaine said to anybody who asked. Laura said the same thing about Richard, but those who had been at practice on Wednesday knew why they weren't there, or thought they did. Laura was surprised that Elaine didn't speak to her at all. Instead, she sat as far away as she could. She hadn't wanted to go to the game, but James said it would look suspicious if neither one of them was there, plus Jamie deserved to have at least one parent present.

Elaine looked so sad that Lydia went to sit next to her. Suzanne sensed more than a stomachache was going on and joined them. "I hope James isn't seriously ill," she said. "Frank told me there was trouble between him and Richard at the last practice. Is that why he's not here?"

"James is sorry for what he said," Elaine explained, "but he'll never admit it. We both think it's best to let the matter drop. Try to forget it ever happened. James was angry at first, but he's calmed down now. He certainly didn't want to talk about it today."

"According to Frank, James said some awful things about Quentin." Suzanne didn't want the matter forgotten. "When's he going to quit resenting Quentin so much?"

Lydia's face twisted into a frown. "Take it easy, Suzanne. This is not Elaine's fault. Don't put her through the wringer."

Suzanne returned the frown. "We hope Quentin will be back on the team next year, but none of us can take another season like this one. James has to straighten up."

The buzzer sounded for halftime. The Terrors were a few points ahead, but the first half had been shaky, with the lead changing many times. "I want to get a few words with Jamie before Paul has his halftime huddle," Elaine said. "Excuse me." She stood up and walked toward the court.

"What's the matter with you?" Lydia asked Suzanne when she was gone.

"Nothing's the matter with me. These parents have to stop being so damn spiteful. We hoped it would happen, but it didn't. Things keep falling apart. Secret meetings. People saying rude things to each other. And then Quentin almost gets killed. But did we come together after that? No! Now we're slugging each other. And Elaine's more upset than she should be about James getting hit. With that guy, I bet it's not the first time."

At the edge of the court, Elaine was looking up at Jamie, her mouth moving and Jamie nodding. Lydia watched them as she listened to Suzanne and wondered what Elaine was saying. "You know what else is odd?" she mused when Suzanne fell silent. "It's not like James to want to forget that Richard hit him. He's not the type to let things like that slide under the rug."

As the second half began, Jeff Colton entered the gym. It wasn't his week to have Malcolm, and it was one of those occasional North Carolina days in February when the temperature climbed to sixty-five degrees, so he'd crammed nine holes of golf into his schedule, which made him late for the game. He first noted the numbers on the scoreboard, then looked around for somebody to sit with. Seeing not a single person who appealed to him, he slid in next to Lydia. "What's going on?" he asked. "James isn't here, and Richard's not here. Is it men's day off?"

"Apparently you thought it was men's day to be late," Lydia said.

"Sorry about that. I couldn't help it. But why isn't James here? He never misses a game."

Suzanne smirked. "If you'd been at practice on Wednesday, you'd know. You missed all the excitement. Richard punched James for making snide comments about Quentin."

"Did James hit him back? Was it a brawl?" Jeff wished he'd been there.

"No, you lunatic. It wasn't a brawl." Lydia shook her head. "It was a sad incident between two men acting like children."

"And now James and Elaine want the whole matter forgotten," Suzanne chimed in.

Jeff was about to ask why when most of the spectators in the gym stood up and cheered. Benny had dropped a three-pointer, giving the Terrors a seven-point lead. The crowd continued to yell as the opposing point guard brought the ball down the court and attempted a quick pass in to one of the forwards. Malcolm managed to get a hand on the ball as it went past him and knocked it toward Frankie, who grabbed it and started toward the other goal. He was two steps ahead of the other players and put in an easy layup. "That's my boy!" Jeff yelled. "Way to steal the ball!"

Things were looking up for the Terrors. A few plays later, Jamie blocked a side shot, causing the rebound to drop into Adam's hands and giving the Terrors an opportunity to score twice with no answering goal. "Slow down!" Paul called from the sidelines. "Take control of the game."

Frankie stood at the head of the key, dribbling while he scoped out the court. "Go three!" he yelled when he passed the ball to Adam. Malcolm rushed to set a pick behind Adam's defender, and as Adam made a move to go around the pick, Malcolm rolled toward the basket, Adam sent him a bounce pass, and Malcolm scored.

When the other coach called a time-out, Jeff was beaming. Two great plays for Malcolm. In the relative quiet of the pause, he remembered James. "What do you mean James wants us to forget Richard hit him? That's not the James I know."

Lydia told him what Elaine had said.

"Something's wrong," Jeff said and leaned back on the bleacher behind him.

Meredith had stopped Elaine as she made her way up the bleachers, but now she was headed back toward Suzanne and Lydia. "You won't get any more out of her," Suzanne said. "She's sewn up tighter than a feather pillow. I'm surprised she's coming back here."

Elaine sat next to Suzanne since Jeff was on the other side of Lydia. In a few minutes, he climbed toward her on the bleacher behind them until he was sitting squarely behind her. "I'm sorry about James," he said. "I guess he's banged up pretty bad." Elaine nodded. "Might do him good to get outside for a few hours. It's like April out there. Tomorrow's supposed to be the same. Do you think he'd be interested in playing a few holes of golf?" If Elaine wouldn't talk, then Jeff would go to the source. Even though James said he wanted nothing to do with politics and refused Jeff's pleas to join the town council, he had a great deal of influence on many people in town, including some on the council. If James's behavior was strange, Jeff wanted to know why to make sure he wouldn't say or do anything that could thwart Jeff's drive to become council president.

"I doubt it," Elaine said. She was sure James wanted to avoid any of the parents from the team, but when Jeff called that night, he surprised her by agreeing to go.

"It's like this," he explained when she questioned his choice. "We can't give Jeff or anybody else a reason to think we have something to hide. We can't call attention to ourselves."

24

Sunday was clear and bright, just as Jeff expected. Since he'd waited so late to get a tee-off time, he had to take eight o'clock in the morning, which was fine with him. He didn't want any stragglers hanging around the clubhouse asking to join their twosome. He wanted to be alone with James so they could have a heart-to-heart talk, or so he hoped. James was definitely not acting like himself. He wasn't even dressing like himself. Jeff wanted to laugh when he showed up at the country club in a green windbreaker and sunglasses. The sunglasses made sense, given his bruised eye, but a green jacket? Jeff would never have guessed the buttoned-down manager even owned such a piece of clothing. It must belong to Jamie. Maybe James was hoping people wouldn't recognize him. He moved through the pro shop with a smile but stopped to talk with nobody, which was unusual for him, and this time hardly anybody spoke to him.

"We missed you at the game yesterday," Jeff said as they walked down the fairway after hitting their first drives.

"I didn't miss anything. We lost again."

"Yeah, but it got exciting at the start of the second half. Benny got hot, and Frankie pulled off a fast break. Jamie made some great defensive moves, keeping them from a lot of scoring. We were ahead by ten points, but then they came alive, and we couldn't shut 'em down. It was a real heartbreaker for the boys."

"Like most of the season." James took a five-iron from his bag. He still had a way to go to get to the green. "I guess we're out of the playoffs now."

"No. I talked to Frank after the game. If we can win next Saturday, we're still in. Right now, our record's seven and seven with the one game left. So, next Saturday's it. Win or die." He paused while James hit his shot. The ball went into the air and came down on the edge of the green. Apparently neither his eye nor his mood was affecting his golf.

"It all comes down to one game," James muttered. "What a wasted season."

Jeff's second shot landed in the sand trap to the right of the green. "Shit," he said. "Shanked it."

The men walked toward the green in silence. Jeff's thoughts were focused on how to get his ball out of the trap, while James was still bemoaning the basketball season. He'd had such high expectations at the beginning, and then everything went to hell. Jeff took a whack at his ball and lifted it onto the green, but it skittered to the far side. James hovered over his ball to line up the putt. It looked dead-on but missed the cup by less than an inch. He tapped it in for a par four and cleared the way for Jeff. Jeff's putt was almost identical to James's, so he ended up with a bogey. The next several holes went smoothly for both players as the sun rose higher in the sky. They had opted to walk the course instead of renting a cart because they expected warm temperatures and Jeff wanted the exercise.

By ten o'clock, they were both feeling the heat. Jeff pulled off his jacket and stuffed it into his pull cart. James lifted his sunglasses and wiped sweat from his eyes with a handkerchief. His left eye and upper cheek looked worse than Jeff thought they would. "Holy shit, James. Can you even see out of that eye?"

"Yes, I can see," James growled. "I'm beating you, aren't I?"

Seizing the opportunity to bring up the subject he came to talk about, Jeff said, "Lydia told me you're not looking to hold Richard accountable for assaulting you. Why not?"

"It won't do any good. Just cause more trouble."

"Since when have you been afraid of causing trouble?"

"Since none of your business." James seized the driver from his bag.

Even though he looked menacing with the club in his hand,

Jeff wasn't afraid. "You know you'd be within your rights if you filed charges against him with the police."

"Of course I know that, but I'm not going to do it. Just hit your damn ball."

Jeff hesitated. The men on the green behind them were the only reason he took a swing. James hit his drive, and they were again walking down the fairway. "You're hiding something," Jeff said. "I know you too well. Any guy with guts enough to call a meeting to fire his son's basketball coaches would not let some jerk get away with slugging him."

"It's okay. It's not like it was a thug trying to mug me. It was Richard."

"The old James would have said that was all the more reason to charge him. He had no reason to hit you."

"Just drop it, or I'll hit you." James had reached his ball. He took a slap at it with his eight-iron and laid it on the green.

Jeff eyed him warily. Now he was sure James had ulterior motives for not pressing charges. "Are you planning to destroy him yourself? You know that could land you in jail."

"Leave me alone, or I'm walking off this golf course right now."

"Go ahead. I'll follow you." Jeff landed his ball very close to James's on the green. James dropped his putt, and Jeff did the same.

When they finished the ninth hole, Jeff said, "Let's take a break. It's not too early for a beer."

"Nope. You dragged me out here. I want to keep going."

Jeff realized he wasn't going to get James to have a chat with him, so he pressed on. James was wound even tighter than he expected, causing Jeff more concern about keeping him under control. He had to try a different tack to find out what was going on. Walking down the tenth fairway, he asked, "Is Elaine the reason you're letting Richard off?"

"What makes you think that?" James's brain buzzed. Did Jeff suspect Elaine's involvement with Quentin?

"I'll bet she's forcing you to keep quiet. I'll bet she's had enough of the things you say about Quentin and his family. Maybe she thinks you finally got what you deserve."

James threw his club into the bag, where it clanged against the other irons. "Keeping quiet about Richard was my idea, not hers." Ignoring his ball in the grass, he yanked the cart toward the cart path.

"I don't believe you." Jeff was behind him, leaving his ball as well to be a happy surprise for the foursome coming up. "You'd never do that. Only Elaine could make you do that."

"Shut up! It's not what you think."

"Then what is it? Tell me Elaine's not involved."

James stomped up the path. He didn't like to be challenged, especially not when he couldn't do anything about it. Suddenly he stopped and turned around. His eye was throbbing with the blood rushing to his head. "I don't ever want to talk about anything involving Quentin Thomas again. I hope he gets well and plays for another team next year. Just not our team. I don't ever want to hear his name again. And I sure as hell don't want it associated with my family."

"What the fuck? Why, James?" Jeff reached out to put a hand on James's shoulder, but James jumped as if the hand were on fire. Jeff had never seen so much suppressed vitriol in another human being. "Why don't you want Quentin's name linked with your family?"

James said nothing. He kept walking toward the clubhouse, his shoulders hunched in a way Jeff had never seen before. There was definitely more going on with him than a punch in the face. What could be worse than that? Jeff didn't wonder long. Since Quentin was involved, it had to be something to do with his injury. What did James's family have to do with Quentin's injury? The thought hit Jeff like a bullet. "You know who hit Quentin, don't you?"

James walked faster.

"If you don't want your family linked to him, it must be somebody in your family," Jeff said. He pictured the four Parkers. His thoughts went from face to face and came to rest on Gloria. She had a driver's license. He was sure he'd seen her driving around town. "It was Gloria," he announced. "Damn, James. She's just a child. No wonder you're so upset."

James scowled over his shoulder at Jeff. "It wasn't Gloria," he said.

"If it was Gloria, and you keep this covered up now, it will haunt her the rest of her life. Word is bound to get out."

"Don't you blame this on Gloria." James stopped, turned, and snarled at Jeff. "Don't you even mention her name in the same breath as Quentin Thomas."

"If it wasn't her, then who was it? I know you know. If you don't tell me, I'm going to go on thinking it was Gloria. And eventually, other people may think so too."

"Shut up! Shut your fucking mouth! Gloria was not driving the car that night. And you know how I know? Because it was Elaine. Elaine was driving the car. She knocked Quentin off his bicycle. And I'll tell you something else. It was an accident, a total accident. She never meant to hit anybody, and after it happened, she panicked. She was afraid to turn herself in. She still is. And she didn't know it was Quentin until that woman from the Copeland church called her."

What woman? The thought zipped through Jeff's mind, but the shock of what James had told him swept that question out of his head. He pictured Elaine—attractive, chatty, well-mannered Elaine. Always doing the proper thing. Always so conscious of what other people would think. She couldn't have done this. "How?" he said. "Are you making this up? Was it really you who hit Quentin?"

"Elaine hit Quentin. And if you tell anybody, I'll kill you. I swear."

Jeff was silent. James began again to walk along the path. When he was almost back to the tee, Jeff called after him, "How can I not tell anybody?" The players arriving on the tee stared at him, but James never looked back. He walked past the pro shop, past the clubhouse, and straight to his car. He shoved his clubs, bag, and cart, all of which he usually stored at the pro shop, into the trunk of his car and drove away, leaving Jeff alone in the parking lot.

When the car was out of sight, Jeff took his clubs and cart to the pro shop. He managed to avoid any conversation with the pro and then went to his car, but he didn't know where to go. He desperately wanted to tell somebody. This was a bombshell that would blow apart the entire town, but he couldn't bear the responsibility of keeping it to himself. How could he be president of town council with a secret like that? At least one other person had to know so if it ever came out, he could say he wasn't the only one. For an hour, he drove aimlessly around town and finally wound up at Lydia's front door. She was strong enough to share the secret.

Lydia had planned to spend the entire day painting her dining room walls, so she was not pleased when the doorbell rang. Malcolm was over at Benny's, and she wanted to make the most of the free time she had. "What do you want?" she asked when she saw Jeff at the door.

"I need to tell you something."

Because his expression was grim, almost frightened, she let him come inside.

"Is Malcolm here?" When Lydia shook her head, he said, "Good. I don't want him to hear what I have to say."

"Okay." Now Lydia was frightened.

"I played golf with James Parker today," Jeff said. "His eye looks like he was hit with a sledgehammer. I kept asking him why he isn't going to file charges against Richard. He got angrier and angrier and finally blurted out that he wasn't calling the police because Elaine is the one who nearly killed Quentin. If he makes a fuss about Richard, then the whole story about Quentin's accident will be raked over again since Richard hit him because he was bad-mouthing Quentin. He wants the whole mess to be forgotten."

Lydia stared at him with hard, unblinking eyes. "I'm going to call Elaine and find out if that's true. It sounds like something James would make up to protect himself."

"No. You can't do that. James threatened to kill me if I told anybody." Jeff hated the pleading tone in his voice.

"You should have thought about that before you told me."

"I can't be the only person hiding this secret."

"It shouldn't be hidden at all."

"Stop with all the *shoulds* and *shouldn'ts*." Jeff's voice rose to a howl. "I think James is right. Outing Elaine isn't going to make Quentin's suffering any easier. Believe me, James will pay any medical bills they need him to if they'll just keep quiet."

"I'm not making any decisions until I talk to Elaine."

"Don't do that."

"Watch me." Lydia disappeared into the kitchen and closed the door behind her. Jeff burst through the door and tried to grab the phone from her hand. She seized a saucepan from an open drawer and waved it toward his head. He backed away just as she said, "Hello, Elaine. This is Lydia Colton. How are you?"

Jeff slunk back into the living room. He wanted to run, but he had to know what Elaine said. He walked in circles on the braided rug until Lydia slipped quietly out of the kitchen. Her eyes were downcast, and her mouth was tight. "It's true," she said as she looked up at Jeff. "She did it, and now she's falling apart. I'm going over there. She needs help."

"Is James there?"

"I don't know, and I don't care. I'm going to see Elaine. And I strongly suggest you keep your mouth shut from here on in." Lydia took her coat from the closet and left.

Elaine was still in her church clothes when Lydia arrived. "Tell me how you know," she said. "Who told you?

"It doesn't matter. Tell me how I can help." Lydia had rarely seen a person look so distraught. Elaine had been sad at the ball-game on Saturday, but now the shadows under her eyes made her look ill.

"Does everybody know? James doesn't want anybody to know."

"Forget what James wants. What do you want?" Lydia sat beside her on the couch.

Elaine took a deep breath. If James or Jamie were in the house, she would never have said what came next. "I want to tell Delia and Marcus the truth. And Quentin."

Now Lydia took a deep breath. Her relationship with Jeff and her friendship with Nancy Galloway had put her in many painful situations but seldom filled her with so much anguish. "You know," she said, "if you confess, you might go to prison."

"Hit-and-run. I know. Whatever happens, happens. I want Quentin's family to know it's my fault."

"What about Gloria and Jamie? They need their mother." Lydia couldn't imagine leaving Malcolm.

"I'd rather go away for a while than have them find out I'm a liar and a coward. Keeping this secret is eating me alive."

Lydia didn't know what to say. Elaine deserved to be held accountable for Quentin's injuries. Thank God she hadn't killed him. And she was brave enough to want to turn herself in. But was that best for everyone? The sound of the garage door opening made it clear that their discussion would have to end. "Think about it," Lydia said. "Talk to James again. Give me more time to think about it. If I can help you at all, call me."

Three days later, Lydia's phone rang. Elaine was on the line. "I have to tell Delia and Marcus," she said. "Will you go with me? I need your help."

25

The meeting was set for five o'clock on Friday afternoon. Lydia invited the people involved to come to her house since she would be the only family member there. Malcolm would be at basketball practice along with James and Jamie. Clarinda could stay late with Quentin and his sisters. It was the best time and place for all. Lydia was nervous. She wasn't sure this was the best action for Elaine, but it was what Elaine had decided. Elaine was the first to arrive. Lydia served her a glass of iced tea as they settled in the living room. "Does James know you're here?" she asked.

"Yes, and he's not happy about it." Elaine took a sip of tea. "He's so angry that he hasn't spoken to me since I told him last night. I'm used to him blowing his top, but this silence is new."

Lydia nodded in sympathy. She'd never known Elaine to be so brave. She was afraid of what would happen next, but Elaine appeared resolute. By the time Marcus and Delia arrived, she was sure Elaine would make it through. She hadn't told the Thomases what the meeting was about, only that it was important. The expressions on their faces showed curiosity and caution. They exchanged pleasantries with Elaine while Lydia brought out more iced tea. She knew everybody would rather have had something stronger, but the meeting was too critical for alcohol. After asking about Quentin and being told he was improving every day, she said, "Elaine asked me to invite you all here today, so I'm going to let her tell you what she needs to say."

Elaine took a large swallow of tea. Marcus's eyebrows pulled closer together above his nose. Delia's heart jogged across her chest. "It's about Quentin," Elaine said. "I was driving the car that hit him that night."

"No!" The word exploded from Marcus's mouth like a puff of smoke. Delia's eyes welled with tears. Lydia wished she were anywhere but in that room.

"It's true," Elaine said, her face like stone. "It was a terrible, terrible accident. I swear I didn't see him until it was too late. I am so sorry." Her face softened. She had rehearsed this speech many times and was sure she could deliver it with sincerity and dignity, yet her chin began to tremble.

"Why didn't you stop to help him?" Marcus's voice was raw.

"I don't know. I honestly don't know. Fear, I guess. Disbelief. I couldn't accept that this was happening to me. I would give anything if I could go back and change it."

"Did you realize it was Quentin?" Delia spoke softly, in her own state of disbelief.

"No, I didn't. I had no idea it was Quentin until Sharon Robinson called me the next day."

Sharon Robinson. Delia remembered her comforting presence in the AME sanctuary the day after Quentin was hit. She wished she were here now. Marcus stood and walked across the room, his hands on his hips. What was he supposed to do? Scream at Elaine? Call the police? Walk out the door and never speak to any of them again? He wanted to do all those things. He wanted to take his family back to a year ago. Back to when they were safe.

Elaine spoke again. "I'll do anything you want me to do. I'll apologize to Quentin. I'll pay your medical bills. I'll turn myself in to the police."

"James won't let you do that," Marcus muttered.

"It's not up to him. It's up to me." Elaine's chin trembled again. She wanted to sound firm, but she was afraid. She could be destroying her marriage. If she went to prison, James would never forgive her. She could never live in Tanner again and certainly never work at the church again. Her life would be ruined.

"This is a lot to take in," Delia said. "We need time to process what we're hearing. I don't know what I want right now, except for this never to have happened."

"Taking time is a good idea," Lydia said. None of them, including her, could deal with the emotional pressure much longer without a meltdown.

"Let's go, Marcus." Delia stood and nodded at her husband.

Lydia retrieved their coats and ushered them to the door. "Thank you for coming," she said. Their grave expressions were their only response.

Out in the car, they sat for several minutes. "I don't know where to go," Marcus said, grasping the steering wheel with such force the color in his knuckles paled. "I can't go home and face Quentin. Not now. Maybe in an hour. I have to come to grips with this myself."

"Let's go get a cup of coffee at Johnny's," Delia suggested. "It's early for the dinner crowd, so we'll have privacy." Marcus put the car into gear.

Two couples were seated in Johnny's new dining room, which he had added on several years earlier. After seeing them, Delia led Marcus to the back dining room, converted from a storeroom, and completely devoid of customers at the moment. They chose a table in the back corner and hoped nobody else came in. The waitress, a local girl named Joyce who had stayed in Tanner after graduating from high school, greeted them heartily. "What can I get y'all tonight?" she asked with a big smile that wavered when she saw their solemn faces.

"Coffee, for now," Marcus said.

When Joyce returned with their coffee, she included a small plate of cookies made by Johnny's wife, who was known for the great desserts she baked for the restaurant. "Just a little treat for y'all," she said.

Delia nodded gratefully, although she couldn't eat a bite. She didn't really want the coffee. Her stomach was growing queasier by the minute. "How can Elaine have done this?" she asked. "I never thought the driver was somebody we know, much less one of the basketball parents."

Marcus stared at his coffee, which he hadn't touched. "I always suspected it was one of them. I know Elaine thinks it was an accident, but maybe her subconscious mind made her turn that steering wheel a little too far to the right."

"She didn't know it was Quentin."

"I'm not sure that's true."

"Marcus! You saw how upset she was. She didn't have to tell us. If the police were going to identify her, they would have done it by now."

Marcus was perplexed. "So why did she tell us?" It made no sense. Unless James put her up to it, thinking the Thomases would be so horrified they'd leave town rather than have to deal with seeing Elaine and being constantly reminded of this awful thing she'd done to them. He put his hands on either side of his head. What had happened to him that he was capable of thinking these awful thoughts? What had these people done to his family?

Delia gently took hold of his wrists and lowered his hands. "We may never know how she came to hit him or why she told us, but it doesn't matter. What matters is Quentin. I don't want him to know that Elaine was driving the car that night. Maybe when he's an adult, but not now."

"You decided that just this minute?"

"Yes, I did." The strong Black woman rose up in her again. Quentin didn't need to be hurt any worse than he already was.

"All right, then," Marcus said. "But what about Elaine? What do we do about her?"

"I can't figure that out yet. I want to go home and see my son."

Marcus left enough money on the table to cover their tab and a good tip for Joyce. Delia took a swallow of her coffee and slipped two cookies into her purse so Joyce wouldn't think they didn't appreciate her kindness. She smiled and waved to them as they left.

Delia was glad she and Marcus agreed not to tell Quentin the truth about the incident when she remembered the doctor had given him permission to attend the Terrors' basketball game on Saturday. He seemed happy about it, but it was hard to tell with him. He'd hardly gone anywhere in the past month. Surely, he wanted to see his teammates and share in the excitement of the game. He was still using a walker, so that would have to go along, but he was nimble with it. He wouldn't look like a total dork. He had ridden in the car a few times and did well in the back with his leg stretched out on the seat next to him. There were steps at the old gym that he would have to maneuver, but Marcus would help him with those. Steps were one of the reasons he hadn't been able to return to school. His life would be better when he was using only a cane.

The Terrors were warming up on the court when the Thomases arrived. Adam saw them first. He stopped in the middle of the drill and began to applaud. The others looked toward the door and started applauding too. Soon the parents and fans who were in the stands stood and applauded. A few of the players let out loud catcalls. Quentin's smile stretched from ear to ear as he made his way around the court. Players on the other team stopped to stare and soon joined in the applause. Frank ran over to the sidelines and slapped Quentin on the shoulder. "Welcome back," he said. "We've missed you."

Paul followed him and repeated the message. "Sit with the team," he added, pointing at the first bleacher. "We've been saving your seat at every game." Marcus and Delia shot each other a wary glance but backed off when Quentin headed straight for the bleacher. Although he had received a warm welcome, they wanted to be sure everybody was glad to see him.

James and Richard were both at the game. James's eye and cheek had turned from purple to green and yellow, and he had shed his sunglasses. Richard sat quietly with Laura and avoided James. He still wasn't sure what James might do to him. Elaine wasn't there.

"Okay, Terrors," Paul said in the huddle before the tipoff, "this game is for all the marbles. Right now, we're seven and seven. If we win this game, we're in the playoffs. If we lose, we're not. What's it gonna be?"

"Don't forget," Frank added quickly, "that this is the first game Quentin's been to since he got hurt. It'd be a damn shame for him to make the effort to come all this way just to see us lose."

"We can do it!" Malcolm shouted and clapped his hand on top of the others' hands in the middle of the huddle.

"Go, Terrors!" the team yelled and raised their hands toward the ceiling. The regular starters took the court as their teammates cheered.

"Don't screw this up," Jamie said to Frankie just before he positioned himself for the tipoff. "It's you and me, Bud. You and me." Frankie nodded, although he resented the implication. When was Jamie going to learn that basketball was a team sport?

Jamie controlled the tip and sent the ball straight to Benny. Frankie made a dash for a fast break, caught a bullet pass from Benny, and laid the ball in the basket. Jamie grinned triumphantly. This was the way he expected the game to go. And so it did as the Terrors built a substantial lead, with Jamie scoring most of their points.

Lydia sat with Suzanne as usual. She watched the game, but she also watched Marcus and Delia, sitting just two rows behind Quentin. What could be going through their minds? This basketball team and Quentin's association with it had hurt him in more ways than one. What would she do if Malcolm were in that situation? Probably take him off the team. But would that be fair to him? About that time, Jamie missed a short jump shot. The look of misery on his face turned her attention to him. What was going to happen to him? He had enough problems without losing his mother for months or maybe years. "Excuse me," she said to Suzanne. "I'll be back in a few minutes. I need to talk to Meredith." Suzanne was so intent on the game that she hardly noticed Lydia's departure.

Meredith was sitting by herself not far from Laura and Richard. "Come with me to get a Coke," Lydia said to her. "I want to ask you a couple of questions. The Terrors are so far ahead, I don't think we'll miss much." Meredith rose and followed her to the gym's small entry area, which was empty of people except for two teenagers behind the refreshment stand with their noses buried in comic books. Not wanting to attract their attention, Lydia motioned for Meredith to stand with her near the door. "Let's suppose the police find the person who hit Quentin. Can they charge him without having Marcus and Delia press charges?"

"Sure they can." Meredith wondered what had brought about this question and the urgency that seemed to accompany it. "In North Carolina, drivers who leave the scene of an accident can be charged with a crime. Whether it's a misdemeanor or a felony depends on the circumstances. Because Quentin was injured, it could be a felony."

"And that means jail time?"

"Possibly up to two years. Why are you asking this? Did the police find the driver?"

"Not yet. I'm just curious."

They walked back into the gym just in time to escape the flood of spectators headed to the concession stand at halftime. Meredith joined Lydia and Suzanne in the bleachers to watch the second half, which took a turn for the worse only a few minutes in. Jamie went completely cold. It was like there was a lid on the basket. Because he was in foul trouble, Malcolm was sitting on the bench next to Quentin. "Oh brother, how I wish we could send you in now," he said, punching Quentin on the arm. "You know this is it for us. We have to win today, or the season's over."

Quentin nodded. To his surprise, he was actually sad the season might be over. Why did he care? His season was over weeks ago. This team meant nothing to him. And yet Malcolm was so anxious, and Malcolm had been good to him. Paul and Frank were working themselves into a frenzy as the Terrors' lead diminished. They were good coaches. They deserved to be in the playoffs. "Y'all can do it without me," Quentin said to Malcolm. "Put this in your shoe. It's always brought me good luck. It'll do it for you too." He handed Malcolm the arrowhead he had brought from Greensboro. Malcolm gave him a puzzled look. "Just put it in between your sock and the laces of your left shoe. It's so tiny you won't feel it, I promise."

No sooner had Malcolm secured the stone in his shoe than Paul called him up as a sub. "Go in for Jason," Paul said. "We need the strongest power forward we have scoring points for us. Shoot whenever you get the chance, but don't foul." Thirty seconds later, Malcolm took a pass from Frankie, faked his guard to the right, and made a beeline from the left toward the basket. Jamie saw what was happening and drew his guard out of the lane, giving Malcolm an open back door. Two points.

"That's it!" Paul yelled.

On the return play, Frankie intercepted a pass and took off in the other direction with Benny right beside him. When a guard caught up with Frankie, he was able to send the ball to Benny, who scored on an easy layup. The quick four points seemed to light a fire under the Terrors. Adam was the next to get a hot hand and dropped a long jump shot. The Terrors on the bench, except Quentin, all jumped to their feet. Their lead was growing again. What Jamie was lacking in offense, he seemed determined to make up in defense. He denied three shots by the opposing center. "Never seen him play such aggressive defense," Frank said. "I like this side of him."

For once, James wasn't screaming at Jamie to score. In fact, James wasn't saying much of anything. Just an occasional "Go Terrors." Laura felt obliged to take up the slack, sending her voice over the crowd at every opportunity. Fortunately, Adam was having a good game, so it was mostly positive comments.

Delia and Marcus sat quietly, applauding only at appropriate times. They both kept an eye on Quentin, alert to any signs he showed of being tired. They weren't sure he could last through the whole game. Marcus occasionally stared at James, wishing he would approach them at some point and, if not apologize, at least acknowledge his wife's role in hurting Quentin. Any such gesture might soften the hatred Marcus felt toward the family. At least he hoped so. He still wasn't sure what to do about Elaine. She should pay for what she did to Quentin. He was almost resolved to call the police.

The seconds on the old gym clock ticked down. With one minute to go, Frank and Paul started elbowing each other with glee.

They had this game. They were going to the playoffs, something they could never have imagined at the beginning of the season. When the buzzer sounded with the Terrors ahead by four, the team, the parents, and all the other spectators on the Tanner side of the court were on their feet. Jason and Carson reached to help Quentin stand, but he brushed them off, saying, "I can do this. I can cheer for our team."

"Will wonders never cease?" Richard whispered to Laura, meaning the win, Quentin's presence, and the fact that James had kept his mouth shut from tipoff to final buzzer.

"What's next?" Benny asked as the team gathered around the coaches.

"Practice. Monday afternoon. We have a division championship to win," Paul said.

26

P aul and Benny were all smiles on the ride home from the game. "We did it!" Benny said as he was nearly bouncing on the back seat. "This'll be our championship year."

"One game at a time," Paul said. "We have some hard games ahead. Everybody has to shine like they did in the second half today."

"We could do it for sure if we had Quentin." Benny's voice lost some of its enthusiasm.

"We can't depend on just one player," Paul said, although he'd been thinking the same thing. "What's wrong with you?" He looked over at Meredith. "You're awfully quiet on such an exciting day."

"Something's bothering me. I'll tell you about it when we get home."

Paul shrugged and went back to laughing with Benny. "So, what is it?" he demanded as soon as they were in the house and Benny had run off to the kitchen to get a snack. "What's eating you? Everything's good for now."

"Everything's not good with the team. Why is James being so nice to Richard after what happened? That's not like him. And why was he so quiet at the game? It's like Richard's knock on his head changed his personality. And where was Elaine? Why wasn't she there today?"

"I can't explain people's behavior. They have a right to act however they want, and frankly, I think James's new personality is an improvement."

"No. Something's going on. Lydia's acting strange too. She asked me what the North Carolina laws are about leaving the scene of an accident. Where did that come from? I asked if the police had a suspect in Quentin's case, and she said no. Explain that."

Paul was beginning to see her point. "How can we find out what's happening?"

Benny came through the living room with two peanut butter sandwiches, a bag of potato chips, and a Coke. "I'll be in the den watching TV," he said. Paul and Meredith said nothing, hardly noticing him. "Okay," he said and kept walking.

After more minutes of silence, Paul said, "I'm going to call Marcus. He can tell us if there's anything new with Quentin. I'll use the phone in our bedroom." And he disappeared up the stairs. Meredith went into the den to sit with Benny and wait for news.

"I'm glad Quentin came to the game today," Paul said when Marcus answered the phone. "Looks like he's on the way to recovery. I hope he liked the reception he got."

"He's doing better," Marcus said. "I think he enjoyed the game."

"It was a good game. The boys did well, but the atmosphere was different, which is one reason I wanted to call and check on Quentin. Has anything changed concerning him and the team that you know about?"

"I heard Richard and James got into a tangle over something James said about Quentin."

"That's true. And James's reaction to that scuffle has puzzled a lot of us. He wants to keep the whole matter quiet, although Richard threw the first punch. And you had to notice he wasn't yelling as much at the game today as he usually does. That's not like him." Paul wished he could see Marcus's face. He had no idea what Marcus was thinking.

Marcus, however, knew what Paul was thinking. Paul sensed a new connection between James and Quentin that went deeper than James's resentment of Quentin as a player or a fistfight with Richard. What exactly did he know, Marcus wondered, and what did he only suspect? Did he know about Elaine and was trying to lead Marcus to the right conclusion? Or did he think Marcus knew more than he was telling and was trying to dig out information? What could Marcus say that would help Quentin the most? He wanted to shout Elaine's guilt from the rooftops. He wanted to hurt Elaine and James's family in the same brutal way James had hurt his, especially Quentin. Maybe if he told Paul the truth, Paul could take care of this unfinished battle for him. But he had never let anyone fight his battles for him before. This was between James and him. Or really, between Elaine and him.

He sat in silence while these thoughts careened through his brain until Paul said, "Marcus, are you still there? Did we get cut off?"

"I'm still here. I'm thinking about James's behavior. This may be the first time I've ever understood why James is acting the way he is." He wanted so badly to tell Paul about Elaine. When did the truth make anything worse? He didn't owe James and Elaine any favors. He wished he and Delia had talked more about this, but she decided unilaterally not to tell Quentin. He could decide what to say about Elaine to Paul. "James has reason to keep his head low," he said. "His wife was driving the car that hit Quentin."

"Holy shit," Paul said. "Elaine? No. That can't be right. What makes you think she did it?"

"She told me. And Delia. She asked us to meet her at Lydia's house on Friday, and she told us." Marcus could still see her trembling chin. The pitiful expression of this woman who could have killed his son.

"Holy shit," Paul said again. "Why? How?"

"She said it was an accident. She didn't know it was Quentin." Marcus's teeth ground noiselessly as he spoke. If she had known it was Quentin, would she have stopped?

"And you believe that?" Paul had a hard time believing anything he was hearing.

"Quentin's hurt just as bad whether she meant to do it or not." Marcus knew that was the right thing to say whether he meant it or not. "And we're still praying he'll be all right."

"I thought you said . . ."

"Of course I said he's getting better. We have to stay optimistic. But nobody knows for sure if he'll recover completely. It'll kill him if he can't play sports again."

Paul was sorry he'd called. This was a case where ignorance truly was bliss. It would be easier to go on coaching this team and being friends with these parents if he didn't know. He slipped farther down into the chair where he was sitting. His shoulders felt so heavy. "What are you gonna do now?"

"I want to report her to the police, but Delia's not on board with that. She doesn't know what she wants to do. I guess she's still stunned by the whole thing."

"If you need . . ." Paul started to say *If you need a lawyer, Meredith and I will help*, but he stopped himself. When the whole town found out what happened, did he and Meredith really want to take sides? For their children's sake, did they want to take sides? "If you need anything, let me know," he finished the sentence. "Until you decide what you're going to do, Meredith and I will keep this to ourselves." Of course, it went without saying that he would tell Meredith.

"Do whatever you have to do," Marcus said. "And any advice you have for me would help."

"Do what *you* have to do," Paul said, wishing again he didn't know anything about the matter. He hung up the phone and immediately went to look for Meredith. "You aren't going to believe this," he said after he pulled her out of the den, led her up to their bedroom, and closed the door.

When he told her about Elaine, her eyes went wide and her nostrils flared. "Why didn't she stop? Even if she didn't know it was Quentin, how could she have left anybody on the side of the road?"

Paul leaned against their four-poster bed and crossed his arms. "I don't know," he said. "But that's in the past. I'm worried about what's going to happen next."

"Elaine will be arrested." Meredith sat in their lone bedroom chair, rubbing her fingers against the rough weave of the upholstery. "Leaving the scene of an accident when somebody's injured is a crime." She paused. "Unless the police never find out." What were the consequences for knowing about a crime and not reporting it? she wondered. She could easily look that up. "How many people know it was Elaine?" she asked.

"Elaine and James. Marcus and Delia. Lydia. Marcus said they met with Elaine at her house. And Jeff maybe. That's all I know." Paul wondered what was going on in Meredith's always churning brain.

"Ultimately, it's up to Marcus and Delia to decide what to do, but any one of us could blow the whistle," she said.

"Marcus may be about to do that."

Meredith had seen so many court cases when people like Clarinda, for instance, had made one terrible mistake and had their lives changed drastically. But Quentin may have his life changed drastically. Was that fair? Now he and Elaine were facing a jury of seven friends, and he didn't even know it. "I'm leaving it up to Marcus and Delia," she said.

Delia didn't want to leave Quentin's side. Somehow, knowing who hurt him made it all worse. Having a nameless monster as the culprit was acceptable. Having a supposed friend be responsible was not. The world seemed more dangerous when evil had a face and a name. She could hate a monster, but could she hate Elaine? Could she recognize evil when she saw it? She spent the entire weekend in Quentin's room or sitting with him in the living room, until he finally said, "Mom, you're crushing me. Gimme some space!"

She could hardly pull herself away to go to work on Monday, but when Clarinda showed up, and Quentin's face brightened, she realized that he and she both needed a break. She called him from school every chance she got until Clarinda sounded annoyed when she answered the phone. *You can't go on like this,* Delia told herself. She knew Marcus's solution was to go to the police, but she was sure the situation was more complicated than that. She needed an objective person to talk to, and she wasn't going to find that among the basketball parents, her family, or her neighbors. Sharon Robinson.

That was her best hope. She called Sharon and arranged to meet her at a café in Copeland at three thirty. The time meant leaving school early, but she had to be home by five o'clock when Clarinda left. A little breaking of the rules was worth the risk in this case.

The café was small with an assortment of unmatched wooden tables and chairs, which gave it an informal, homey feel. Carvings of initials and stick figures in the tabletops suggested it was a hangout for teenagers, which proved true when a gaggle of girls in leggings and oversized sweaters swept through the door about the time Delia arrived. The atmosphere couldn't have been more different from the quiet dining room with the white tablecloths where she and Marcus had discussed what to do about Elaine on Friday. Sharon was already there, sitting at a table for two against a back wall. *Why did she pick this place?* Delia wondered.

"There was so much urgency in your voice that I figured you wanted to discuss something about Quentin. I wanted to have young people top of mind as we talked." Sharon answered her question without even hearing it. "So, what's up?"

"I know who was driving the car that hit Quentin, and now I have to decide what to do about it." Delia explained about Elaine and the complications her involvement created. "If it was some man I don't know, I'd want them to put him under the jail for hurting my baby and leaving him to die. But Elaine's a mother like I am. That makes me concerned for her and also scares the hell out of me. Who else do I know that's capable of doing something like this? Am I capable of doing it?"

"Let's put your fears aside for now," Sharon said. "Does Elaine have to be punished in order for you to know Quentin has gotten justice? Do you want her to go to prison?" A waitress stopped by and took their orders for Cokes and fried onion rings. "The onion rings here are the best," Sharon said as Delia struggled for an answer to her question.

"Of course, I want justice for Quentin, but who gets to decide what that is? Shouldn't it be a professional judge?"

"That's the way our legal system works—if you want to turn it over to them."

"Why wouldn't I?"

"Because there are wider repercussions to this case than fall under the purview of the courts. You recognize that, don't you? And that's causing your dilemma." Sharon folded her hands. Her ebony eyes felt to Delia as if they were looking straight into her soul.

"I worry about the kids," Delia said. "Not just Elaine's kids, but all the kids who are friends with her kids and with Quentin. How is knowing that Elaine is a criminal going to affect them and their relationships? We're all supposed to be examples for them."

The food and drinks arrived. Both women took the opportunity to eat and drink in silence.

After finishing an onion ring, which was amazingly good, Delia said, "There's also a problem because our family is the only Black family on the basketball team."

"So?" Sharon put another bite of onion ring into her mouth.

"So, if we decide not to tell the police about Elaine, I don't want it to be a case of the Black people giving in to the white people like we've had to do for so many years. It's important that we stand up for ourselves."

"Does anybody besides you and Marcus know Elaine was the driver?"

"Yes. At least one other person, and possibly more."

"Then it may not be up to you. Somebody else may go to the police. Elaine may even do it herself."

Other teenagers had swarmed into the café while Delia and Sharon were talking. Some were Black, and some were white, but most didn't sit at segregated tables. "Children are our only hope for the future, aren't they?" Delia said. "A lot of them haven't learned to hate."

"Do you hate Elaine?"

Delia remembered her thoughts about how hard it was to hate a person she knew. A person like her.

"Can you forgive Elaine?" Sharon asked.

Delia remained silent. There was a huge gap between not hating someone and forgiving them.

"Go home. Keep talking to Marcus. Talk to the people who know. The Lord will tell you what to do."

Delia left the café wondering why she came. She was no closer to peace than she had been when she arrived.

Lydia was loading the dishwasher after dinner Tuesday night when the doorbell rang. She had just sent Malcolm upstairs to do his homework and didn't appreciate the interruption. Annoyed and yet curious, she opened the door and found Tom, swaddled in a heavy wool coat and a red cashmere scarf. "May I come in?" he asked.

Lydia jerked him inside and greeted him with a kiss. "What are you doing here? And why didn't you call?"

"I wanted to surprise you, and I've been really busy since I landed in Charlotte this morning." He unbuttoned his coat and removed his scarf. "Mom fell and broke her hip last night, so I took the first plane out this morning. She's okay, just driving the nurses at the hospital crazy. For somebody who's almost seventy years old, she's still got a mean bark."

Don't I know it? Lydia thought and then wondered why Nancy hadn't called her. She hoped it was a sign of Nancy's independence.

"Anyway, she's going to be in the hospital for a while, so I'll probably stick around a few days, at least. Take some of the worry off Nancy."

Maybe Nancy wasn't so independent after all. Lydia was sorry to hear that. She reached for Tom's coat and scarf and hung them in the closet.

"So, what's new and exciting in Tanner?" he asked.

Lydia longed to tell him about Elaine. He may have asked about Tanner, but he had no interest in the town outside of the mill and his family. He didn't care about the other townspeople and how they treated each other. He could give an objective answer to her questions about Elaine and the police. He wouldn't be callous, but he also wouldn't be sentimental or care what anybody else thought. But maybe his lack of interest in her friends was the reason not to tell him. If they decided not to expose Elaine, the fewer people who knew, the better.

"Not much," she said.

27

Over at the Parkers' house, James and Elaine sat in front of the TV, staring at the screen but not paying attention. Their time together had been like this since her meeting with Marcus and Delia. James was still angry with her for telling the Thomases about her involvement with Quentin, even though he had been the first to reveal the truth when he told Jeff Colton. There were times when he regretted his explosive outbursts, and that was one of them. Now he had to clean up the mess with Elaine fighting him every step of the way. "I can't sit here another night waiting to see if the bomb is going to drop," he said.

"I thought that's what you wanted. For nothing to happen." Elaine was frightened and frustrated with James's attitude in the matter. She had done what her conscience told her to do—she had told Quentin's parents about her guilt. Now she was resigned to wait and let events unfold however they would.

"No," James said. "I want the matter resolved. I want to know for sure that you won't be charged with a crime and that no one else will know about this. I want a pledge from everybody who already knows that they'll keep it secret."

"You'll never get that."

"I can try. And I'm going to start with Marcus and Delia. We need to meet again, with both of them this time. Just the four of us."

Elaine sighed. She wasn't sure she could face Delia again. But James would not let this go until he was satisfied he had done everything he could to make it end the way he wanted it to end. "Okay," she said. "I'll invite them over Friday night. But just for coffee." She didn't want them to stay long enough to eat anything.

"Why do we have to go over there?" Marcus demanded when Delia told him about the invitation. "I'll be happy if I never see those people again."

"You don't have to go. I'll go." Delia had asked her doctor to increase her dosage of antidepressant, and she was feeling more in control. She was almost at the point where she just wanted it all to be over, no matter what the outcome was.

"I can't let you go alone," Marcus said, so they both showed up at seven thirty as requested.

Neither of them had been inside the Parkers' house. Delia noticed the brocade draperies first, which she thought were rather dour and inappropriate for the size of the living room. Marcus saw them as the mark of a man who assumed he was on the way up. James greeted them at the door, unsmiling but gracious. "Elaine will join us soon," he said as he gestured for them to sit on the couch. From the couch, Delia studied the painting above the fireplace mantel. Its field of yellow daisies beneath a clear blue sky was the brightest spot in the room. *Elaine put that there,* she thought. As the idea settled in her brain, Elaine came into the room. Delia stared at her, trying to see the woman who chose the painting instead of the woman who injured her child. She couldn't.

"Why are we here?" Marcus asked.

Elaine looked to James to answer. He stood next to the chair nearest the couch. "Elaine told you how sorry she is about what happened to Quentin. It was all a terrible accident, and she wishes every day she could go back and change it. But she can't. So now we need to look ahead and figure out what's best for everybody." He paused as if he expected a reply, but Delia and Marcus were silent. "I've told you we'll pay your out-of-pocket medical expenses."

"You bet you will," Marcus muttered.

"And that girl you have staying with Quentin, we'll pay for her too. Whatever you need. But there's more at stake than money. People's reputations are at stake. And their future happiness."

"What about Quentin's happiness?" Delia asked. "If he can't walk or run like he used to, he won't be happy."

"We pray for him every day," James said. "At the game on Saturday, he looked like he's healing just fine." Elaine motioned for him to sit down, but he continued to stand.

"Exactly whose happiness and reputation are you worried about?" Marcus asked.

"Everybody involved." James's face tightened with the stress of appearing earnest. "This is hard to say, but if word gets out that Elaine was driving the car, her future in Tanner is ruined. She won't be able to hold her head up anywhere. We'll have to leave town. If not for her sake, for our kids. How can they continue going to school here when everybody knows what their mother did? And if, God forbid, she ends up in prison, they won't have a mother."

"So, what do you want from us?" Delia knew there had to be a downside after all this buildup. She'd heard this type of argument before and was waiting for the punch line.

Elaine squirmed, wishing James would quit towering over them. He put his hands on the back of the chair in front of him as his expression grew even more rigid. "We are asking you, please, to keep Elaine's involvement just between us. We'll do whatever we can to help your family, but our family's life and future depend on you."

Delia had never seen James act so humble. This must be a whole new world to him. Marcus couldn't help taking pleasure in the situation. They sat silently, studying each other. James began to fidget. *Why didn't they say something?*

"This is how I see it," Marcus said finally. "You're asking a lot of us. We're going to need you to do a few things in return." Each of the others looked at him in disbelief. No one had seen this coming. Not even Delia. Marcus stretched his legs out in front of him and clasped his hands behind his head. "First, James, you have to apologize to Quentin for all the mean things you've said about him since he joined the team. Not just a quick 'I'm sorry.' You have to explain what you said and why you said it. Second, you have to apologize to Paul and Frank for holding a meeting behind their backs and trying to get them kicked out as coaches. They work hard and deserve more respect than that."

James stopped fidgeting while a look of confusion rose on his face. This couldn't be happening to him.

"And that's not all," Marcus continued. "You have to stop yelling at Quentin, Jamie, any player on the team, and the coaches for the rest of the games this season and next season and any other season when Jamie plays basketball. I'm going to tell Jeff Colton the same thing, so you'd better make sure he keeps his mouth shut at the games if you don't want to put Elaine's future in jeopardy."

"And if I do all that, you'll help me protect her from the police and any angry people in this town." James's voice was hard but without his usual bluster.

"I'll do what I can, but I can't promise nothing else will come of it." Marcus stood so he was looking at James eye to eye. "Delia and I will keep our part of the deal. And you'd better do the same. If either one of us hears or sees you say or do anything we don't like, we'll go straight to the police."

Quicksand seemed to be pouring in on James as he sank deeper and deeper. He didn't like what Marcus was saying, but he had no choice. He needed Quentin's family's cooperation to save his family. Before he agreed to anything, though, he had to make sure the secret was really safe. "Who else knows about this besides the Coltons and us?" he asked.

"I told Paul," Marcus said. "And I'm sure he told Meredith. So that's two more you have to worry about."

"I can deal with them," James said. He would tell Paul that Marcus agreed to keep silent as long as James paid any medical expenses they had because of the incident. Paul didn't need to know all the details of the arrangement.

"So, you accept our offer?" Marcus asked.

James nodded.

"Don't forget the rules, because I'll know if you break one. I have friends among the parents, and I have friends at the mill. As long as Foxrow Mills stays in Tanner and we have jobs there, I'll know, so do not say anything at work against Quentin or the basketball coaches." Marcus wasn't sure any of that was true, but he hoped it was.

"I understand," James said. He didn't like being the underdog, but he was so grateful that Elaine most likely wouldn't go to prison and his family wouldn't be ostracized, which meant his position at the mill was safe. He looked at Elaine for her reaction. She had hardly moved since the discussion began. She sat like a ragdoll thrown into the corner. But now her face took on an expression of relief.

"Thank you, Marcus—and Delia." Her words were soft but filled with emotion. "I promise on every Bible you can find that I didn't mean to hurt Quentin. And I'm ashamed that I was such a coward, afraid to come forward as soon as it happened. You're demanding that James change his behavior as a price for your silence. What about me? I'm the one who almost killed Quentin. Can I do anything to make this right?"

Delia sat up straighter and looked hard at Elaine. "I'm mad at you, Elaine. Damn mad. I'm mad because you hurt my child, and I'm not sure I can forgive you no matter what you do. But you're a mother like me, so you know the person we have to focus on is Quentin. He's the victim. No matter how much we worry about ourselves and act like we're worried about other people, he's the one we need to help. What if he never runs again? There's a chance that all the money in the world can't fix his broken bones completely. Not all the kindness and encouraging words, either.

"Marcus is looking at the big picture, trying to make James act like an adult instead of a spiteful, self-centered ass and stop him from hurting any other children with his hateful comments. I'm proud of Marcus for that. But all I really care about is my child. He's the one who continues to endure the pain, the days lost from school, the loneliness of being at home, the uncertainty of not knowing what's going to happen to him. You know, Elaine, if we took this case to court, Quentin would surely get an award for pain and suffering. That's what I want from you. I want payment for pain and suffering. Something that is his and his alone."

"Like what?" James asked.

"I don't know. I just now realized Quentin deserves this. Boy, does he deserve this. I think it should be a fund that Quentin can draw on when he needs to or maybe if he just wants to."

"He could use it for college," Marcus said.

"If that's what he wants," Delia replied. "He'll need some guidance, but I want the decision to be ultimately his."

"How much money are we talking about?" James asked.

"I don't know. I'll have to do some research on what pain and suffering awards usually are in a case like this. Meredith can help me. Maybe we can set up a kind of trust."

James shook his head slowly. "Marcus and I already agreed on the terms of our deal."

"But I didn't," Delia said. "And it sounds like Elaine didn't either."

"I think a fund is a good idea." Elaine looked up at her husband. "Think, James. What if Jamie were in Quentin's place? We'd want all of this and probably more for him. I don't want to go to prison, but I'll have a hard time living with myself if I don't do something to help Quentin."

Marcus sat down next to Delia and took her hand. "If this is what you want, we'll get it." Then he turned to James and Elaine. "We'll need time to figure out the particulars of a fund. Taxes and ownership and all that. Plus, what happens when Quentin turns eighteen."

"All right," James said, "but in the meantime, you'll protect this secret as closely as we will. Does that suit you, Elaine?"

Surprised and pleased that he asked her consent, Elaine said, "Yes."

"In that case," James said to Marcus and Delia, "I would like y'all to leave."

Marcus and Delia stood. Only Delia said goodbye as they left the house. Inside their car, with the doors and windows closed, she said, "Good lord, Marcus. Did we do the right thing making all those demands?"

"They're no less than we deserve and a lot more than they deserve."

"Was I out of line demanding money for Quentin? He deserves compensation for what he's been through."

"No, ma'am." Marcus smiled at his wife. "You were not one bit out of line. Money can't always fix things, but it can sure make them easier to bear. And, if Quentin wants to play basketball in this town, things have to change. If we can use our advantage to make a difference, then I'm gonna do it. Shutting up some rude bigots is a small step. Still, it's a more important step than throwing a terrified woman who made a mistake into jail. Yeah, I've decided it probably was an accident—an accident and poor judgment. Thinking anything else is beating ourselves up over something we have no way to prove."

"What about Laura? I'd like to shut her up and then some." Laura's saccharin kindness in their relationship and snide comments at the games still made Delia cringe.

"If James and Jeff restrain themselves, maybe Laura will too. She won't want to be the only loudmouth in the stands."

"I wouldn't bet on that. She didn't stop yelling just because James was quiet at the last game, but we'll see," Delia knew there'd be no way of knowing until next season, assuming Quentin was playing again.

Lights were bright in the living room windows when they arrived at home. Because she knew enough about the situation to suspect Marcus and Delia's visit with James and Elaine was not a pleasure trip, Clarinda had volunteered to stay with the kids for free. She didn't want them, especially Quentin, waiting at home alone for their parents' return because she didn't know what their parents' state of mind would be. She and Quentin had developed a blossoming friendship in their days together. She would miss him when he went back to school.

"Welcome home," she said to Delia and Marcus.

"Thanks. How is everybody?" Delia replied.

"Doin' fine," said Quentin, who was sitting on the couch watching TV and eating popcorn.

"The girls are getting ready for bed," Clarinda said.

"That's good." Delia sat next to Quentin. She wanted to hug him, but that would embarrass him, so she had to be content with patting his knee. "Thanks for doing this," she said to Clarinda.

"I like doing it. The girls remind me of Lucy."

"Any news about when you might get her back?" Marcus asked.

"Not yet, but Meredith has been my cheerleader through all of this, and she says working here has given me lots of points." Clarinda patted Quentin on the shoulder. "You know, man, I've enjoyed taking care of you, being your buddy. When you go back to school, I'm thinking about applying to the practical nursing program at the community college—if I can get financial aid."

Quentin took an unexpected interest in the conversation. "When am I going back to school?"

"Soon," Delia said. "Practical nursing's a great idea for you, Clarinda. You'll have to find a job to support Lucy and you while you're in school, but we'll give you a good reference for being a caretaker."

"Maybe you could be a nurse's aide while you're in school," Marcus suggested.

"But I'll still need somebody to watch Lucy."

"Some hospitals have daycare, and she'll be in kindergarten next fall." Delia hoped Clarinda could make this work.

"I'll look into it," Clarinda said. "See you on Monday."

After she left and Rosalie and Camille went to bed, Marcus and Delia sat with Quentin. When the show he was watching ended, he sat quietly for a while. Then he asked, "When do y'all really think I can go back to school?"

Marcus smiled. "It's been five weeks since the accident. Your doctor said you'd need to stay home about six weeks, so I'm guessing next week's the week. See what he says at your appointment. I bet he gives you the all-clear. You seem fine to me. And we want you out of the house." He chuckled.

"How do you feel about it?" Delia asked. "Are you ready to go back?" The question had so many levels of meaning. Delia wanted Quentin to sort through them on his own.

"Right after it happened, I would have said no. Not in a million years. I never want to go back to that school. It would never be my real school. But since I've been staying home, I've missed some of the people there. Most of the guys on the team are cool, especially Malcolm and Frankie. After the cheer they gave me at the game last Saturday, maybe they really want me back." Quentin shrugged his shoulders. "I'll give it another try."

Epilogue

Change comes slowly, especially to small towns. Before it can become part of a town's heartbeat, it must be nurtured like a living thing—fed frequently and protected from the cold.

Nearly eight years passed before Foxrow Mills was sold to a manufacturing conglomerate. And three years passed before Lydia Colton married Tom Galloway. When Malcolm graduated from high school in 1989, he and Lydia moved to Connecticut to live with Tom, taking the beat with them and yet leaving it better for their having been there. After Caroline Galloway died in 1992, Tom and Lydia became Nancy's guardians and moved her to Connecticut too. They sold Foxrow farm to Jeff Colton, who was elected president of the town council in 1987 and served until he was elected mayor of Tanner ten years later.

James and Elaine Parker left Tanner in 1990 when rumors of selling the mill were no longer just rumors and Jamie had completed a successful high school basketball career and joined the team at Wake Forest University in Winston-Salem.

Quentin Thomas's leg healed well enough for him to join the junior varsity basketball team at Tanner High School in the fall of 1985. He quickly moved up to varsity, and by their senior year, he and Jamie worked out an amicable relationship that allowed them to lead the Tanner team to the state championship. The University of North Carolina at Chapel Hill offered Quentin a full basketball scholarship, and he played a major role when the team won the NCAA men's championship in 1993.

Frank Jessop joined the Kiwanis Club on his own, and he and

Suzanne spent the rest of their lives in Tanner, keeping time to the town's beat, which kept them united with Laura and Richard Campbell, despite their different views of the town and life in general. Although Paul Westover never coached another basketball team, he and Meredith also remained part of Tanner's ongoing rhythm.

The old gymnasium was not so fortunate. Backhoes descended upon it in 1995. Its cavernous space and light-filled windows were soon only a memory to those who had honored the gods of basketball within it.

Acknowledgments

Since I joined my first writing group, The Kansas City Writers Group, in 1989, followed by The Two Bridges Writers Group in New York City, the Maryland Writers' Association, and the Main Line Coffeehouse in Pennsylvania, I've learned two things: (1) to produce a professional novel requires a team, and (2) talented, kind, and helpful writers live in many different places. For *Circle of Adversaries*, I am grateful to the Main Line Coffeehouse, who took me in five years ago and provided me with friendship, literary insight and advice, and laughs.

They also gave me two of my early readers, Merry Jones and Kimberly Leahy, who helped with many aspects of *Circle*, especially plot and character development. Thanks to them, several of the people in the circle are more complex and relatable.

Other appreciated readers included Martha Newland, my expert on all things southern, and Nathan Whitney, who made sure my descriptions of youth culture in the 1980s were correct.

For detailed information about child custody laws and social services procedures in cases of child abandonment, I was fortunate to have help from Tracie Murphy, MSW, director of Randolph County, N.C., Department of Social Services. Thank you to her and to Cathryn Davis, Randolph County risk manager, for bringing us together.

When I needed legal advice, I turned to The Authors Guild, the nation's oldest and largest professional organization for published writers. I am grateful to Legal Counsel Darryl Jennings for his timely and thorough response.

Thank you again to Duke and Kimberly Pennell of Pen-L

Publishing, my guides to the publishing industry who have always led with knowledge and understanding. I'm also grateful to Kimberly for the novel's interior and back cover design, Eliza Whitney for the front cover design, and editor Lori Draft.

Special thanks to the most important members of my team: my sons, Nathan and Andrew, who encourage me every day with their love and concern; my sister Martha Newland, who is always there when I need her, and my grandchildren Parker, Harlow, Julia, and Hayes, who brighten my days and give me hope for the future.

Reading Group Guide

1. Is it possible to stand up for your rights and not infringe on someone else? By insisting that their sons get more playing time in basketball games, are the parents in *Circle of Adversaries* infringing on Quentin's rights?

2. Why do you think Laura is so eager to have the Thomases join her church when she obviously doesn't want Quentin on the basketball team?

3. Is being the best player on the team good for Quentin, or would he be less vulnerable if he weren't?

4. Should Paul and Frank tell the Thomases about the meeting at James's house? Why or why not?

5. How many microagressions against African Americans did you notice? How often do you witness microagressions in everyday life?

6. Which approach to solving the team's problems do you think is best? What would you have done?

7. Is Paul right to assume he's expected to tell Meredith about Elaine's guilt? Should spouses feel this way about each other?

8. Should Lydia have told Tom about Elaine's guilt? Could he have given her an objective perspective on involving the police?

9. The basketball parents want justice for their sons in basketball and for Quentin when he's hurt. Also for Elaine. What is justice in each case and who should get to decide?

10. What is the difference between justice and revenge?

11. How do the parents' feelings about competition, self-image, racial differences, and success influence their perceptions of justice? Are they aware of these influences?

12. What goals, influences, and prejudices shape your perception of life?

13. Who or what is the main character in the novel?

14. Which character do you identify with most? Which one do you identify with least?

15. Which characters act as you expect them to act? Which ones do not?

16. Do you think this group of adults can continue to be friends?

About the Author

Although Sally Whitney has spent most of her adult life in other parts of the United States, her imagination lives in the South, the homeland of her childhood. "Whenever I dream of a story," she says, "I feel the magic of red clay hills, soft voices, sudden thunder storms, and rich emotions. The South is a wonderland of mysteries, legends, and jokes  handed down through generations of family storytellers, people like me."

Sally is a fan of stories in almost any medium, including literature, theater, and film. She'd rather spend an afternoon in the audience across from the footlights than anywhere else, and she thinks DVDs and streaming movies are the greatest inventions since the automobile. She loves libraries and gets antsy if she has to drive very far without an audio book to listen to.

The short stories she writes have been published in literary magazines and anthologies, including *Best Short Stories from The Saturday Evening Post Great American Fiction Contest 2017* and *Grow Old Along With Me—The Best Is Yet To Be*, the audio version of which was a Grammy Award finalist in the Spoken Word or Nonmusical Album category.

Her first novel, *Surface and Shadow*, published by Pen-L Publishing in 2016, tells the story of a woman who risks her marriage and her husband's career to find out what really happened in the suspicious death of a cotton baron in Tanner, North Carolina in 1972. In Sally's second novel, *When Enemies Offend Thee*, published by Pen-L in 2020, a woman originally from Tanner returns to the town after thirty years away and is raped by a former high-school classmate in a bizarre attempt to settle an old score. When police refuse to charge him, she vows to get even on her own.

In nonfiction, Sally's worked as a public relations writer, freelance journalist, and editor of *Best's Review* magazine. Her articles have appeared in magazines and newspapers, including *St. Anthony Messenger, The Kansas City Star, AntiqueWeek*, and *Our State: Down Home in North Carolina*.

She's a member of The Authors Guild and has been a fellow at the Virginia Center for the Creative Arts.

Sally currently lives in Pennsylvania with her cat, Ruth. When she isn't writing, reading, watching movies, attending plays, or pursuing her most recent interest, playing pool, she likes to poke around in antique shops looking for treasures. "The best things in life are the ones that have been loved, whether by you or somebody else," she says.

YOU CAN FIND SALLY AT
SallyWhitney.com
Facebook: SallyMWhitney
Instagram: SMWhitney65

Don't miss these fine books
by Sally Whitney

WHEN ENEMIES OFFEND THEE

Viciousness can lurk beneath even the most serene of surfaces.

Recently widowed, Clementine Loftis returns to her hometown in North Carolina looking for comfort and peace. Instead, she finds an angry former high school classmate who sexually assaults her in a bizarre attempt to settle an old score.

When her lack of evidence prevents police from charging him, Clementine vows to get even on her own. After her first attempt doesn't pan out, she escalates her effort. When that fails, she escalates again . . . and again.

Clementine's determination to make her attacker pay for what he's done drives her to walk a fine, dangerous line between vengeance and justice, making her question who she really is and whether she can ever again be the woman she wants to be.

When Enemies Offend Thee is a provocative thriller that will have readers questioning their own friendships, loyalties, ethics, and the possibility of redemption.

Praise for *When Enemies Offend Thee*:

"When Enemies Offend Thee is a riveting tale of crime, retribution, and healing. Sally Whitney is to be congratulated for creating a protagonist rarely seen in contemporary fiction: a dynamic, sexy older woman."

~ Patricia Schultheis, author of *St. Bart's Way and A Balanced Life*

GET YOUR PRINT OR EBOOK TODAY AT
WWW.PEN-L.COM/WHENENEMIESOFFENDTHEE.PHP

SURFACE AND SHADOW

What are you willing to risk to break free?

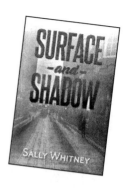

Smothered by her husband's expectations and the rigid gender roles of the 1970s, Lydia Colton sees a chance to rediscover and unfetter herself—if only she can find out the truth about a wealthy man's suspicious death.

According to history in the small town of Tanner, North Carolina, Howard Galloway died from accidentally drinking poison moonshine, leaving his twin brother, Henry, sole heir to the family's cotton mill and fortune. When Lydia hears that some people suspect Henry killed Howard, she impulsively starts asking questions and is soon tangled up in the Galloway secrets, which no one—least of all the Galloways—wants her to pursue.

Lydia's husband, Jeff, warns her that enraging Henry, the richest and most prominent employer in town, could jeopardize Jeff's career in Tanner, and soon Lydia and Jeff's marriage is at risk. But attempts by Jeff and other townspeople to thwart Lydia only make her more determined to solve the riddles she's uncovered.

Will revealing the truth save or destroy her?

Praise for *Surface and Shadow*:

"While *Surface and Shadow* offers the compelling tensions of a mystery story, its deeper probing involves the unknowns of the central character, Lydia Colton. As she delves into the lives of others connected with the circumstances of a strange death from a half century before, Lydia comes to realize that she is also confronting the secrets of her own identity. The answer to one mystery is inseparable from an illumination of the second. What started as a concern about a long ago death becomes the source of lives renewed, for Lydia and for others. The resolution satisfies the reader as much as it does Lydia."

~ Walter Cummins, Editor Emeritus of *The Literary Review*

Dear Reader,
If you enjoyed this book enough to review it for Goodreads, B&N, or Amazon.com, I'd appreciate it!
Thanks, Sally

Find more great reads at
Pen-L.com